STAND WITH ME, EARL

A Very Fine Muddle
Book Three

Kate Archer

ARE YOU SIGNED UP FOR DRAGONBLADE'S BLOG?

You'll get the latest news and information on exclusive giveaways, exclusive excerpts, coming releases, sales, free books, cover reveals and more.

Check out our complete list of authors, too!

No spam, no junk. That's a promise!

Sign Up Here

www.dragonbladepublishing.com

Dearest Reader;

Thank you for your support of a small press. At Dragonblade Publishing, we strive to bring you the highest quality Historical Romance from some of the best authors in the business. Without your support, there is no 'us', so we sincerely hope you adore these stories and find some new favorite authors along the way.

Happy Reading!

CEO, Dragonblade Publishing

Additional Dragonblade books by Author Kate Archer

A Very Fine Muddle
Romance Me, Viscount (Book 1)
Be Daring, Duke (Book 2)
Stand With Me, Earl (Book 3)

A Series of Worthy Young Ladies
The Meddler (Book 1)
The Sprinter (Book 2)
The Undaunted (Book 3)
The Champion (Book 4)
The Jilter (Book 5)
The Regal (Book 6)

The Dukes' Pact Series
The Viscount's Sinful Bargain (Book 1)
The Marquess' Daring Wager (Book 2)
The Lord's Desperate Pledge (Book 3)
The Baron's Dangerous Contract (Book 4)
The Peer's Roguish Word (Book 5)
The Earl's Iron Warrant (Book 6)

PROLOGUE

THERE HAS NEVER been a question in the minds of the *ton* that a young lady must be guided very carefully. Her character must be formed by strict supervision and direction. Her judgment must be cultivated with precision to ensure there is never any danger of a misstep in society.

The looks of the lady should be comely, but her appearance will be only the decorative icing on a cake of serious reflection and modesty.

Any matron who would nurture and raise such a feat of young womanhood must be disciplined, careful, orderly, and cautious.

Unfortunately, Miss Eloise Mayton, dear aunt and guide to the five Bennington daughters, had never been informed of these facts.

The lady was unsteady and impractical and prone to approving the most rash ideas and plans.

But then, Miss Mayton saw little reason to change her course now. So far, everything had worked out rather well. The two eldest girls were married, and if there had been false suitors, hired pickpockets, an ill-advised kidnapping, or any other less than well-considered plan, that was all to be forgotten.

At least, forgotten by Miss Mayton. She had little time to reflect upon such trifles. Her thoughts were far too taken up with reminiscing over her history of tragic romances on the continent when she had been young and beautiful all those many years ago.

The dear lady had been crossed in love as no other lady ever had—poisonings, hangings, deadly falls—so many gentlemen in love with Miss Mayton had come to a highly romantic and rather final end. She had come very close to becoming a baroness or countess so many times, but fate always stepped in to thwart her.

The Bennington daughters had grown up on her stories and were thrilled by them. They quite naturally presumed they would themselves be the recipient of such deadly passion.

They must only keep their lovestruck gentlemen alive long enough for them to understand their desperate love was requited. That was where their poor aunt had so often gone wrong.

For all that, though, the notion of a gentleman tearing his hair out and threatening to do a violence to himself in the throes of passionate love was found to be very interesting.

And so, with those genial ideas, the five sisters would descend upon London to find their true loves.

CHAPTER ONE

The Angel, Basingstoke
1804

VIOLA BENNINGTON, THIRD daughter of the Earl of Westmont, had spent the preceding months dreaming of copper-haired Lord Baderston.

She could hardly attend her sister Rosalind when she visited them in Somerset to tell them of her wedding trip with Conbatten. Though, from what she could remember, the sailing had been positively ghastly and everything else had been positively lovely.

Viola found she could pay little mind to her sister Beatrice's cajoling of her husband, even though they were neighbors and often at the house. Van Doren was still up in arms over Rosalind's kidnapping and had composed a thousand lectures about how nothing of the sort could ever happen again.

As time moved dreamily on and the gunshots of the hunting season rang out, she was hardly cognizant of any of it. Her thoughts were too taken up by Lord Baderston.

Her paintings, an art she had taken up during last season, seemed always to drift to a portrait of that young earl, no matter what she had initially intended. She spent hours mixing red and brown to get the color just right on his wonderful copper-colored hair. It was so hard to capture, though—some things produced by nature were too perfect to be replicated.

Viola had not, of course, had any extended conversation with Lord Baderston yet, having only met him once in the park. At least, no extended conversation where he was actually present. She'd had quite a few in her thoughts, though.

Perhaps she did not know him intimately well yet, but he had everything to recommend him! His hair was divine. He had an equally charming face—rugged and ruddy, as if he spent his life out of doors. He had such a strong and determined chin, and at the same time he seemed terribly friendly. He had already expressed an unusual fondness for ham, which everybody knew Viola was exceedingly partial to. That was one thing they had in common, and Viola was certain there were many more to be discovered.

They really were off to a good start. The season was coming and she would see him at parties. He would ask to be put on her card and he would show himself to be just the sort of man she looked for. Beatrice had even speculated that he'd be so keen as to be waiting nearby the doors at Almack's to see her arrive.

All Lord Baderston had to prove, to be entirely perfect and hers forevermore, was abject loyalty.

Complete and unwavering loyalty was Viola's absolute requirement. Beatrice may have had her very long list of unattainable attributes and Rosalind may have insisted on courage, but to Viola, loyalty was the hallmark of a true heart.

After all, had it not been *she* who'd patiently waited for two weeks for a very early infatuation to come round and tell her he loved her? It was true that she'd only been eight when the feeling struck but considering her tender age, she'd stayed with it remarkably long.

Was it not *she* who stood by and defended her pony, Alice, even though Alice hated all living beings, including herself? How many times had Alice attempted to bite her hand or kick her, then hang her head in shame, certain she would be sent away. Alice was not sent away though, she was given an apple and counseled to try to do better. Alice depended upon her and Viola would love her no matter how hideously she behaved.

Was it not Viola who, at the age of nine, pronounced slices of ham superior to all other meats, and then stayed firm in that opinion? It had not always been easy, either, as sometimes she got a stomachache from it.

She must have a gentleman's true heart to match her own true heart. There could be nothing more frightening than a person whose opinions on things might change from day to day. Especially not a husband. Was his wife to wake one day and discover she was no longer preferred? No, she could not bear that.

Viola Bennington must have loyalty in any and all circumstances. If she were to burn the house down, though it was far more likely that Cordelia and her footlights would accomplish such a thing, her lord must stay loyal. If she spent all his money on baubles, though she was not particularly fond of shopping, he must stay loyal. If she was found to be a murderess, though so far she had always called for Lynette when there was a spider to be disposed of in her bedchamber, he must stay loyal.

And perhaps, along with loyalty, she must have some shade of red hair too. Just like that early infatuation, the tinker's boy who had passed through the village. He had a marvelous head of red hair and when he'd passed by in his cart he'd winked at her.

Viola had spent many a private moment during the two awful weeks she was in love with him thinking he would come back for her and they would marry. She would not even mind riding round the countryside in a tinker's cart, as long as he was beside her.

The boy never did come back, which Viola must assume her father would be grateful to know if he had been aware of her attachment. He had eventually faded from her thoughts, but his red hair never had. There was something original and romantic about it, as if it capped off a passionate nature. There was something about it that stirred her.

And then there had been Lord Baderston sporting a shade she had never dreamed of. Not too bright, but a most pleasing copper.

Now, the Benningtons were on their way to Town. It was to be her season, and Lord Baderston would be waiting for her.

At least, she hoped so. There was always the outside chance that some other lady with a fondness for copper-colored hair and ham slices had swooped in. But Viola would not allow her thoughts to drift in that direction for too long. It was too distressing to think of.

The Angel in Basingstoke had only taken six days to reach. Some other caravans may have made the trip from Taunton to that location in fewer days, but it was quite a good pace for the Benningtons.

Whenever the family was on the move, it seemed there were no end of delays to be encountered. Sometimes Viola had to get out and walk from eating too much ham, and then Juliet often needed to stop to write an ode to an inspiring vista.

They had been delayed at the outset when they'd stopped at *The Lamb* at Hindon as they had encountered a most unpleasant fellow. They had instantly felt it their absolute duty to manage him. Once they had managed him, they'd spent two days there, settling the result of the affair.

A certain Mr. Ladle, who had recently lost his wife, was determined to rid himself of that lady's most precious possession. A lovely bird named Chester had kept poor Mrs. Ladle company through what must have been a most tedious marriage.

They had encountered Mr. Ladle attempting to convince the innkeeper that his guests would be amused by having Chester on the scene. He was said to be a scarlet macaw and that sort of bird was known to captivate and entertain travelers.

The innkeeper did not see the charm of the idea. Or the charm of Chester. He told Mr. Ladle that not only would he not pay five pounds for the bird, but he could not *be paid* five pounds to take the thing.

This was all very distressing to the Benningtons. Or at least to the sisters and Miss Mayton, if not their father who was still outside, directing the arrangements for the horses.

What would happen to Chester? He could not survive in the out of doors and they would not think it past Mr. Ladle to put him there. For one, Chester was a tropical sort of bird and could not tolerate the weather. For another, he'd been the indulged pet of the long-suffering Mrs. Ladle and would have no idea how to fend for himself.

Chester would constantly give away his location to predators by his brightly colored red, yellow, and blue feathers. His tail feathers were so majestically long that Viola did not see how they could be hidden in any hidey-hole.

And then, Chester did have things to say for himself. Viola could just imagine a fox or stoat walking by who had somehow not noticed Chester. Then that creature would suddenly hear the bird talking to himself. She had already heard him say a number of things: *Charming Chester. Biscuit. Bad man.*

The much-aggrieved Chester was just now lunging at Mr. Ladle through the bars of his cage and screaming, "Bad man, bad man, bad man."

"Shut it!" Mr. Ladle said, rattling Chester's cage.

In retaliation, Chester reached a claw out between the bars and scratched Mr. Ladle's hand.

"Hand over that bird at once," Viola said, thinking she'd best get the bird in hand before her father came in to put a stop to it.

Mr. Ladle had turned at the sound. He looked over at Viola, Cordelia, Juliet, and Miss Mayton. Seeming to take their measure, he said smoothly, "Of course, miss, this here bird is yours for only ten pounds."

"Bad man!" Chester cried.

"Yes," Viola said to the bird, "I believe you are right, Chester. Now, Mr. Ladle, you must know that Mrs. Ladle is very ashamed of you. You do realize that she can see what you're doing from heaven, as can *God*."

Mr. Ladle had apparently not considered there might be eyes upon him and glanced all round as if Mrs. Ladle or God might be spotted hiding behind a door at the inn.

"Indeed," Juliet said. "I cannot imagine what poor Mrs. Ladle and God think about this."

"Nothing very pleasant, I'm sure," Cordelia said.

Mr. Ladle took this very hard, and Viola was certain that when he set out to sell the bird he'd not factored in both God and Mrs. Ladle watching him do it.

"I don't mean no harm," he whispered, "it's just…the thing don't never shut up."

"Well," Miss Mayton said, "I am not surprised by it. Chester does not seem to care for you particularly. I must presume he has been calling you a bad man for quite some time."

"*She* taught him to say that," Mr. Ladle muttered. "I know she did."

"The best you can do now," Viola said, "if you wish to have Mrs. Ladle's gaze averted from you, is to hand Chester over to us and begone."

Mr. Ladle seemed to consider the advice. Then, thinking better of having his dead wife staring at him from heaven all the time, he shoved the cage into Viola's arms and fled out the doors.

As they were all cooing at Chester, who seemed a deal more sanguine after seeing the back of Mr. Ladle, the earl came in from the inn yard.

"Look, Papa," Juliet said, "we've got a parrot!"

If the earl was not quite as overjoyed at this turn of events, he was not as irate as some other fathers might be. The Earl of Westmont was a rather even-tempered man who only lost his equanimity over a house fire.

He stared at Chester and said softly, "Of course you have."

THAT EVENING, AS so often occurred when the Benningtons journeyed, they encountered a rather genial fellow traveler. This gentleman's name was Mr. Thomas Lawrence and he was speedily identified as *the* Thomas Lawrence—the most famous portrait painter in England.

Considering that Viola had so recently taken up the art herself, and brought with her a portrait she'd been working on that may or may not have been Lord Baderston, the earl was pressed to invite the gentleman to dine with them.

The table had been laid and the courses arrived with an inn's usual organized rapidity. Viola found Mr. Lawrence a pleasant enough person, though she had expected a famous portrait painter to be something more. Perhaps more flamboyant or eccentric, or so taken up with his art that he ignored the niceties of society.

She'd often found she was just that eccentric herself whenever she was gripped by a sudden feeling of inspiration and ran to pick up a brush.

As it was, Mr. Lawrence was seemingly usual in all respects. His only eccentricity at all was his aversion to birds.

They had not the heart to leave Chester by himself in their rooms after his harrowing afternoon, and so his cage currently sat on a window seat nearby the table.

Mr. Lawrence was seen to be often glancing toward the cage as if he were afraid Chester might let himself out of it.

It was true that Chester had occasionally interrupted the table's conversation with one of his own comments, but what bird would not be full of nervous energy after having his cage rattled by Mr. Ladle?

In any case, Chester had quieted quite a bit after receiving a few biscuits and a handful of almonds.

"Mr. Lawrence," Miss Mayton said, "we have painter in our own family sphere. Lady Viola took it up just last year and is prodigiously talented."

"Excellent. Who do you study with, my lady?" he asked Viola.

"Study with?" Viola said, rather surprised by the question. "Well, we did all have a drawing master years ago. But he was always putting charcoals in our hands and so we never got anywhere with it."

"You see, Mr. Lawrence," Cordelia said, "Viola was all along a painter, not a sketcher. She knew it as soon as she picked up a brush."

"She took right to a brush like it had been in her hand all along," Juliet said, nodding.

"Do you say, then, that we speak of a sudden, prodigy sort of talent?" Mr. Lawrence said, beginning to look very intrigued.

The earl coughed and said, "Now, I would not go so far—"

"Practically a phenomenon," Miss Mayton said. "After all, when I think where our Viola was when she began, and where she is now, well, it makes one's head spin."

"I would be interested in seeing something of this," Mr. Lawrence said.

"I really do not think—" The earl said, brows knitting.

"Now, Papa," Cordelia said, "do not be modest on Viola's behalf. Mr. Lawrence, it so happens that the painting that our sister is just now in the midst of creating is in our carriage. Viola let it dry for five days so we might take it with us."

"It is, naturally, only in development," Viola said, as a waiter came round with a syllabub.

Mr. Lawrence nodded. "And so, you might not wish anyone to view it just yet. That, of course, is understandable. To the untrained eye, a portrait not yet finished can seem rough and confused."

"Yes, that is it exactly," the earl said with enthusiasm. "It simply is not ready."

"However," Mr. Lawrence continued, "to the *trained* eye, it provides a view to what it will be when the last paint stroke has been applied. I would be delighted to see it."

The earl fumbled with his spoon and it clattered onto the table. "Now, I—"

"An honor, indeed," Miss Mayton said. She turned to one of the waiters and said, "Might you fetch it from our carriage? You will know it as the one of the earl's coaches—the one with the dark blue velvet seats. The painting is just inside, wrapped in brown paper."

"Do not put the boy to such trouble…" the earl said.

"It is no trouble at all, my lord," the fresh-faced waiter said, eagerly hurrying out to do Miss Mayton's bidding.

This was really something. Mr. Thomas Lawrence was moments away from viewing one of her own works!

"While we wait," Juliet said, "I suppose you'll want to hear the ode I composed today?"

The earl was pouring himself a large glass of port from the bottle the waiter had so helpfully left on the table. "I am not sure—"

"You are a poet, Lady Juliet?" Mr. Lawrence asked. "I prodigiously admire those who can write such moving phrases, though I have no talent for composing myself."

"I am inspired by what I see around me, Mr. Lawrence." Juliet stood and said, "Ode to Chester."

> *Bright colored bird, cruelly treated*
> *That rogue of a man must be defeated*
> *Mr. Ladle was firmly and handily managed*
> *And so Chester was forthwith put in our carriage.*

Viola and Cordelia led the applause. Though, Viola was beginning to wonder if her father was unwell, as he looked pale and had been late to it.

Mr. Lawrence looked a bit stunned. He no doubt pondered how Juliet could have so quickly composed the ode about Chester, as he'd already been informed that they'd only rescued the bird that very afternoon.

Chester, very much liking to hear his name upon a person's lips, shouted, "Charming Chester!"

The young waiter hurried back in with Viola's painting. She hopped up, carefully untied the string, removed the paper wrapping, and propped it on the mantel.

Mr. Lawrence had stood and applied his quizzing glass. It

suddenly fell from his hand and swung on its chain, making lazy arcs through the silence.

"Now, if I may explain where I am with this," Viola said.

"Please do," Mr. Lawrence said quietly.

"The blue in the background is the sky. And those, there, will be trees, though I'll have to make them bigger. You see this part here, I am aiming for a copper color, that will be hair. I haven't got to the face yet. So, at the moment, the hair is bigger than the trees. That will have to be fixed."

"She's getting very good with proportions," Cordelia said.

"Viola is really something, is she not, Mr. Lawrence?" Juliet asked.

Mr. Lawrence staggered back to his chair and sat down heavily. "I cannot argue that it is something," he said, "though *what* precisely, I am not certain."

"Naturally," Viola said, "I do not have any professional aspirations. I really look at it as being skilled at sewing or some other household matter. It will be handy to see a blank wall and be able to fill it myself."

"Viola has already painted a portrait of the Duke and Duchess of Conbatten," Miss Mayton said.

"Really? The duke?" Mr. Lawrence said.

Viola nodded. "He was quite pleased with it."

"Really?"

"It's even got its own room," Juliet said. "Conbatten insisted it go into what he's named his family room. It is for family only and nobody else is allowed in there. One of my odes is in there too."

"I see," Mr. Lawrence said, glancing at Viola's painting. "So it is not for public consumption. Very wise."

"Mr. Lawrence," Miss Mayton said, "I hope we find in you a lover of literature?"

"Literature? Yes, as it happens, I am a rather enthusiastic reader."

"Excellent," Miss Mayton said. "I have been reading to everybody in the evening. It helps to pass the time."

The earl said, "It is not particularly highbrow, but it is a cracking good tale."

"It is *The Harrowing Homecoming at Harrowbridge Hall*," Juliet said. "There are two dukes returned from abroad, but only one of them is real. How is the gentle governess to decide between them?"

"Well, I…" Mr. Lawrence trailed off.

Miss Mayton said, "Chapter Two."

The gentle governess was all aflutter. The two dukes, only one of which was real, were determined on a contest to prove their legitimacy and win her love. The nature of the contest was confusing—it was a battle of doing things that only a duke could do. What were those things, though?

The first duke said, "I propose dismissing the butler. A duke will do it in a certain way."

The second duke said, "I could dismiss a butler in my sleep!"

"Call the butler forth!" Duke One said.

Mr. Crayden, the aged butler, hobbled into the solarium. "Your Graces," he said, as his eyesight had got so bad that he did not know which was the real duke either.

"Crayden," Duke One said, "pack your bags and depart at once!"

"Nonsense," Duke Two said. "Crayden, you are a rogue and a thief. I will issue no reference and you will be escorted down the drive this instant!"

"I change my answer!" Duke One said. "Crayden, you are a scoundrel! How dare you steal the silver? Out with you!"

"Steal the silver?" Crayden said weakly. "My eyes are so bad I don't even know where it is anymore."

The two dukes turned to the gentle governess. "Well?" Duke One said. "What is your verdict? Which one of us dismissed the butler like a duke?"

"Yes, gentle governess, who dismissed him best?" Duke Two asked.

Mr. Crayden turned and began to shuffle out of the room. "I'd best go pack my bags. If I can find them."

"No, Mr. Crayden," the gentle governess called. "You are not really let go. It was just a contest. By the by, I have never witnessed a duke dismissing a butler. Do you know who did it best?"

Miss Mayton laid down her book. "So, Mr. Lawrence, we can see where this is going—the two dukes will have a battle for the ages and one of them will be revealed as false." She sighed and said, "I do find the poor aged butler so poignant, though."

"He'd be lucky to get out of that house, if you ask me," Mr. Lawrence said quietly.

Miss Mayton picked up the book again to read further, but Mr. Lawrence practically flew out of his chair. "I am sorry, I must bid you good evening for an early start on the morrow."

He practically fled the room and Viola began to think that maybe he did indeed have his little eccentricities, as any famous portrait painter would.

It was a shame though, as to cap off the evening, Cordelia performed her Desdemona death scene she was so known for.

Though Mr. Lawrence was not there to appreciate it, dear Chester found Desdemona's dying most thrilling. He squawked and paced and generally was a very attentive audience.

Viola sighed contentedly. It seemed wherever the Benningtons traveled, they must bring joy to whomever they encountered.

CHAPTER TWO

ROLAND TREWELLIAN, EARL of Baderston, avoided his mother's gaze. The dowager countess paced the drawing room, as it seemed she had been doing for months.

"My son," she said, "I simply do not understand your reluctance to engage yourself to Lady Clara. She comes with thirty thousand and we have known her people forever."

Roland felt as if he and his mother were strapped to a wheel—just going round and round on the subject of Lady Clara.

His mother had all along presumed he would marry Lady Clara and he had been remiss in not challenging that idea for the past three years. He'd never agreed to it, but he'd allowed her to make those little comments that she thought it must be so without a challenge.

She was an argumentative sort of lady and it was generally prudent to leave her to argue with herself.

Then, without his knowledge, she'd invited that family to a house party. He'd not found out about it until they were at the gates.

What an awkward visit! He and Lady Clara were constantly thrown together in the stupidest manners possible. They had eyes upon them at every moment.

Everybody was waiting for him to declare himself. Toward the end of the visit, Lady Clara's father had begun to be rather surly.

Roland would have very much liked to pull the man aside and explain the facts of the case to him. He'd had no hand in the invitation and would have stopped the dowager from issuing it had he known of it.

Of course, that was impossible to do without insulting his daughter in some manner and causing a rift between the two families.

The days had dragged on and Roland had sighed with relief at the end of each evening, when his bedchamber door would be closed and the only person looking at him was his valet.

Markson, perfectly aware of the straits he was in, would arrive with a large glass of brandy to assist him in recovering from a long and tedious day.

Lady Clara and her parents had since departed.

In response to his mother's constant questioning as to why he had not proposed, he'd finally had to confront her with the truth. He would not wed Lady Clara.

This news had not been taken at all well. Particularly since he would not account for his reasons.

He did have his reasons, though. Or, he might better say, *one* reason.

Lady Viola Bennington. He must return to Town and meet with that lady again.

He had only encountered her very briefly the year before, as she'd not yet been out. But what he knew about her! What he'd thought when he saw her!

Lady Viola's sister, Lady Rosalind, had told him all about her sister when they had danced at Almack's. Lady Viola was said to be partial to his particular color of hair and that was no small thing. He'd been called Lord Gingerbread at school and he had not liked it. His friend, Hastings, had informed him that the usual lady preferred black, brown, or fair hair.

He could not know why it was so, but it seemed it was so. He wondered if it might be because Henry the Eighth had been a redhead and had proved himself a rather unpleasant and unreliable husband.

Roland had assumed he'd have to find a lady who would put up with his unfortunate hair. But now, here was a lady who actually sought it out.

Forearmed with that idea, he'd then seen her that day in the park. She was achingly lovely and seemed so genial. And, Lady Rosalind had said Lady Viola was a very loyal person. She'd said that once Lady Viola decided to be for a person, she was for that person forevermore.

He rather liked that idea. He valued loyalty quite a bit himself.

Of course, there had been the matter of his feelings about ham. Lady Rosalind had very specifically said that Lady Viola was excessively fond of ham, and she hoped he was too.

In truth, he had not ever held that meat above all others. However, he was prepared to do it!

He'd eaten more ham over the last months than he ever had in his life. When Lady Viola quizzed him about it, as he supposed she would, he would be able to be truthful about his consumption of that item.

"Now, Baderston," his mother went on, "I think you might have the wrong idea about marriage. It is to be built on practicalities. You do not suppose your father and I were carried to the church by our feelings, do you?"

"You were not?" he asked. This was a rather new idea. He'd always noticed that his parents had acted toward one another in a painstakingly polite fashion that felt rather distant. He had supposed though, that there had been something more lively between them in their youth.

"Certainly not," the dowager said. "If I had allowed myself to be carried away by my feelings, I would have collapsed after a particular earl went and married somebody else. I did not collapse. I very sensibly took rational steps. As I could not have *that* earl, I had the sense to see I must have somebody and took on another earl. Your father."

That was ghastly and he dearly hoped his father never knew it. He also wished his mother would stop telling him things he did not need or want to know. It was rather sickening to imagine her a lovestruck young lady who was thrown over, and then looking about herself in a calculating fashion.

He knew no end of older gentlemen who would be the right age to be the culprit. Did they know they'd thrown her over? Or had they not noticed her favor and just chosen some other lady? If they did know of her preference and that she would take it hard, what must they think when they encountered *him*?

They were probably grateful to see they had escaped having a son with red hair.

"I expect you to do your duty, Baderston. I expect you to engage yourself to Lady Clara this coming season. I expect it, her father expects it, and the lady herself expects it."

Roland did not answer. He had no intention of engaging himself to Lady Clara, nor did he think she particularly wished for it. Though, she was likely to do her parents' bidding, as she had several seasons to her credit.

What he *did* have every intention of doing was to seek out Lady Viola at the earliest possible moment.

After all, should things proceed the way he hoped, he was certain his mother would approve of the lady. What was there running against Lady Viola? Absolutely nothing!

There had, of course, been certain stories about the Bennington family gone round. If one wished to be nitpicky about it.

There had been talk that Lady Beatrice had entertained a slew of suitors and then threw them all over for Lord Van Doren. But was it to be that lady's fault that she'd had so many gentlemen circling round?

Then, the rather more alarming bit of gossip that Lady Rosalind had somehow managed to get herself kidnapped by design. But, she'd married Conbatten and he was a duke, so those whispers came to an end rather quick.

And of course, people did whisper about Miss Mayton—the

lady in widow's weeds who'd never married and who told bizarre stories from her years on the continent. It seemed that anybody falling in love with Miss Mayton was swiftly prompted to kill themselves. None of the stories made sense, but then Miss Mayton was getting up in years and sometimes an older person did go a little funny in the head.

Was Miss Mayton to be condemned simply for falling prey to the ravages of age?

Other than those trifles, there was nothing that could be pointed to. Lady Viola was of good family and by all reports her dowry was more than sufficient to please his mother.

"Remember, Baderston," the dowager said, "the most important thing is to keep our family name as it has always been. Absolutely unsullied. I refuse to countenance ever hearing a whisper of gossip about a Trewellian. Lady Clara and her family are a known commodity and therefore a safe choice."

Roland did not answer. He felt as if safety were the last thing on his mind just now. He would leave for London on the morrow, though he had a great urge to jump on his horse this very night and highwaymen be damned.

Lady Viola Bennington might be there even now.

⇉≫≪⇇

TATTLETON REALLY COULD not understand how the family had managed to find a parrot between Taunton and London.

The Bennington caravan had been going along quite nicely, if not slow as molasses, when one morning the ladies strolled out from the inn with a parrot in a cage. He was promptly informed the bird was called Chester.

As if he cared what the bird was called! Was a butler to be expected to engage with such a creature?

He was the smallest bit mollified to understand that this newfound avian would *not* be making its way to the servants' hall, as had a certain pregnant dog and four unruly cats in previous seasons.

This Chester was to take up residence in the drawing room.

He must suppose this would be more work for the maids. They already had a job of it scrubbing paint splatters from the floor after Lady Viola began painting portraits in that location.

Or whatever it was she painted.

He'd seen the alleged portrait of Lady Rosalind and the Duke of Conbatten, given them as a wedding gift. Was it a portrait, or had she just tripped with a paint bucket?

Now, there would be who knew what else ending up on the floor. Lady Juliet had already informed him that they would need a large supply of biscuits, almonds, a variety of seeds and, if at all possible, worms and snails.

Was he to start digging the garden for worms and snails now?

And then, this Chester had the audacity to speak!

It was very disconcerting to walk by its cage and hear a nasally voice say, "Bad man."

Where did the cheeky thing find the nerve to pronounce him a bad man?

Mrs. Huffson hurried into the kitchens. "Well, Mr. Tattleton, here we are again in Town. I suppose we hold on to our hats and see what happens this time."

Tattleton sighed. This time. If the two last times were anything to go by, he'd be less holding on to his hat and more clutching at his heart.

"There now," the housekeeper said, always being very attuned to his moods, "there is every chance that nothing at all untoward will occur. We could find ourselves positively bored by the sensible routine of it all."

Over their heads, they heard screeching from the drawing room. "Bad man! Charming Chester!"

Tattleton gazed dolefully at the stairs. "I have little hope of it, Mrs. Huffson. Desperately little hope."

THE BENNINGTONS HAD arrived at Portland Place and Viola and her sisters had seen that Chester was settled in the drawing room.

First, they'd let him out of his cage for a while so he could stretch his wings. He quite enjoyed himself, flapping across the room to land on the mantel, then crashing onto the window seat and clawing his way up the curtains, then coming down and waddling across the floor in the most charming manner possible.

Naturally, he did not yet know the room well, so there were a few items knocked over and a bowl chipped. Then of course, his claws were rather sharp, which was not at all his fault and just as nature intended, though they did make some holes in the silk curtains.

Chester was lured back into his cage with a biscuit when he seemed to get tired of flapping round. He very happily went inside and Viola was certain he felt safe there after all the upheaval in his life over the past days. The poor thing had seemed delighted to see the last of Mr. Ladle, but he'd not taken to the swaying of the carriage at all well.

At one point he'd fallen off his perch and laid still and they very much feared he was dead. They'd stopped the coach and he'd eventually struggled upright again, however he swayed back and forth though the carriage remained at a stop. It had taken him some minutes to regain his equilibrium and steady himself.

Getting Chester comfortable in his new home had helped to pass the time as they waited for their dear brother Darden. The earl had sent a note to the Young Bucks Club, a club Darden had founded—his family had arrived and he was expected to dinner.

Viola looked up as they heard the familiar crash of the front doors. They all knew it would be Darden, as he never came softly into the house.

He was in the drawing room in moments.

"Darden!" Juliet cried, launching herself at him.

Not to be left behind, Viola and Cordelia followed suit.

"Hello, my sisters," he said, muffled by the yards of muslin just now engulfing him.

"Our dear brother," Cordelia said.

"Our best brother," Juliet said.

"We have missed our brother," Viola said.

"And guess what, Darden," Juliet said, "we've got a parrot!"

"Of course you do," Darden said laughing.

"We rescued him from a very unpleasant man named Mr. Ladle," Viola added.

"How else would it be?" Darden asked.

"His name is Chester," Cordelia said.

"Very fitting. Do let me breathe now," Darden said, untangling himself.

Juliet took him by the hand and led him to the birdcage.

Chester was very charmingly preening his feathers. The bird looked up and said quietly, "Bad man."

"No, Chester," Viola said, "not all men are bad. You only think so on account of Mr. Ladle. You'll see that our dear Darden is quite a different sort."

Chester did not look entirely convinced, but he did not repeat the condemnation.

"Oh, guess what else?" Juliet asked. "You'll never guess."

"Let's see," Darden said, laughing, "you've picked up a tiger along the way too, and he's just now below stairs devouring the servants."

"Do not be ridiculous, Darden," Cordelia said. "If we'd found a tiger, we'd have built a proper cage and informed Lady Castlereagh of it. She is the only one who has one, as far as I know. I should not like to think how worried she would be if he wandered off."

"You mean, how worried we'd *all* be if he wandered off," Darden said.

"I knew you would not guess. While we were at The Angel," Juliet said, "we dined with Mr. Lawrence. The famous one who paints portraits."

"He was positively stunned when Viola showed him her latest painting," Cordelia said.

"Practically speechless," Juliet said.

"I bet he was," Darden said, rubbing his chin.

The earl came in, escorting Miss Mayton. "There you are, my boy," he said jovially. "I could hear the doors crashing from above stairs."

"Father, Miss Mayton, how good it is to see you again."

Miss Mayton blushed, as she always did have a soft spot for Darden.

Tattleton came to the drawing room doors. "You may go through whenever you wish, my lord."

"Well, we should not tarry, then," the earl said. He walked with his son toward the dining room and Viola overheard him say, "I suppose you met Chester. Calls me a bad man on a regular basis."

Darden put his arm around his father's shoulders. "He doesn't like me either," he said, laughing.

They had settled themselves round the table and Viola was struck by how empty it seemed now that both Beatrice and Rosalind were married and were gone from the house.

"Darden," Juliet said, "you will be so pleased to understand that Viola already knows who her particular gentleman is."

"Again?" Darden asked. "Last season, Rosalind said she was in love with an unknown gentleman on horseback. Then we all found out it was the duke."

"Oh, we knew it was the duke all along," Cordelia said.

"Did you?" the earl asked.

"Of course we did, Papa," Viola said. "When Rosalind went to Almack's he was there and she discovered who he was. You do not suppose she would have kept it from us?"

"She managed to keep it from me and your brother," the earl said.

"Well, now," Miss Mayton said, in a bid to stop the earl from wondering why he'd not been informed of last season's goings-on, "I am pleased to tell you that this circumstance is no mystery to anybody."

"So?" Darden said. "Who is the fellow?"

"Lord Baderston," Viola said. "I wonder if you know him."

"Baderston?" Darden asked. "Yes, of course I know him. He's a member of my club, just recently admitted through his friendship with Harveston."

"A member of the YBC?" Viola said, very encouraged to hear it. Darden only had the best gentlemen in his club.

"Well, Darden?" the earl asked. "Is he suitable in every respect?"

"Suitable? Yes, he's very suitable—he's an earl from an old family, the Trewellians."

The earl nodded, satisfied.

"But," Darden said slowly, "there has been talk about Baderston. There has been talk of a match between him and Lady Clara. I understand Lady Clara and her parents were even there for a house party over the summer. I know nothing firsthand, but heard it mentioned at the club."

"A house party!" Viola cried. Who was this Lady Clara and what was she doing at a house party at *his* house?

"That is what is said," Darden said, "that she and her parents were there for a fortnight."

"But was there an engagement announced?" Miss Mayton said.

"No, nothing as of yet, I do not think," Darden admitted.

"There now," Miss Mayton said. "A young lady's parents may drag her anywhere, but good luck to them trying to drag her to an altar. Even a weak-minded young lady will often put her foot down at *that*."

"Oh, Aunt," Viola said, "you do not think he asked and was refused? I could not bear it. I could not bear to be chosen second. I could not imagine going along wondering if my husband was forever regretting what he could not have."

"If I may inquire, my dear," the earl said to his daughter, "how is it you know of this Baderston and have developed such strong feelings for him when you have not yet been out?"

"Rosalind introduced us when we were in our carriage in the park," Viola said.

"It was a very short introduction," Miss Mayton assured the earl.

"And he has red hair," Juliet said, as if that point would clarify things in the earl's mind.

"It is really more of a copper color," Viola said. "The most charming shade I have ever seen."

"And that is somehow significant?" the earl asked, puzzlement overtaking his features.

"Of course it is, Papa," Cordelia said in an indulgent tone. "Because of the tinker's boy Viola wished to marry."

"What tinker's boy!" the earl exclaimed.

"Do not trouble yourself, Father," Viola said. "He never came back for me and I quite gave him up ages ago."

"But she's been dreaming of red hair ever since," Juliet said.

The earl's brow wrinkled. "So you say, then, that you would rather have been born with Cordelia's shade?"

"No, Papa. Cordelia's auburn suits her and my strawberry blond suits me. It is the *gentleman's* hair that strikes me. Now, Lord Baderston's hair is a bit lighter than Cordelia's but not so light as to make it surprisingly bright. You see?"

"Well, I hardly think a gentleman's hair color..." the earl drifted off.

"Lord Darden," Miss Mayton said, seeing the earl would never comprehend a woman's feelings on the matter of hair color, "have you arranged for Viola to attend Almack's on Wednesday? We feel certain he will be there."

"Yes, of course, it's all arranged. Voucher and tickets secured."

"Darden is the dearest brother, is he not, Papa?"

"Yes, yes," the earl said distractedly, looking as if he were still trying to work out why a certain hair color had become a vital point to his daughter.

"Excellent," Miss Mayton said. "We shall go and we shall see that dear Lord Baderston only has eyes for Viola."

Viola nodded gratefully at her aunt. It must be so. She'd thought of Lord Baderston for all these months! He'd been cemented in her mind. Certainly, she would not now discover that he preferred Lady Clara.

Who was this lady, anyway? Did she prefer red hair? Did she adore ham as much as Viola and Lord Baderston did? Did Lady Clara have anything at all in common with the gentleman?

Viola stopped her thoughts from running away from her. She must believe that all would be well. It must be.

The earl, seeming to have recovered himself from this most recent conversation with his daughters, said, "I wonder, Miss Mayton, if you would carry on reading to us tonight?"

Miss Mayton nodded. "Lord Darden, we are reading *The Harrowing Homecoming at Harrowbridge Hall.*"

Darden laughed and said, "It sounds suitably harrowing."

"You will not believe what has gone on so far, Son," the earl said. "The duke has been in Egypt ever since his wife died, four years ago. Now he's returned, but there is another gentleman who also claims to be the duke! The gentle governess does not know who, between them, she really loves. They have been competing for her love in the most energetic ways possible. Will she fall in love with the duke? Or will she fall in love with a charlatan?"

"Just at this moment," Juliet said, "they are having a contest of things only a duke could do."

Darden snorted. "I suppose there is no chance that some family member or friend can have a look at both men and pick out the real duke?"

"Sadly, no," Miss Mayton said. "The children were too young when the duke left, the butler is nearly blind, the rest of the family are dead, and…well, the duke never did have a lot of friends.”

“Of course,” Darden said.

“I will paint while you read, Aunt,” Viola said. “I have a mind to start a new canvas and paint Chester.”

“Very good thought, my dear,” Miss Mayton said. “Goodness, Beatrice and Van Doren will soon come to open their house across the street, and we expect to hear from Rosalind any day. We are well on our way to another jolly season!”

Viola had every hope of it. She would walk into Almack’s and Lord Baderston would be there, waiting for her. He must be there. That was the only thing that would make her jolly.

CHAPTER THREE

ROLAND HAD NEVER felt anxious about encountering a lady in his entire life. He did now, though.

He'd arrived to Almack's on the very early side and bided his time until he could approach Lady Jersey. Then, he'd made his request—he would wish to be given leave to put himself down on Lady Viola Bennington's card.

Lady Jersey, having been in the world long enough to know when one ought to wonder about something, had a series of questions.

"How is it, Lord Baderston," Lady Jersey said, "that you know Lady Viola? She is not yet out and she is not from your county."

"Well, it is not so much that I know her," Roland said. "It is just that her sister, Lady Rosalind, now the Duchess of Conbatten, did extoll her virtues quite compellingly."

"That is all?"

"I did see her in the park one day last year," he said. "She was out with her sisters."

"And from that, you have somehow surmised that you have much in common?"

"The 'much in common' is to be discovered, though I imagine it will come to that," Roland said. "I do know that we both prefer ham and are loyal sort of people."

"Ham."

Roland probably should have left out the part about ham. Now that he'd said it out loud it did not sound as compelling as it had when he'd been thinking about it.

"I rather wonder, Lord Baderston," Lady Jersey said, "that you are not intent on securing Lady Clara's card at the first opportunity."

Of course, she *would* wonder—his mother kept up a correspondence with the lady and would have confided her plan. Roland wondered who else the dowager had informed of it.

Rather than answer outright, he just shrugged. Though he'd not said anything, Lady Jersey was astute enough to see where the wind was blowing on that particular subject.

"A shame," she said quietly. "Very well, I give you leave to approach Lady Viola."

It had been an uncomfortable interrogation, but he'd got what he wanted. She'd given him leave.

He should not mind being uncomfortable, as he was certain there would be ample opportunity for it in the coming weeks. At least, if his mother had anything to say about it.

The dowager, who did not particularly care for either London or parties, and who should have been resting comfortably in the dower house in Dorset, had come to Town.

He'd always kept her bedchamber in the London house just as she'd left it, for her particular use. But that was just a courtesy. She was not supposed to actually turn up to use it!

What a talk they'd had about it. He'd tried every reason he could think of to thwart her and stop her from coming. She would not be moved and was determined. What could he do? Was he to bar the lady from his house?

It was very tempting, but he did not do it.

She'd be on her way to Almack's by now. Roland had claimed he must set off on his horse and could not escort her in the carriage because his animal needed exercise.

The dowager had not believed it, but she could not find a way to stop him.

Now, he was lurking by the front doors near a column. He would step behind it if he caught sight of the dowager, and step in front of it if he caught sight of Lady Viola.

THIS WAS IT. They were in the carriage and on their way to Almack's. Viola glanced down at her marvelous dress—a lilac silk with a netting overlay in a shade darker.

Rosalind and Beatrice were right, a dress such as this could give a lady courage.

She did need courage at this very moment.

Viola had discovered, as Lynette had dressed her, that it was one thing to daydream about a gentleman, and another to consider actually encountering him.

Daydreaming had felt quite safe, while reality felt quite fraught. Daydreaming had allowed her to direct what everybody would say and do—what *he* would say and do.

Now, she was to discover what he would say and do on his own, no longer the marionette of her imagination.

That, and knowing she was minutes away from walking into Almack's and being examined by the patronesses, sent a shiver running down her spine.

The earl patted her hand. "You are very quiet, Viola, which makes me think you are anxious regarding this first outing."

"I am, rather," Viola confessed.

"Put your nerves aside," Darden said. "The Benningtons always stack up rather well, in my experience."

"That is very true," Miss Mayton said. "All of us must be admired wherever we go. I do remember how solicitous Lady Jersey was to see me in my widow's weeds last season."

The earl and Darden glanced at each other as if they were surprised to hear it.

Her aunt had continued on with wearing black, having several new gowns in bombazine made for her. Just now, she rustled with every shifting.

Viola could not know what Lady Jersey had thought of her aunt's mode of dress. It was not usual that a lady who'd never married now dressed in mourning for a husband who had never been. Of course, she knew that. But then, there was a certain romance to the idea too. Miss Mayton was in mourning over a loss—quite a few losses actually—and it hardly mattered that there had never been a meeting in a church.

"Here we are," the earl said as the carriage rolled to a stop. "Be of good cheer and light heart, my dear. By the time you get home this night, you will laugh at the nerves that assault you now."

Viola hoped that was true. It would be very uncomfortable to go about always feeling as if your heart was about to fly out of your body.

A footman helped her down to the ground.

In what seemed to be time moving both faster than it ought and slower than it ought, vouchers were examined, tickets handed in, and into the foyer they went.

Viola's breath caught. There he was, Lord Baderston, looking even more glorious than she remembered.

It was just as they'd all imagined—he'd been there waiting for her. She was sure of it. His eyes had locked on hers and he hurried forward.

"Lady Viola," he said, the warmth of the timbre of his voice sending the blood to her cheeks.

"Lord Baderston," she said with a curtsy. "You know Miss Mayton, and Darden too, I think."

Lord Baderston bowed. "Miss Mayton. Lord Darden."

"And this is my father, the Earl of Westmont."

"My lord," Lord Baderston said. "A pleasure to know you."

Viola's father nodded graciously at Lord Baderston.

"Lady Viola," Lord Baderston said, "I have taken the liberty of retrieving your card. It can be a long walk to the cloak room."

Viola smiled. And would also like to pinch Darden, as he seemed as if he were holding back laughter over the idea of the long walk.

"That was very considerate, Lord Baderston," she said.

"I wonder," he said, "if I might step forward to escort you into the supper later this evening?"

"That would be most pleasant," she said.

Goodness, what was she saying? Most pleasant? It would be divine. It would be just as it ought to be. It would be perfect. Of course he must take her into supper. How else could it be?

Lord Baderston wrote his name down. As he handed her card to her and she slipped it on her wrist, a feminine voice was heard behind her.

"There you are, Baderston."

Viola turned her head, certain she would see the wretched Lady Clara who'd had the temerity to attend a house party at the lord's estate. Instead, it was a woman of late middle age.

"Mother," the lord said.

His mother! Viola felt rather sick. For all the time she had dreamed of Lord Baderston, she'd not for a moment considered his family. He had a living mother, and that lady would need to approve of her.

The gaze of the patronesses suddenly seemed as nothing. It was this lady who must be pleased.

Lord Baderston cleared his throat and said, "Dowager Countess of Baderston, may I introduce you to the Earl of Westmont, Miss Mayton, Lord Darden, and Lady Viola Bennington. My mother so rarely comes to Town, Earl, that I must presume you are not acquainted."

"On the contrary," the earl said. "Though it has been very many years gone by, I do recall our meeting several times over one season, Countess. We were all very young and full of fun then."

The dowager countess nodded, though she looked exceedingly cold about it. Viola would almost think the lady had reason to dislike her father.

That, of course, would be nonsense. Nobody in the wide world disliked her father.

Viola noticed the lady's eyes drifting to her wrist and the card that was on it. She glanced down herself—Lord Baderston's name down for supper was clearly visible.

The dowager countess frowned. "Have you yet seen Lady Clara?" she asked her son.

"Lady…uh…no," Lord Baderston said, looking decidedly uncomfortable.

The dowager countess turned to the earl. She said, "I only mention Lady Clara as we had the very good fortune of seeing her and her parents on our estate over the summer. We are all very fond of Lady Clara."

"I have not the pleasure of knowing her yet," the earl said. "Darden, I suppose you are acquainted with Lady Clara?"

"Yes, certainly, a genial lady," Darden said noncommittally.

"We do find her so," the dowager said. "And of course both she and her family are above reproach. Sticklers for propriety is how I would describe it—they never put a foot wrong. Some people simply have the right instincts for it."

Viola could feel her face growing red. It was one of the downfalls of her sort of coloring. Some ladies could hide their feelings, but hers raced to make a loud and public announcement.

Lord Baderston's mother seemed practically enamored with Lady Clara and far less so with her. She'd hardly given Viola a glance after they'd been introduced.

"Baderston, do escort me inside," the dowager said. She nodded to the earl and put her arm out for her son.

Lord Baderston did not look very enthused to be pulled away, but Viola supposed he had no choice. He bowed and took his leave, escorting his mother with her head held high.

"That was rather chilly," Miss Mayton said.

"Chilly?" Darden said with a laugh. "It was more like we'd accidently wandered into an icehouse."

"Yes," the earl said thoughtfully. "I had not thought…"

"Does she not like me?" Viola asked. "Why? She does not know me at all. Goodness, she must not like the look of me, as that is all she's had to go on."

"That cannot be," Miss Mayton said. "Everybody likes the look of you. I expect she is just an ornery sort of creature."

"She does not seem so ornery about Lady Clara," Viola pointed out. "She seemed very approving of that lady."

"Perhaps it has been the dowager that has pushed the idea of an engagement to Lady Clara," Darden said quietly. "I did notice her looking at your card—perhaps she expected her son to secure Lady Clara for supper."

"And she sees me as some kind of interloper!" Viola whispered back. "What shall I do?"

"Nothing," the earl said confidently. "Allow time to smooth over any difficulties, as time usually does. If I recall correctly, the dowager has always been a rather headstrong creature, but she will be sensible in the end."

"Father is right," Darden said. "Chin up, Sister, and let us proceed to face the patronesses. After all, Baderston will not be the only gentleman on your card this night."

Viola nodded. Of course, Darden was right, Lord Baderston would not be the only gentleman on her card.

It was just that he would be the only one who mattered.

ROLAND HAD ESCORTED his mother into the ballroom. Once he was a safe distance from Lady Viola and her family, he heatedly whispered, "What on earth was that performance?"

As he so rarely ever said anything heated to the lady and she was accustomed to delivering the heat from her end only, she looked at him in surprise.

"Excuse me?" she said haughtily.

"Do not pretend you do not know of what I speak. That was positively rude. I would know the cause of it."

"I do not care for the earl," she said sharply.

"Why? You haven't seen the fellow in nearly a quarter of a century. I've never even heard you speak the man's name."

"One does not need to speak of someone to dislike them. I have my reasons, and they are private."

Roland felt a real temper beating in his chest. He would not stand for this. It had been one thing to imagine his mother would have to be pulled away from the idea of Lady Clara and pulled toward the idea of Lady Viola.

He'd imagined she'd be irritated and argumentative over it. He had never, though, imagined she would be downright insulting to anybody over it. At least, not in public to the very person her ire was aimed at.

And for what? What could the earl possibly have done twenty-five years ago?

If he knew his mother, it was some ridiculous slight that she'd allowed to simmer on a low boil for all her adult life. Nobody could hold a grudge like she did—she still fumed that Lady Alicia had enticed away their cook, and that had been ten years ago.

Another thought occurred to him, as much as he wished it had not. Was it possible that the Earl of Westmont was the same earl who'd thrown her over all those years ago? It was a ghastly thought, and if true might cause all sorts of difficulties.

But no, that would be too coincidental. He must not build a house of problems with wisps of ideas.

"I won't stand for it," Roland said resolutely. "If you cannot behave with courtesy to the Benningtons, you can pack up and go home."

"Do not you dare—"

"It is my house," Roland said, "and those are my demands."

The dowager got rather red in the face over that idea. She was not used to being crossed. She was not accustomed to Roland asserting his rights.

Until now, there had been little reason to cross her or assert his rights over her.

Until now.

"Ah!" his mother said, suddenly smiling and all enthusiasm, "Lady Clara. Goodness, we have had our eye out for you, it is wonderful to see you again."

Roland turned to find Lady Clara standing there.

"Lord Baderston was just saying he would be destroyed if he'd missed the opportunity to take your first," his mother plowed on.

What was she doing?

"As it happens," Lady Clara said, "I have just arrived." She held her card out.

He was entirely boxed in. Poor Lady Clara could not know that his mother was inventing words out of the air.

Roland reluctantly took her card and penciled his name in for the first. There was simply nothing else he could do.

"I do hope you enjoyed your visit to our humble estate over the summer," the dowager said.

"I would hardly style it as humble, Countess," Lady Clara said.

"Well, perhaps not," the dowager conceded. "Though the size of the place did not awe you—you seemed quite at home."

Lady Clara blushed at the heavy hint. Roland seethed.

Seeing he had nothing to say to that comment, Lady Clara curtsied and moved on.

Quietly, he said, "Do not ever do that again. You are leading Lady Clara down a starry path that will go nowhere and she will not thank you for it. As for Lady Viola, I will make your excuses to her by claiming you have been unwell. Now, either go home or go to the card room. I have been shamed and will not be so again."

Watching the thoughts run through his mother's mind as they crossed her features reminded him of a caged animal calculating a way out.

Roland thought if feelings could take substance, hers this moment would burst her hair into flames.

She turned and swept from the ballroom, leaving him to plan out exactly how to repair this first ghastly meeting between Lady Viola and his mother.

And how to gently hint to Lady Clara that there was nothing between them.

THE EARL, MISS Mayton, and Lady Viola had been waved off as they departed for Almack's and now Tattleton stood by the drawing room doors, pretending that nothing at all was amiss. It was a butler's duty to always appear as if things were just as they should be.

Even when they most decidedly were not.

Just now, the noise in the room was deafening. It was one thing for Lady Cordelia to act out Desdemona's death scene from *Othello* in her usual energetic fashion. He'd become accustomed to it, though he was not certain that any Desdemona on a real stage did so much running to and fro and shouting, or setting things on fire with knocked-over candles.

Now, however, the bird must add in his own dramatic comments. The wretched creature was pacing its perch and doing everything in its power to mimic Lady Cordelia's words.

"Murder! Farewell!" it screeched.

He would consider himself lucky indeed if a shouting lady and screeching parrot were all he had to worry about.

That was not all, though.

Lady Viola had come to Town already entirely fixed on who she must marry.

It made no sense! She had only encountered the fellow very briefly last year, and now he was to be held above all others?

And for what reasons, exactly? He had red hair and liked

ham?

Though Tattleton, himself, had never been married, he could not think that was enough!

It was so likely to go wrong, and then what? Was Lady Viola to set out looking for another red-haired gentleman with a penchant for ham?

How many other redhaired eligible gentlemen could there be?

He was very afraid that there would not be many. Or any.

Tattleton thought himself very naïve indeed to have imagined that the launching of Lord Westmont's daughters was to be an easy stroll through the garden. What a fool he'd been three years ago, before they'd actually begun.

He'd been so full of confidence. He'd imagined that the ladies, being comely, pleasant, and well-funded, would walk into a ballroom somewhere and then walk out of it again engaged.

It should have been that easy! But no, the plots and intrigues of the last two seasons had defied even the wildest imagination.

"Murder, murder, murder!" the parrot screamed.

Tattleton took in a deep breath. He was a butler. Whatever else went on around him, he must keep his composure.

"Murder!"

That bird should really stop screeching about murder. It was beginning to give him ideas.

Of course, he would not act on them and actually wring its neck.

Though, there was no harm in soothing himself by imagining the thing lying lifeless in its cage, claws pointing skyward and silenced forevermore. Perhaps it would be felled by some kind of bird disease. Maybe it was already very old. After all, how could they tell? What did an old bird look like?

As if the bird could read his thoughts, it shouted, "Bad man!"

Tattleton glared at it. *Prove it, you wretch.*

CHAPTER FOUR

VIOLA WAS USUALLY of one mind at any given moment. This night was such a jumble of thoughts. Her head could not settle anywhere.

She had been relieved to see that wherever Lord Baderston's mother was, it was not in the ballroom.

However, the more she lived with her reception from that lady, the more uncomfortable she got with it.

What would he say about it? Would he acknowledge it at all? How important was the lady's opinion? Why did she seem so set on Lady Clara?

Darden had since pointed out Lady Clara and she seemed very usual. She was of average height, dark hair and dark eyes. Her dress was exceedingly pretty, but that could not be the whole of it.

The dowager had spoken of Lady Clara's propriety—was that a hint that she viewed the Benningtons in a less flattering light?

But then, what did Lord Baderston himself think? Did *he* favor Lady Clara?

She had wondered if Lady Clara was particularly amusing, but Darden said he could assure her that she was not.

Viola did not know what sort of hold Lady Clara had on Lord Baderston. And what sort of hold she had on his mother, for that matter. She could not, however, ignore what was in front of her eyes.

Lord Baderston had taken Lady Clara's first dance. Why would he do it if he had no regard for the lady?

The reality of the situation Viola had put herself in began to crystallize in her mind. She'd built a fantasy over the months, conveniently leaving out anybody who was not Lord Baderston. It had been a little childish, really.

That fantasy she'd built had included his developing feelings, though she had no real notion of whether they were there or not. His mother and Lady Clara had not made an appearance in those daydreams at all.

Lord Baderston had, of course, seemed to be waiting for her at the door. And then he did fetch her card and give the lovely excuse of it being a long walk.

But those two things might only point to a mild inclination, or curiosity. Countered with a mother who did not look kindly upon her and another lady seemingly approved of…well, it all felt a little doomed at the moment.

Viola took a breath and remembered that both Beatrice and Rosalind had experienced their own moments of feeling doomed. They had persevered on and the doom had gone up in a puff of smoke, as if it had never been.

Though, this particular doom was coming before they'd even danced together one time. It felt rather soon to be doomed.

Now, Lord Baderston was walking toward her, his lovely hair glinting in the candlelight. He really was charmingly handsome. His eyes were a deeper color than his hair, brown but still showing a hint of copper. He had a delightfully strong jaw and his complexion just the slightest bit ruddy. Who could not like the look of his features?

And then the rest of him! He was so well-proportioned. Her head reached just below his own, as if God had made him perfectly for her. His shoulders were broad and his build lean.

"Lady Viola," he said, holding out his arm.

As he led her to the line so they might take their places, he said, "Sometimes, Lady Viola, I find the best thing is to be direct, and to do so quickly."

Viola's heart sank. His serious tone. It was coming. He was to communicate that he would not be paying her any more attention, as his mother did not approve. Or that he had suddenly recalled his feelings for Lady Clara.

How odd though! Did gentlemen go round informing ladies that they'd been put off of them? It had been her understanding that they just quietly drifted away, not that they made an announcement about it.

"My mother has been unwell," Lord Baderston said. "She should not have come to London. She was too unwell to travel, and then Town has never agreed with her, and she does not care for balls and parties. It's all made her unusually prickly. That is no excuse, I know. I have informed her of that fact. But, you see, she's just not a particularly agreeable woman and she does sometimes let her moods get the better of her. In any case, I do hope you did not take offense."

Viola was rather stunned. "Offense? No, I was more…frightened."

"Do not be, I beg you. You will find her in better spirits when next you meet."

Could that be true? What a relief it would be if that turned out to be the case.

Viola felt herself lighter than she had been all night.

"And the rest of your family?" Lord Baderston asked. "Do you suppose they thought anything particular about the encounter?"

Viola smiled. "Well, Darden did say it felt like accidently wandering into an icehouse."

Lord Baderston colored. "Darden. And I having just joined the YBC."

He did seem very regretful over his mother's cool reception of her. And he did seem very sure it was an anomaly. Certainly, those were very positive signs.

"You really should not worry over it, my lord," Viola said. "The Benningtons take most things in stride and do not nurse pricked feelings."

"No?"

"No."

"Truly?"

"Truly."

Though she said it, Viola was not entirely certain she would soon forget the dowager's stance. However, Lord Baderston had just given her so many reasons to account for it and she should try to believe him. He claimed the lady had come through the doors already very out of sorts.

There were such ladies, she knew. The Benningtons had been blessed with Miss Mayton, who was never out of sorts. But that was not the case with every lady in their neighborhood. There was one particular spinster, Miss Fairweather, who suffered from arthritis and could be positively rude at times.

An ill temperament was not confined to women, either. What about Mr. Graydell, forever threatening people over his coveys? According to Mr. Graydell, his coveys were the center of the known world and every man in the vicinity was trying to get at them. No amount of sense and logic could convince him otherwise.

Viola resolved to look upon this night happily. Lord Baderston had waited for her, fetched her card, and taken her supper. She would not be thrown off by a person's mother who was not in a very good frame of mind to begin.

It became far easier to shake off any misgivings when Lord Baderston led her through the dance. How expert he was! There was something about his arm, it was very strong and there was a confidence to it.

Dancing with him was so different than what she had experienced at home. There, at the small parties with neighbors that she'd been allowed to attend, she'd be partnered with some callow youth who might not be very light on his feet and would spend the entire time looking embarrassed. The last she'd seen him, young John Haven had even had rivulets of sweat running down his face, such was his terror to be faced with a woman.

Lord Baderston smiled at her as they danced the figure of eight. She smiled back. He really was marvelous.

As the other dancers took their turns, she and Lord Baderston stayed smiling at one another.

Viola felt as if it would be very difficult to stop from smiling. She looked at him. He looked at her.

It was an odd sensation and she realized she had never before stared directly at a man's face for an extended period, other than her relations.

There was something intimate in it.

Viola was hardly cognizant that the dance had come to an end until Lord Baderston bowed and then held out his arm.

He led her into the dining room. Beatrice had told her that at any other ball, the dining room would be a lively place filled with people and food. Almack's would be rather more sedate, as nobody was in a hurry to secure its offerings or thrilled when they got them.

That did seem to be the case, as she could see several people looking morosely at their dry cake or stale bread and sour glasses of lemonade.

Perhaps nobody had told them to eat ahead of time, the poor creatures. Viola had eaten a full dinner earlier, and then a plate of biscuits just before leaving the house.

"Ah," Lord Baderston said, "I know just where we should go."

He led Viola to an older lady sitting near the far end of the room.

"Lady Hightower," he said, bowing. "May I introduce Lady Viola Bennington?"

"Another Bennington girl on the scene, eh?" Lady Hightower said. "Well, I am delighted. Your sister married my very good friend, Conbatten."

Viola curtsied. Lord Baderston pulled out a chair for her to sit next to Lady Hightower, while he took her other side and motioned for a footman.

"Indeed, my lady," Viola said, "we are delighted with the duke. Of course, we were all very grateful to you when you took Rosalind into your carriage after she was accosted by a pickpocket in the park last year."

Lady Hightower laughed and seemed to find amusement in it. "If I recall, it was your sister's darkest hour. At least, that is how she described it to me."

Viola felt herself going pink. It was clear enough that Lady Hightower did not consider having a handkerchief taken in the park to be a particularly dark darkest hour. At least she did not know the real circumstances of *that* encounter.

To change the subject, she said, "I recall Rosalind praising your musical evening last season."

At the mention of her musical evening, Lady Hightower almost had a look of alarm.

"Naturally," the lady said, "I will extend you an invitation this year. But, I wonder, Lady Viola, do you happen to play in a…similar style to the duchess?"

"Oh, no," Viola said, "nobody can play as Rosalind does."

"No, I would not think so. It was most surprising."

Viola nodded. "We all think so. One never does know where it's going—one minute a reel, the next a funeral march, the next a fugue. I am afraid I am far more pedestrian and can only read the sheet in front of me and play that."

Lady Hightower let out a breath, as if she'd been holding it. "That will do very well, I think."

A footman placed a slice of dry cake and a glass of lemonade in front of Viola. Lady Hightower leaned toward her and said quietly, "It is no accident that Baderston has steered you this direction, Lady Viola."

"It is not?"

To her other side, Lord Baderston laughed and said, "I only prayed that you had brought your interesting reticule with you, Lady Hightower."

Lady Hightower moved the tablecloth with her finger to reveal the largest reticule Viola had ever seen. It was somewhere between the size of a usual reticule and something a maid might use to carry things back from the grocers. It sat on the floor by her chair.

She picked it up and opened it to reveal a large corked bottle filled with a thick, white liquid of some sort.

"Sugar syrup," Lady Hightower said softly. "It can be used to good effect on absolutely anything that arrives at table in this place."

She uncorked the bottle and poured some of the mixture over Viola's cake and then added it to her lemonade for good measure.

"You see, Lady Viola," Lady Hightower said, "I arrive, I trounce Lady Agatha at piquet, she leaves in a pique over piquet, I pour sugar syrup on my dreadful cake, and I consider it an evening well spent. I believe the patronesses suspect me of adulterating their grim menu, but nobody dares confront the oldest bat in the rafters."

Viola found Lady Hightower to be an absolute delight. "Of course, I could not dare it myself," she said, "but I prodigiously admire it."

"You? Not dare it? Now, that does not sound like a Bennington lady to me."

As much as Viola was enjoying the conversation, Lady Hightower's attention was speedily sought on her other side by a gentleman friend hopeful of her sugar remedy.

Viola turned back to Lord Baderston, who was looking very amused.

"Oh dear," she said, looking at his plate, "you did not get any."

"I do not need any. I'd much prefer ham."

"As would I," Viola said. "Of course, we have the penchant for ham in common."

"I expect we probably have a lot in common."

"I think we must," Viola said, delighted with where the conversation was going. "Do you like to look at paintings?"

"I adore it," Lord Baderston said.

"Then I must tell you, I have taken up painting and have had the honor of meeting Mr. Thomas Lawrence."

"The famous portrait painter?"

"The very one," Viola said. "He was terribly interested in my work and even asked to see a piece I'd been working on."

"Gad, that's remarkable."

"I did get the feeling that he viewed it as very original," Viola said. "Now, what are your thoughts on *Othello*?"

"I find it one of Shakespeare's better plays," Lord Baderston said.

"I think so, too. I especially like Desdemona."

"Poor Desdemona."

"My sister, Cordelia, does a terrific Desdemona. Do you enjoy poetry, Lord Baderston?"

"Indeed I do," he said. "Wordsworth is doing some very interesting things these days."

"Wordsworth," Viola said with a sigh. "But do you not think he goes on rather long?"

"Long?" Lord Baderston said, knitting his brow. "Well, now that you point it out, I think you might be right about that. Yes, now that I look at it that way, his poems can go on a bit long."

"Just so," Viola said, nodding approvingly. "My younger sister, Juliet, writes very charming odes and they are only four lines."

"I see, yes, just four lines does seem better," Lord Baderston said.

"What would you say about the idea of loyalty, my lord?" Viola asked, eager to get to the most important point. "Would you not agree that it is a thing that must be demonstrated, rather than just talked about?"

"Demonstrated, yes, that does sound right."

"It must be proved, is what I have always thought."

"Proved must always be superior to just talked about. A person might spout off about any number of things, but until they are proved, well…"

"That is precisely it!"

And so they went on happily, comparing all the views they held in common. It was lovely that they liked so many of the same things, but the crucial idea had been settled between them.

He'd flat out said it—he understood that he would have to prove his loyalty to her and he seemed very prepared to do so.

Sitting next to him felt…well, she had a great urge to touch his hand. She had the feeling he would like to touch her hand too. There was a pull between them. It was as if the fates had searched the world over to discover Viola Bennington's perfect person and here he was, delivered to her.

Certainly, there could be nothing between him and Lady Clara. Certainly, he had never wished to hold that lady's hand.

Certainly, she hoped.

ROLAND TROTTED HIS horse through the streets, weaving round carriages that made their way home in the early hours of the morning.

What a night!

Of course, it had started off with a painful bump by way of his mother's rude behavior and meddling. She had been unconscionable in her behavior to the Benningtons, and then she'd topped it off by foisting Lady Clara upon him.

Lady Clara, herself, had made him uncomfortable in some way. She mentioned the visit over the summer several times and made comments about the house that would be better spoken of by the house's mistress.

He'd got a queasy feeling that perhaps the dowager had some sort of tête-à-tête with Lady Clara. If that was so, his mother would have misled the lady. He was sure of it. Furthermore, he knew in his heart that Lady Clara was not in love with him or even particularly attracted to him. If she did wish to go forward with an engagement, it was as calculating as his mother had been in marrying his father.

For all that had happened, though, the night had not ended on a bad note. No, not at all.

He'd made his mother's excuses to Lady Viola as best he could. What a lady she was to tell him he ought not to dwell on it! He thought many a lady would have been in a pique and would wish to have nothing further to do with the Trewellians.

Lady Viola was so gracious—a lesson his mother would not be harmed in learning.

After his apology, it had all gone swimmingly between them. Lady Viola was everything he'd imagined she would be. So beautiful, so graceful on the ballroom floor, so charming and genial. Her hair was a delightful cascade of varying shades running from blonde all the way to tawny with gold and red glints. Her eyes were a deep shade of blue and so lively and sparkling.

There was something in her smile that touched him, as if it were meant for him alone. It had made him imagine being alone with her. And perhaps made him think of things he ought not think about before a vicar put his signature to it.

They'd had a thorough conversation at supper, getting to know one another.

What an amount of ground they'd covered; he did not suppose he'd ever had another conversation like it.

He'd been able to work in his new love of ham very smoothly. Then he'd heartily endorsed the idea of liking to look at paintings.

Roland had not had the first inkling that Lady Viola was so talented in that area. To think, she'd come to the notice of portrait painter Mr. Thomas Lawrence. It was a striking idea. He could not say he had ever spent any great amount of time staring at paintings, but he was prepared to do it.

There had been a few points in the conversation where he'd not been entirely certain where his opinion ought to land. He'd been asked what he thought of *Othello*, and he'd thought he better say he preferred it. Else, why would she have mentioned it?

That had seemed right, though Lady Viola appeared to have a special place in her heart for Desdemona so he probably should go back and read that play again. As far as he recalled it, the play was about a crowd of hysterical people bent on revenge, murder, and suicide.

Then had come the subject of poetry and he'd really thought Wordsworth would be a safe choice. Who did not like Wordsworth? People were always talking about that fellow and spouting off quotes.

As it turned out, Lady Viola found the gentleman on the verbose side. She thought his poems were too long. Her sister wrote poems of four lines, which he assumed were special in some way, as Lady Viola had mentioned them.

What famous poet did she like, then? Was there a fellow known for brevity? He would have to ask around and find out.

But those few questions were easily remedied. He would stare at paintings and learn to like it, reread *Othello*, and dig up a poet who kept things short.

If there had been any moment in their exchanges that might have been concerning, it had been her opinions on loyalty.

He was all for it, of course. But Lady Viola seemed determined on the idea that it must be proved.

How did one go about proving loyalty? Naturally, had there been some crisis on the horizon and people choosing sides over a matter, he would march firmly into Lady Viola's camp.

But there was no such crisis looming. How was one to demonstrate loyalty when everything went along so well?

Perhaps he ought to ask Conbatten about it. He supposed Conbatten had been asked to prove his loyalty to Lady Viola's sister and had thought something up that was suitable.

Whatever it was, he would very happily do it in service to

Lady Viola. He would see her in two days' time, at Lady Rawley's theatrical evening, so perhaps he might have opportunity to prove it then?

After all, it *was* rather loyal to attend Lady Rawley's theatrical evening. He'd never consider going if Lady Viola had not mentioned she would go. It was always a painful thing to watch. Not only were Lady Rawley and her friends particularly unskilled actors, but they'd taken to rewriting poor Shakespeare's plays to suit their liking. He'd gone once, years ago, and had been very surprised to see that Romeo and Juliet lived happily ever after.

None of that mattered, though. Lady Viola had explained that Miss Mayton very much enjoyed the evening last season and had even been called upon to step into a role after Lady Agatha had been taken ill. They were very much looking forward to it this year, as it was to be *Much Ado About Nothing*.

He would dig out that invitation and accept first thing in the morning.

And to think, Lady Viola preferred his hair color above all others.

Very suddenly, his life had become extraordinary.

CHAPTER FIVE

V IOLA COULD NOT be more satisfied with her circumstances. She was beginning to be puzzled by how much trouble Beatrice and Rosalind had been put to in securing their own loves.

Everything to do with Lord Baderston was falling into place very effortlessly.

Of course, there were some small matters that had not yet been ironed out. She must find a way to ingratiate herself to the lord's mother, but certainly that was not insurmountable. After all, as far as Viola knew, everybody she was acquainted with liked her. Why should the dowager countess be any different?

Then, on occasion, Viola did wonder about Lady Clara. The dowager certainly favored her and Lord Baderston had taken the lady's first dance at Almack's.

She would remind herself that she must not fret over these things when there was so much else that had gone well.

Lord Baderston had said he would attend Lady Rawley's theatrical evening on the morrow after Viola had said she would go.

No, it was more than that. He'd said he never did attend, but if she were going then so would he.

She might wish the intervening hours that must be gone through to pass by speedily, but she also knew there would be much to entertain and occupy her this night.

Van Doren and Beatrice had arrived to their own house on Portland Place and Rosalind and Conbatten were now installed in Grosvenor Square. All four would come to dinner.

"What a jolly time we will have this evening," Juliet said, lounging in the drawing room and waiting for her two eldest sisters and their husbands to arrive.

"Murder!" Chester shouted from his cage.

They all pretended they did not hear him. Chester had acquired the unfortunate habit of screeching "murder" after listening to several renditions of Cordelia's Desdemona. It was agreed between them that when he said something pleasant, like "charming Chester," they would give him an almond. When he shouted about murder they would ignore it. They hoped this would lead him away from thoughts of murder, though he did get very excited when Cordelia began her speech.

"I've written an ode to jolly times," Juliet said. "It's called *Ode to Jolly Times.*"

Juliet cleared her throat.

Conbatten and Rosalind, Van Doren and Beatrice
Joined in matrimony and sealed with a kiss
Now they come merrily through our door
All charming but for Van Doren, the tragic bore.

Viola laughed and said, "That is so apt, Jules. Do not recite it in front of Van Doren though. Beatrice has enough on her hands to manage him and I am sure our Rosalind would not care for lecture number one hundred and nine regarding her kidnapping."

"Yes, I suppose you're right," Juliet said. "Though how he thinks we could have predicted our plan would go wrong is quite beyond me."

Just then, Cordelia came in with a bag of almonds for Chester.

"Murder!" he cried.

"Oh goodness, Chester, I am afraid you've taken the word

murder to be a request for almonds. It doesn't mean that at all."

Despite their vow that they should not reward Chester for shouting about murder, Cordelia fed him a handful of nuts.

They all three leapt up as Tattleton strode through the door.

In a marvelously stern and dignified tone, he said, "His Grace, the Duke of Conbatten and Her Grace, the Duchess of Conbatten."

Viola thought Tattleton had grown rather fond of announcing the duke.

They exchanged greetings and Juliet did not waste a moment before inquiring if her wedding present—an ode called *When the Love is True*—had been properly hung yet.

"As you are aware," the duke said, "I early concluded that such an important piece of literature must be housed in a special room. I have spared no expense in remaking the music room into what we now call the 'family room.' Carpets were replaced, paper hangings selected, and the finest furniture installed. All done for the family, as I will never allow an outsider through its doors."

"It's marvelous, Juliet," Rosalind said. "And Viola, the portrait you painted of us is hung in there too."

"Any gift from the Bennington family will find its way to that place of honor," Conbatten said. "I will never house these remarkable gifts anywhere else."

Soon after, Beatrice and Van Doren, being just across the road, were led into the drawing room.

After greetings were exchanged, meaningful looks were passed between the sisters. Juliet said, rather forcefully, "Conbatten, Van Doren, come and meet Chester while we wait for everybody else."

Clever Juliet. As she had not asked those two gentlemen whether they cared to meet Chester or not, they were stuck with it.

Viola slipped off to the far end of the room with Beatrice and Rosalind while Juliet and Cordelia informed Van Doren and the duke of everything they knew about Chester. And probably some things they didn't, but thought must be true.

Viola, Beatrice, and Rosalind sat themselves in a cozy corner. Viola said, "Now, before I tell you of my progress, you will tell me of your own. Rosalind, how does Conbatten treat you?"

Rosalind leaned back and looked very dreamy. "He is wonderful. You would be surprised to know how many times danger has lurked round me, but Conbatten always spots it. Just now, on our way over here, he noted a carriage driven by an intemperate coachman and he threw his arms round me lest our own carriage was forced into a sudden swerve to avoid it. It seems he is always saving me from something or other."

"Now, I did wonder," Viola said, "if all those stories that go round about him are really true."

"The bath," Beatrice said, laughing.

"Yes," Viola said, "the idea that he takes a bath at precisely ninety-eight degrees."

"Oh yes, that is perfectly true," Rosalind said. "I often join him in it."

"Do you?" Viola said, intrigued by the idea.

Rosalind nodded. "I wear my best diamond necklace and we have all of our important marriage conversations in it while we drink champagne."

"What are important marriage conversations?" Viola asked, wishing to be prepared for what they were comprised of.

"Well, I might say that I was thinking of changing the wallpaper in the dining room and Conbatten will say I must have whatever I wish. Or I might say that I adore the emerald ring he just bought for me, and he'll say he's decided I'd better have a necklace to match it."

"That's rather smashing," Beatrice said. "I wonder if I could talk Van Doren into a bath."

"He is such a curmudgeon," Viola said, "except when it comes to you. I imagine you could talk him into anything. I trust he remains very solicitous of you?"

"Exceedingly so," Beatrice said. Then she dropped her voice

very low. "I expect that care to only increase very soon. I am with child and past the danger, but he does not know it yet."

Viola and Rosalind grasped their sister's hands. "Wonderful!" Rosalind exclaimed.

Viola glanced down to her sister's midsection. It was indeed looking rather thicker than it ever had.

"He does not notice, though?" Rosalind asked. "When you…well, when you are…less dressed?"

Beatrice giggled. "He *has* noticed my recent expansion, but I have been clever about it. I fret to him that I am eating too many cakes, and really, I am eating everything in sight these days. He says I may grow as big as a house and he will not mind it. I will tell him soon, I just wished to get to Town first. I feel wonderful, but if he'd heard the news in Somerset, he'd never have allowed me into a carriage."

"Good thinking," Viola said.

"Now Viola, we can wait no longer," Rosalind said. "Have you seen Lord Baderston?"

"I have," she said. "He is everything wonderful and I will see him on the morrow too. He took my supper at Almack's and we had an in-depth conversation about our opinions on things. We are so similar!"

"And he understands your ideas about loyalty?" Rosalind asked.

"Yes, and he seemed quite eager to prove his loyalty."

"How will he, though?" Beatrice asked. "We all saw how much trouble Rosalind had to go to so that Conbatten could show his courage. I will not even refer to my own adventures in love, as they are too ridiculous to recount."

Viola nodded, as she'd had the same thoughts herself. Her sisters had not had an easy time of it and how *was* Lord Baderston to prove his loyalty?

"I cannot be certain yet," she said, "but it is early days. Certainly, something must come up."

Beatrice rubbed her chin. "Hmm," she said. "It is difficult to think of something. Everything is so perfect between you."

"Yes, perfect…" Viola trailed off. As much as she would push two particular ladies out of her mind, Lord Baderston's mother and Lady Clara were very insistent on pushing their way back in.

"What are you not saying, Vi?" Rosalind asked.

"Well, one thing is, at Almack's, you see Lord Baderston's mother was there."

"The dowager?" Rosalind asked. "I understood she never came to Town. At least, I did inquire of Conbatten any facts he might know about Baderston and he mentioned that. He also said it was well she did not, as she was not a very happy woman."

"She is here," Viola said, "and it is true that her temperament seems less than genial. Lord Baderston told me that himself, after apologizing for her."

"Apologizing! Goodness, what did the lady do?"

"Rather what she *said*. When we were introduced, she was very cold. And curt. And held a very high opinion of some other lady." Viola paused, then said in a whisper, "And it even seemed as if she did not like Papa."

"The woman must be mad," Rosalind said. "Everyone likes Papa."

"Do not worry, Vi, she's bound to come round," Beatrice said. "Now what is the other problem? You said the dowager is *one* problem."

"Yes, well I suppose I wonder about this other lady. The dowager is very approving of her, and Lord Baderston took her first dance."

"Perhaps he had no choice," Rosalind said. "Perhaps that was the only one that was open?"

"That seems unlikely though," Viola said. "Would all the other gentlemen have passed on it?"

Just then, their tête-à-tête was interrupted by the earl, Darden, and Miss Mayton coming into the drawing room.

"We'd best rejoin the party," Beatrice said. "Juliet and Cordelia have kept our husbands examining that parrot for long enough. Poor Van Doren, he is not at all fond of the idea of a bird in the house."

"Chin up, Viola," Rosalind said. "It will all come right, I am certain it will."

Viola nodded and did put her chin up. What else could she do?

TATTLETON HAD EXPRESSLY ignored the wretched bird when announcing that the family might go through to dinner. That little heathen might scream murder all it liked, with no reaction from him.

He would not condescend to notice the creature. He was a butler, not a zookeeper.

A bird like that, with a brain the size of a pea, could not be expected to understand the gravity of this particular dinner.

It was not just the immediate family anymore. The Benning-tons had expanded their intimate circle.

He was used to serving Lord Westmont, Miss Mayton, occa-sionally Lord Darden, and the earl's daughters. Then of course, Lord Van Doren, being a neighbor in Somerset, had often been on the scene. An earl, two viscounts, and four ladies.

How things had changed. Now, they had a duke and duchess on hand. A *duke*. There was nobody placed higher but for the royal family. His Grace, the Duke of Conbatten, was now a relation.

Tattleton had already noted the duke look approvingly at the wine he'd selected. He'd managed to discover, through a vast network of servants, that the duke had been exceedingly admiring of a certain dry Tokay he was served at Lady Hightower's house last season.

It had not been easy to find, but he'd contacted every wine merchant in the city until he'd located one who had the stuff.

Now, with great aplomb, he served it as if it were a mere trifle. After all, it would be very un-butler-like were he to allow the perspiration of the effort to be seen on his countenance.

"Excellent wine, Earl," the duke said. "I believe I had something similar at Lady Hightower's last season."

"The dry Tokay," Rosalind said. "I remember how much you liked it."

The earl sipped his wine and said, "Yes, it's very good indeed, though I do not recall having it in my cellar. Tattleton, is this a new acquisition?"

Tattleton nodded gravely.

"If you would, Tattleton, please inform my valet of your sources," the duke said. "He's gone half mad trying to get the contact out of Lady Hightower's butler."

Tattleton delivered his most restrained and dignified nod.

He could not care less what else was said at the table. His wine selection had been noticed by the duke and he'd been tasked with advising the duke's valet.

His victory was complete.

ROLAND SHOULD NOT have allowed himself to be caught in the library. Though the house in Town was large by London standards, it was much smaller than his house in Dorset. It gave him the feeling that his mother was round every corner. No, not just the feeling—she *was* round every corner.

He ought to have had his correspondence sent up to his bedchamber and dealt with it there.

The dowager had been lying in wait downstairs and as soon as he'd gone in, she'd followed him, and shut the door behind her.

"Baderston," she said, "I have heard the most alarming things about the Bennington family."

Roland did not answer.

"I see from your lack of questions that you already know to what I refer," the dowager sniffed. "Apparently, during Lady Beatrice's season there were fellows lining up on the pavement at Portland Place. They were all from a certain club."

"The Young Bucks Club, of which I am currently a member," Roland said.

"Young bucks?" the dowager sputtered. "You consider yourself a young buck now? What next? Will you style yourself a Corinthian? Or worse, a dandy?"

Roland did not respond. Though, had he answered, he would have pointed out he was far more suited to the Corinthian's life than he was to Brummel's careful stylings. Give him a horse and some fences to clear any day—his clothes were his valet's problem.

"And then, as if a line of gentlemen callers was not disturbing enough, along comes the next sister—Lady Rosalind," the dowager said.

Roland attempted to keep his expression neutral. Though the talk had been tamped down quickly, there *had* been some alarming stories gone round.

"Lady Jersey told me, quite confidentially, that it is said that Lady Rosalind arranged her own kidnapping so that the Duke of Conbatten could rescue her. It's all hushed up now, at the queen's direction."

Of course, Roland had heard that precise thing too, and it *had* been hushed by the palace. Queen Charlotte seemed to favor Conbatten and would not allow the talk to bloom for long.

He really did not know how much, if any, of the original story was true. Darden, usually so voluble, was very quiet on the subject.

"And then," the dowager rushed on, "Lady Jersey tells me that the woman named Miss Mayton, the bizarre lady who attends entertainments in widow's weeds, has never even been married! Is that really a proper guide for young ladies? No wonder one of them arranged to be kidnapped."

Roland felt his cheeks color just a little bit over Miss Mayton. He did not know what else the dowager knew about that lady, but all of society took her to be quite the eccentric. Her preposterous stories had raised eyebrows—he'd heard just that morning that at Almack's she'd entertained her whist partners with a tale of a Swedish count who'd been despairing of his love for her and somehow come to a bad end.

"Did you know," the dowager said, "that this Miss Mayton tells some rather delusional stories about herself? She claims she nearly married a French fellow, but he hung himself in his garret, believing his love was unrequited. Now, I ask you, what reasonable person knows somebody who lives in a garret?"

"It seems to me," he said, "that since Lady Jersey has so much to say about the Benningtons, it is a wonder she still sponsors them all at Almack's."

The dowager's lips tightened. "She does so because Lady Rosalind went and married the duke, giving her protection forevermore. And, I believe Lady Jersey has…a blind spot regarding those girls' distasteful father."

"The Earl of Westmont?" Roland asked. "What can you possibly have against the fellow that is significant? You cannot tell me he's ever done anything to seriously injure you."

"Can I not?"

"If you can, which I highly doubt, then I would know it," Roland said resolutely.

"It's none of your business," the dowager said curtly.

"I am going to the stables to have a look at Tempest's foreleg."

"We have not finished this conversation. Barnard tells me you have no engagements this evening. We will dine together and discuss these distressing matters further."

"Barnard does not know everything," Roland said. "I will be out."

It was perfectly true; he would be out. He would not, however, inform his mother that he was set to attend Lady Rawley's theatrical evening solely because Viola Bennington would be there.

He also did not care about what talk went round about Lady Beatrice or Lady Rosalind or Miss Mayton. They were not Viola Bennington. Viola Bennington was a charming lady who would never cause talk. She could not be measured by anybody else's yardstick.

"I see," the dowager said. "I had been willing to forgo my own plans to attend you, but as that is not to be, then I will be out too. However, Baderston, you cannot be 'out' forever. We will discuss this further."

The dowager swept out of the room and Roland thought he'd better have a quiet word with Barnard. If the dowager asked his butler again for his calendar, he was always to be out.

Roland sighed. He would like to make his mother happy, as anybody would. The problem was, she was never happy. Even when she claimed a thing would make her happy, she never seemed very happy to get it.

He was well aware that she was so set on Lady Clara because she viewed the lady as being very pliant. The dowager always wished to dominate, and certainly that was what she wished for in a relationship with a daughter-in-law. Lady Clara had deferred to her on all matters when she had visited the house.

This was a problem he would have to solve himself. He would not allow a lady, whoever she turned out to be, to become the mistress of his estate, only to find herself browbeaten by the elder woman in the dower house.

Roland had hopes that the lady who would eventually come to his estate might be Viola Bennington. He had not stopped thinking about her since he'd met with her at Almack's. Really, he had not stopped thinking about her since he met her last year in the park. He could not imagine there would ever be another like her.

It was funny, really. Until he'd met Lady Viola last season, he'd convinced himself that he was in no hurry to marry. Would not thirty, which was some years off, be the right time?

He'd looked at the whole thing as a chore and a duty. Heirs must be had.

Now, he felt as if his future happiness hung in the balance. Roland realized that he'd used his parents' marriage as the example of the wedded state. It had not looked like something to run to, but rather just a thing that must be done, like patching the roof or auditing the wine cellar.

Everything was different now. Viola Bennington had changed everything.

If things were to proceed as they had so far...well, he would not countenance an unpleasant situation made so by the dowager.

Roland shook himself from his reverie. His mother could be managed, one way or another. In the meantime, he would see Lady Viola this very night.

CHAPTER SIX

VIOLA AND MISS Mayton had set off very early, on account of Lady Rawley sending an urgent note earlier in the afternoon.

It seemed that Lady Marie, who was to be part of Lady Rawley's theatrical, had been suddenly called away by an old aunt's grave illness in Kent. Lady Rawley recalled how helpful Miss Mayton had been last season, when Lady Agatha had been struck down with a stomach complaint—might she condescend to step into the breach again?

Lady Rawley wrote that there was only one line to be memorized and she dearly hoped Miss Mayton would take pity on her.

Very naturally, Viola's aunt had written back with alacrity—it was no sooner asked than it was accepted. It would be her honor to provide whatever little service was needed.

They would arrive early to fit the costume and review the line before the other guests arrived.

"Goodness," Miss Mayton said, gripping the invitation in her hand as the carriage rumbled along, "this is all very exciting."

"Cordelia was beside herself," Viola said. "How she would have wished to be called upon for such a duty."

Miss Mayton nodded. "I was able to soothe her by pointing out that I will have done two favors for Lady Rawley now and we are very much *in* with that lady. Next year, when it is Cordelia's time to come out, I have high hopes for the theatrical. Just think, if I am called on again, I can accept and then at the last-minute claim I have twisted my ankle and cannot proceed."

"But Cordelia could," Viola said, marveling at her aunt's cleverness.

"Naturally, as she would have helped me to practice."

"Do let me see the invitation for this evening," Viola said, "so I may picture where your name would go on it, in place of Lady Marie."

Miss Mayton handed over the sheet.

In this exciting new idea of Much Ado About Nothing, things proceed as expected, until the final question must be answered. After all the trials poor Hero has been put through, will she still consent to marry Claudio? Or, will she turn to someone else? If so, who? What does her father think of the goings-on? (Heads are spinning as Hero finally sets forth the path to her own destiny!) All will become known in the most dramatic terms in a final revealing moment.

Cast: Hero played by the incomparable Lady Margaret Rawley

Claudio played by the indomitable Mrs. Jemima Robinson

Hero's father Leonato, played by the indubitable Lady Agatha Montfried

Beatrice played by the indispensable Lady Marie Hedwedder

Viola laid the paper in her lap. "Lady Marie was to be indispensable. Now it is you who have become indispensable, Aunt."

Miss Mayton nodded contentedly.

Viola was thrilled for her, naturally. Of course, the play would be interesting. But the really interesting thing about the evening would be Lord Baderston.

Would he sit near her? Would he instantly perceive that she was, for all intents and purposes, unchaperoned, as her aunt was preparing to take the stage?

Perhaps the chairs would be situated very close together and he might accidentally brush her hand.

What a delicious thing to wonder about.

ROLAND'S VALET, MARKSON, had been more than a little surprised to discover that Lady Rawley's invitation to a theatrical evening had been accepted.

Roland supposed most earls never knew if their valet was surprised by any matter, as the fellows would keep that sort of thing under wraps and only mention it at the servants' table.

Markson, however, had been a boyhood friend. They had run through the woods and fished and wrestled throughout childhood. Markson was meant to be a tenant farmer, just like his father, but he'd never taken to it.

Markson had been observant and clever, though, and it had seemed to him that nobody did less work than a valet. He'd slipped his way into the house as a footman and then made the very astute move of ensuring that Roland's mother was the recipient of a constant stream of compliments.

He and Markson used to laugh about it. Markson would get himself in the countess' presence somehow and then shake his head and say softly, "A shame it ain't my place to speak of it."

The countess would naturally press him on this thing that could not be spoken. Then Markson would say something along the lines of, "My lady, it's just that I was in the village on my day off and everybody was talkin' of when you went by in the carriage last Wednesday and how there was not a more regal looking lady anywhere. They'd dare any county to claim there was."

The countess became very fond of Markson and he was promoted to Roland's valet when he was of an age to have one.

"I remember you did complain, though," Markson said now, "that Lady Rawley's theatricals were a torture. The last time you went, Romeo and Juliet both lived on very happily and had several children."

"Romeo named his eldest son Romiet, as a combination of *Romeo and Juliet* so, yes, I did complain. Rather bitterly, if I recall," Roland said. "This evening, Lady Rawley is set to massacre *Much Ado About Nothing*. My guess is, it will be much ado about something entirely ridiculous."

"Shakespeare won't like it. You won't like it. Why go?"

"Because a certain Viola Bennington is going."

Markson laid his forefinger along the side of his nose. "I understand you now. A bit of fun, is she?"

"A bit of fun!" Roland said. "Do not ever refer to Lady Viola as a bit of fun. She is nothing of the sort."

"Ah well, if she's a lady and she ain't fun, I reckon the dowager is all in for her."

"Actually, the dowager is anything *but* all in. And anyway, Lady Viola is fun, she is just not a bit of fun. At least, not in the way you mean it."

"Does that mean Lady Clara is off, then?"

"Lady Clara was never on."

"But Lady Viola is on?"

Roland nodded. "Lady Viola is very much on. I only hope she views it the same way."

"And the dowager don't like her already. Well! Let the fireworks fly then!"

VIOLA FOUND LADY Rawley an amusing woman—she spoke of the theater in exceedingly lofty terms and made several references to "treading the hallowed boards."

For all that though, one could not help but like her. The lady's gratitude to Miss Mayton for "bravely stepping into the breach" was very touching.

Viola wandered the as-yet empty drawing room while Lady

Rawley rehearsed the theatrical with her friends and Miss Mayton.

The seating was set up round the stage, in groups of four chairs, each grouping with a small table placed in front where one might put things down.

The actors were dressed in yards and yards of white lawn, but for Mrs. Robinson, who was in some sort of soldier's uniform. Miss Mayton's skirt was far too long, but there was nothing to be done about it at such a late hour.

Viola could not say precisely what was to take place in this new play, or if it was even a complete play. As far as she could tell, the whole thing would center round the end, when Hero arrives to wed Claudio for the second time, so perhaps it was only a dramatic scene.

It was all rather strange, as Mrs. Robinson, who was to play Claudio, had just been fitted with a small pigskin sack of something or other under her helmet.

Why was Claudio wearing a helmet to his wedding to Hero? What was in the sack?

The footmen had been in and out a dozen times and had three sideboards set up. It was very elaborate with all sorts of sweets and savories.

The first board held lamb tartlets, sliced roasted beef, dressed rabbit with boiled onions and herbs, stewed duck with peas, turbot in a mushroom sauce, and loveliest of all, sliced ham. Lord Baderston would be so pleased to see the ham, as he did like it as much as she did.

The second board was heavy with sweets: Portugal cakes, seed cakes, iced pound cakes, macaroons, custards, ices, nuts, and dried plums.

The third board was crowded with bottles of wine and champagne, a punch bowl, and a tea and coffee service.

Whatever was to be experienced this night, nobody would go hungry.

Lady Rawley had paused in her running to and fro across the

stage and took a deep breath. "My fellow thespians," she said, "we are ready to surprise and delight our audience with an original styling of the illustrious bard's work. Shakespeare was a great man of his time, but we humbly make those little changes that may elevate his already lofty words."

"Goodness," Miss Mayton said, swimming in her white muslin.

Viola suppressed her laughter. She could not imagine what Shakespeare would think upon finding that his words were to be elevated by Lady Rawley and her fellow thespians.

"Now," Lady Rawley continued, "my guests will arrive timely as we will begin the performance at nine o'clock and everybody will wish for refreshment beforehand. Let us follow their wise lead and raise a glass of the noble grape to steady us."

Lady Rawley was entirely an original. She was a bit of a dear, really.

She was also not wrong about how the evening was to kick off—her guests did begin to arrive in a steady stream. As most of them made their way directly to the sideboards, Viola got the idea that it was one of the particular draws of the evening.

Viola did her best to attempt to be subtle in where her gaze was going, but she could not help but keep her eye on the door.

She looked for lovely copper-colored hair and an easy smile. She looked for Lord Baderston.

Viola blinked when she caught sight of a person completely unexpected. And unwished for.

The dowager countess, Lord Baderston's mother.

Viola quickly turned away and hoped she had not caught the lady's attention. For all Lord Baderston claiming the lady would be in better spirits when she was next encountered, Viola had found herself not entirely convinced of it.

But then, why was she worried about the dowager being in the same room? It was not as if the woman would wish to seek her out and this was not the sort of party where everyone must be introduced.

Oh, but Lord Baderston would come and his mother was here. He might find he must attend her.

Viola was feeling exceedingly deflated upon considering that Lord Baderston would be taken up with ensuring his mother's comfort.

Well, at least she would see him, if not spend much time talking to him.

"Lady Viola," she heard behind her.

Viola turned slowly. She curtsied and said, "Dowager Countess."

⇶⇶⫷⫷

ROLAND ARRIVED TO Lady Rawley's house in good time and hurried into the drawing room to find Lady Viola.

The last person he'd expected to find was his mother. Worse, the lady was talking to Lady Viola. Why? What was she up to?

He made his way over, determined to interrupt whatever it was she was doing.

"Lady Viola, Mother," he said. He looked at the dowager and said, "I did not know you would attend this evening."

"Nor did I, until I had a second look at your calendar and found this added," she said cooly.

Blast. Now she was snooping into his calendar and following him round London.

"Lady Viola was just going to accompany me to a chair, Baderston. Do get us plates—bring the lamb tartlets and a dry wine, if you please."

Roland would really like to escort Lady Viola away in another direction. She was looking particularly smashing in a cream silk dress edged with seed pearls. What she was *not* looking, however, was comfortable in the dowager's presence.

Seeing as he could not steal Lady Viola away without somehow causing a scene and embarrassing her, he nodded and marched to the sideboard.

There was indeed a generous supply of lamb tartlets, which he'd fully expected there would be since the dowager was particularly skilled at sizing up a sideboard.

There was also ham, and Roland would not for the world allow Lady Viola to believe that he'd forgotten her fondness for it. In fact, he would get ham for himself too. It would make a statement. Of some sort.

He commandeered two footmen, as he could not carry three plates and three glasses at once.

From past theatricals, Lady Rawley had seemed to realize that it was a near impossible feat to eat from a plate and drink from a glass with no table to set things down on. She'd since arranged things more comfortably, with the rows spaced further apart and a small table in front of every four chairs.

As he led the footmen back, he noted his mother had set things up rather diabolically. Lady Viola was seated at the end of the row, with his mother on the other side. There would be no opportunity to sit next to her.

The dowager looked down at the plates set in front of her—one of lamb tartlets and one of ham.

Before she could comment, he said, "Lady Viola, I remember your fondness for ham, as I am very fond of it myself." He looked determinedly at his own plate of ham to better make the point.

Lady Viola nodded. "You are very kind to remember it, Lord Baderston."

"You can sit there, Baderston," the dowager said, pointing to her other side.

Roland sighed. He had dearly hoped to find himself sitting by Lady Viola. He'd imagined they might whisper to each other throughout the performance. He might even accidentally brush her hand. He certainly had not the slightest interest in actually watching the play. He'd only come to be near Lady Viola. Now he found the dowager was to be between them.

"Elegant ladies and esteemed gentlemen," Lord Iverson said

from the stage. "If you would take your seats we are set to begin."

Roland smiled. Lord Iverson had announced the beginning of the ill-fated *Romeo and Juliet* scene too, years ago. He supposed the fellow was a keen admirer of Lady Rawley's theatrical stylings. Or perhaps just an admirer of Lady Rawley, as they were both widowed.

The lady herself was helped up to the stage and following her was her troupe of actors. Just like the last time, there was Lady Agatha and Mrs. Robinson.

But the last lady, trailing a dress that was far too long…Miss Mayton.

Gad, he'd been so taken up by finding Lady Viola with the dowager he'd not even thought to wonder where her chaperone was.

To his right, his mother said, "Is that your aunt, Lady Viola?"

"Indeed, yes, Dowager Countess," Lady Viola said. "She was entreated to step in at the last minute, as Lady Marie was called away from Town."

The dowager pursed her lips, though Roland could not guess why. Lady Rawley's attempts at playacting were faintly ridiculous, but there could be nothing shocking about Miss Mayton taking part in it.

The dowager then leaned toward Lady Viola and said something else, but she'd lowered her voice and he could not hear what it was. It seemed she was whispering in a rush, as if she must hurry to communicate her thoughts.

Whatever it was, he did not think it was particularly pleasant, if Lady Viola's expression were anything to go by. She had looked at the dowager with her eyes wide and then quickly averted them to the stage.

He would have to speak to the dowager later about that. If it were another episode of rudeness, he would pack her bags.

"My friends," Lady Rawley said, "I give you *Much Ado About Nothing*, as I imagined in my own mind how that unfortunate situation, had it been real, might have played out."

As Roland watched the scene unfold, he began to think that nothing particularly rational had occurred in Lady Rawley's mind while she'd been imagining.

Hero was just now preparing to meet Claudio at the altar for try number two and had very alarmingly hidden a sword in the folds of her wedding dress. Claudio, for his part, was inexplicably wearing a helmet to meet his bride.

As Hero reached the side of her betrothed, Claudio apologized profusely for believing a pack of lies about her. He was also very sorry that she'd supposedly died of grief over it. He was, according to him, very pleased that she was still alive.

Hero's father, Leonato, laughed and said, "I hath been thinking—all's well that ends well, the end justifies the means, forgive and forget, where there's a will there's a way, what's done is done, and so on and so forth."

Hero spun toward her father. "Father!" she cried. "Hath you the carelessness to pledge me to this faintheart of a boy? Hath *I* the folly to wed such an unsteady man? I will take Benedick instead."

Roland set down his glass of wine. That certainly hath been a twist.

Miss Mayton, playing Beatrice, stepped forward. "I hath already pledged to him, cousin."

"Then I hath at least my revenge on Claudio!" Hero cried.

She raised the sword from the folds of her dress and struck poor Lady Agatha, playing Claudio, over the head.

Ah, so that was the reason for the helmet.

The players all stood there staring at one other, as if somebody had forgotten a line.

Claudio blinked hard at Hero, as if to remind the lady of something or encourage her on.

Hero nodded and then hit Claudio over the head again. There was a sudden spurt of red liquid that rained down on the coat of his uniform.

Lady Rawley's audience gasped.

Claudio cried, "I hath been killed for being of faint heart!" He dropped dramatically to the floor and the other actors bowed to the audience.

Roland drained his wine. Did he just see what he thought he did? It was all rather…well, it was…He gave up. He did not know what it was.

Lady Rawley's guests, finally understanding that they'd *not* just witnessed Lady Agatha bleeding from the head, although she did seem a bit stunned, took up an applause.

The dowager suddenly grabbed hard at his arm. At barely a whisper, she said, "I am feeling exceedingly faint from this display. Escort me out."

Roland saw that she was pale and small beads of perspiration had formed on her forehead. He leapt up and took her arm.

"Lady Viola," he said, bowing as well as he could under the circumstances. He supported the dowager to the front doors, hoping the fresh air would prove conducive to her condition.

A chair was fetched and her carriage called for. Lady Rawley's butler offered to fetch a vinaigrette, but the dowager refused. Rather, she stayed draped over the chair, softly moaning, and Roland wondered if she would fall to the ground at some point.

He would have to send for a doctor. He'd never seen the dowager in such a state as this.

Roland made arrangements for one of Lady Rawley's grooms to bring his horse home so he might ride in the carriage, lest the lady faint in the vehicle. Fortunately, it was not too long a time before the dowager's coach arrived.

He helped her into it, feeling a little guilty about all the sharp words that had passed between them recently. She could be meddling and tiresome, but she was still his mother, after all.

She settled herself in the seat and Roland climbed in after her. The carriage set off.

He said, "We will be back at the house soon."

The dowager suddenly sat up and took on an entirely different mien. "It is a miracle. I am very suddenly well," she said.

The scheme the dowager had just enacted came to him in a flash. She had faked the whole performance and was not the least bit ill.

She was a far better actress than Lady Rawley and her friends.

"Yes, I see you understand me," she said.

"You must stop this ridiculous interference at once," Roland said.

The dowager shrugged, as if he'd said nothing at all.

"What was it you said to Lady Viola just before the performance started?"

"Nothing of consequence, as she is of no consequence."

"I will warn you once more—continue on with your rudeness to Lady Viola and you will find yourself back in the dower house before you can blink. Furthermore, if you press me far enough, you will find your time in the dower house grim indeed, as invitations to the main house will dwindle to nothing. It will be a lonely existence, as you are not well-loved in the neighborhood."

The dowager stared at him. "I do not believe London is doing anything wonderful for your temperament."

His temperament? She made comment on *his* temperament?

Perhaps she was right, as Roland was very close to losing his temper just now. He took in a long, slow breath. Arguing with the lady never produced any particular results.

No, he would have to be more clever, more strategic.

She could not do anything substantial to ruin his chances with Lady Viola. She only had her words. She had no power to stop him from doing what he wished to do. He was free to continue his pursuit and she could not always know where he would be.

In fact, he would move his calendar to his bedchamber so that she would never know where he would be. He would put a second, false calendar in its place. She'd already had one look at it, so its entries must be similar, but wrong. He would move the dates for parties and routs a day forward, so she always arrived twenty-four hours too late. He would invent parties. He would leave at odd times. He would dodge her until he could get her into a carriage back to Dorset.

He would not be stopped or bend on this matter.

"You are very quiet, Baderston," the dowager said. "I do not like it."

Roland smiled. She had no idea what else she would not like that was to shortly come her way. He would send her on one long and never-ending goose chase.

If that was not sufficient, he would send her back to Dorset.

CHAPTER SEVEN

VIOLA JOGGED UP the stairs to her bedchamber with Miss Mayton on her heels. Even in her aunt's moment of glory, having just emerged victorious from her stint as Beatrice in *Much Ado About Nothing*, the dear lady had instantly perceived that all was not well.

In the carriage, Viola had admitted that she was discomfited, but asked not to be pressed to relay the cause until she could be at home with her sisters. It was not a tale she would prefer to tell twice.

Her sisters were in her bedchamber waiting for her. Cordelia sat up and Juliet laid down her pencil on seeing the door open.

"We stayed awake," Cordelia said. "I spent the past hour imagining Lady Rawley's theatrical evening."

"And I spent the hour trying to think up an ode to it," Juliet said. "Though, so little rhymes with Rawley! The closest I've got to is doily."

"Viola," Cordelia said, "what is the matter? You look distressed. Did the play not come off?"

"Oh no, the play came off wonderfully," Viola said. "Miss Mayton was a triumph as Beatrice. But there were other things that happened…"

"She's told me nothing about it yet," Miss Mayton said, settling herself in a chair.

Just then, Lynette came in to help Viola undress.

"Do tell us, Vi," Juliet said, "Lynette will not repeat anything she hears."

"Certainly not," Lynette said, looking taken aback that such a thing even needed to be mentioned. "I hear very little, and what I do goes into a sturdy locked box in the back of my mind."

Viola nodded, as of course they all knew Lynette played things very close and did not reveal their secrets below stairs.

As Lynette helped her out of her dress and into her night-clothes, Viola took a deep breath.

"Lord Baderston's mother was there. You will remember that Lord Baderston said I should find her in better spirits the next time we met. Well, that was not at all the case. She made her views on me very clear. Very clear, indeed."

"But what could she have said?" Cordelia asked.

"She said that he did not have any serious intentions, my family was an endless source of distasteful gossip, he would never stand by me, he would jump when she told him to jump, and I was not to think a preference for ham would do me any good."

"That's outrageous!" Juliet cried.

"So I thought too," Viola said. "I wondered if I should inform Lord Baderston of what she said, but I could not decide if that were right or not. It ended up not mattering anyway, as he escorted his mother home soon after the performance ended. She was right—she told him to jump, and he did."

"I do not know what you should do about it," Juliet said. "How could you bear living so closely connected to the lady? How could you stand up to it when the woman in the dower house was so spiteful to you?"

"That does not bother me much, really," Viola said. "What bothers me is, where does Lord Baderston fall? If he were to stand by me against all others, I might face down the queen herself. But if he were not…"

Cordelia tapped her chin with a forefinger. "You are left to parse the truth of her words. Does Lord Baderston have serious intentions toward you, would he stand by you? That is the question."

"Just so," Viola said. "Would he stand by me? I would have thought so, but she claims he would not. What if we were to wed and then something unfortunate happens. Perhaps I accidentally burn the house down—does he stand by me? Or if he is unduly influenced by her and she turns him against me? How am I to know what he would do?"

"This is a fine muddle," Miss Mayton said. "Our Viola requires loyalty above all else, and Lord Baderston's mother has implied he could not be trusted for it."

"What did she mean about distasteful gossip?" Juliet asked.

They all shrugged their shoulders, as nobody had the first idea of what she could have been talking about.

Miss Mayton said, "That is the nature of gossip though, is it not? Whatever it is, it is never entirely true. Everybody knows it. It is, now that I think of it, much ado about nothing."

Viola had not known that, exactly. She had assumed that most of the things she'd been told in whispers in her own neighborhood were entirely true.

"But then," Cordelia said, "why do people insist on doing it?"

"It is amusing, I suppose," Miss Mayton said.

"I must have my questions answered," Viola said, "even if the answers will break my heart."

"You must know if Lord Baderston loves you," Juliet said.

"Yes, Jules, but even more than that. If he loves me, would he be loyal?" Viola said. "Loyalty is the glue of love, it's what makes it stick. I could not bear to live a life always wondering if my husband's feelings were somehow changing."

"You must test him to find out," Cordelia said.

"I think if he defies his mother, that must say something," Juliet said hopefully.

Viola sighed. "Defying his mother would be about her, not about me. How do I know he would stand by *me*? Cordelia is right, his loyalty must be tested, but I cannot for the world think of how to do it."

"It seems like the dowager really does not care for gossip, as she did mention it," Cordelia said. "And Miss Mayton has pointed out it's rarely true. Perhaps you might send round some little piece of invented gossip about yourself and see what he does. Something harmless. She would use it to condemn you, but what would *he* do? That would involve both her *and* you."

"That is true, Cordy," Viola said.

"There now," Miss Mayton said soothingly, "devising a plan must always put one's mind at ease. It gives one a direction to travel, as it were."

"Well, we do not have a plan yet," Viola said. "We still must think of some little idea to send round. It must not be too outrageous, but then not so innocuous that nobody bothers to repeat it."

Juliet nodded. "It must be just right."

Lynette had finished brushing out Viola's hair and braided it. "Lord help us all," she muttered.

"Don't worry, Lynette," Cordelia said. "Our plans *can* be daring, I'll be the first to say so, but they do always work out wonderfully well."

"In the end," Juliet clarified.

Yes, Viola thought. They always did work out in the end. The evening had felt so heavy and dark and full of misery coming her way. But now, there was a direction to travel, as her aunt had so aptly put it.

Far in the distance of those miles to be traversed, happiness was like a glowing light leading her forward. It was small and out of reach at this very moment, but at least it was there.

She would not give up hope. If she had learned anything from Beatrice and Rosalind, it was to never give up hope.

TATTLETON SAT DOWN heavily at the servants' table. Everyone

had already gone to their bed, but for Lynette who was still above stairs with the ladies, and Mrs. Huffson, who often waited up for him so they might share a brandy together.

"So you say, then, Mr. Tattleton, that something is amiss, but you do not know what?"

"That is what I say, Mrs. Huffson. I have known these young ladies since they came into the world, and I know their expressions. Lady Viola looked decidedly downcast when she and Miss Mayton returned from the theatrical evening."

"Perhaps Lynette will be able to tell us when she comes down."

"Lynette tells us nothing but platitudes. She will say Lady Viola is only tired, or some such nonsense. They've got her on their side—she keeps their secrets better than a queen's page."

"But, what on earth could have happened at a theatrical evening?" Mrs. Huffson said. "I understand that Miss Mayton was to have some small part in it, do you suppose she was a failure?"

"There is every chance of it, though that is not what upsets Lady Viola. Miss Mayton swanned into the house like she was Sarah Siddons taking a turn as Lady Macbeth. Whatever her performance was, and I will hazard a guess it was bizarre, Miss Mayton is thoroughly satisfied with it."

"Then Lady Viola will be satisfied too," Mrs. Huffson said. "The ladies and Miss Mayton are peas in a pod."

"Don't I know it. It's as if they're all having the same fever dream together. Have you seen Lady Viola's latest painting? Have you heard Lady Juliet's latest ode? Have you noticed that there is a parrot in the drawing room?"

Mrs. Huffson nodded slowly. Never one to criticize, she said, "They all do support each other wonderfully well in their endeavors."

"This is something else, though. Something untoward happened at this theatrical that has nothing to do with Miss Mayton's dreadful acting. I very much fear it's to do with the redhaired fellow Lady Viola is so set on."

"Oh dear," Mrs. Huffson said, "I do hope Lady Viola is not on the verge of having her heart broken."

"That is the least of our worries!"

"It is?"

"By far the least," Tattleton said, nodding gravely. "It may have escaped your notice, but whenever there seems to be a difficulty regarding a young man, a plan is formed."

"Oh my."

"Say it, Mrs. Huffson. Look the truth straight in the eye and say what the problem is with the ladies' plans."

Mrs. Huffson looked round the room as if somebody else might be coerced into answering the question. She fiddled with her glass and then said quietly, "The plans are always very bad."

"That is correct. They are the authors of bad plans, including last season's kidnapping. We must brace ourselves, Mrs. Huffson. I am certain another bad plan is in the offing."

ROLAND FELT AWKWARD in the extreme to call on Conbatten. He was acquainted with the duke, though he could not say they were fast friends.

Did Conbatten have fast friends? He had a wife now, as he had married Lady Viola's sister, and he seemed very pleased to have her. It appeared that he doted on the lady and he was often caught smiling at her, which was not a thing he was known for. But did he have close gentlemen friends?

Roland did not know; all he was certain of was that the duke's name came up quite a bit at the YBC. It seemed it was always a matter of debate over whether to approach the duke about joining their club. Darden was to have asked him ages ago, as Conbatten was now his brother-in-law, but somehow it had not occurred. The members still fretted that the duke would not accept. Or that he would accept and then what would they do?

They spent most of their time in the coffee room joking and laughing—did Conbatten joke and laugh?

He must go forward with the visit though. Conbatten had won Lady Viola's sister, Lady Rosalind, and that made him the only person who might have some helpful hints on how he was to prove his loyalty to Lady Viola. Of course, there was Lord Van Doren, who'd married the eldest sister, and he must know something about it too, but Roland did not really know him. He had a reputation for being exceedingly prickly, so Conbatten seemed the best choice.

In any case, there was no turning back now without looking like a terrible goose. He'd been led into Conbatten's drawing room and left to wait there.

As he looked around, he thought he could detect the new duchess' influence. He'd been in the room once before, a few years ago, when Conbatten had thrown a large dinner. It had been far more austere and there certainly had not been any pillows embroidered with flowers.

The doors flew open and, much to Roland's surprise, it was not Conbatten who came through them. It was the duchess.

"Your Grace," he said bowing.

"My dear Earl," the duchess said, coming forward, "let us not be so formal between us, you'd better call me duchess." She paused and laughed. "Though, goodness, that always sounds so foreign when I say it."

"Duchess," Roland said. He was at a loss as to how to proceed. He had really planned to talk to Conbatten.

"Now Lord Baderston, I have ordered a tea tray and you must stay and have a chat with me, even though you have come to see the duke. He is at Tattersall's just now, looking at a horse that he believes must suit me wonderfully."

"It would be my honor to stay for tea, Duchess."

"Excellent. We will talk of trivialities and once the tea has been laid and the door shut, I have high hopes you will confide in me."

Roland was entirely nonplussed. What should he do? Dare he ask the duchess any probing questions about her own sister?

It did seem as if she were a willing ear. Though, how did she know he had something to confide?

As he was wondering about it, the duchess prattled on about this and that. Mostly about Conbatten. It seemed the duke was forever saving her from some sort of danger. Just the day before, he'd removed his coat and thrown it over her head until she was safely in the carriage, as a hornet had been spotted in the vicinity and he would not have his duchess stung. This day, he was looking at a horse with the express idea that he must find one that would not dare throw his lady.

Roland did not have the first idea how Conbatten would make such arrangements with a horse. One generally did not know that a horse was prone to spook or had an unwieldy temperament until it resided in one's stables. The seller certainly would not mention it.

The duke's butler arrived, leading in two footmen with trays. Under his grave stare, they laid the service expertly, the duchess all the while nodding her approval. The footmen were blushing by the time they were through and Roland got the idea that they were very keen to please their mistress. She seemed rather indulgent of them.

The doors closed and she poured him a cup. "Here we are in a confidential conversation," she said. "I am delighted to find you here and hopeful that you have something to say about Lady Viola."

There it was. She had opened the door. All he need do is walk through it.

"Well," he said slowly, "naturally you did represent Lady Viola exceedingly well when you described her to me last season."

"She is rather perfect, is she not?"

"Indeed, yes, everybody would say so."

"But do you say so?"

"Me? Oh yes, I assumed that was understood."

"It is understood now, Lord Baderston, and I feel it gives me leave to say something personal to you. If there were any little questions you might have regarding my sister? I do know her so very well."

Roland gulped his tea. It was scalding in his throat, but it gave him a moment to think.

"Well," he said slowly, "I did wonder, you see, Lady Viola did mention, very strongly, really, that loyalty is her primary requirement. Now, of course, I am a very loyal person. However, the rub seems to be in proving it."

The duchess nodded knowingly. "Is that not always the case?"

"Is it?" Roland was rather confused. He had not known that this proving of loyalty was a regular thing.

The duchess leaned forward and said quietly, "I will tell you a secret, as I believe I can trust you. I required the very same from Conbatten."

"Did you?" Roland asked. He'd been right, Conbatten *did* know how this whole proving loyalty thing worked.

"Oh yes, only *I* required courageousness. Well, I can tell you, it was no easy feat. I eventually had to arrange my own kidnapping to give him a proper opportunity. You may have heard it whispered about for a time."

"Oh, I never listen to gossip…"

"Absolutely everybody listens to gossip, but it is no matter," the duchess said. "The queen made it known that she did not like that particular circumstance talked about and so it was quickly forgotten. She's very fond of Conbatten, you know."

"I see," Roland said, "but I am at a loss over what I am to do, Duchess. Am I to wait to hear that she's been kidnapped? Or keep my eyes open for kidnappers and stop them? Who are they? How will I recognize them?"

Peals of laughter filled the drawing room. "Goodness, none of that," she said. "Viola values the quality of loyalty and that would be unlikely to require such derring-do. I cannot speculate on what might come up that *would* require loyalty, I can only say—be at the ready. When Viola requires you to be firmly in her camp, then make it known that you are firmly in her camp."

"Of course I will, there is no other camp I would consider!"

"Just as I'd hoped."

"There is one thing…you see…my mother…she can be…less than accommodating. She's had the idea of another lady in mind, which I assure you is her idea alone. So what I am saying is, perhaps to defy my mother and stand firmly in Lady Viola's camp would show the right amount of loyalty?"

"That would certainly be a start, Lord Baderston."

A start. Well, a start was at least a place to start.

CHAPTER EIGHT

ONLY AN HOUR ago, Viola was being dressed for Lady Hightower's musical evening when Rosalind hurried into her bedchamber.

"Vi, there you are," her sister said. "I was so hoping to catch you before you went out. Lord Baderston came to see me today."

Viola spun round, nearly knocking Lynette over, who was valiantly wrestling with her buttons.

"He did?" she cried.

"Well, actually he came to see Conbatten, but my dear husband was out acquiring the perfect horse for me. Her name is Mabel and she has been thoroughly lectured about never daring to throw me."

"Rosalind! Do tell me what Lord Baderston wanted before I burst into a thousand bits."

Rosalind threw herself onto the bed. "Well, it is just this—he thinks you are perfect and he is standing at the ready, prepared to prove his loyalty at the first opportunity."

Viola sighed. It was as if a weight had been lifted from her shoulders. Though, as soon as it lifted, a small bit of that weight settled back down again.

"His mother, though," she said. "She does not like me at all. She's come right out and said so in the most horrible terms and she said he would jump when she told him to jump. Then, she did tell him to jump, and he jumped."

Rosalind waved her hands as if it were of no consequence. "Oh yes, he mentioned his mother. He wondered if standing up against her would accomplish proving his loyalty. I said it would be a start."

"Yes, that is true," Viola admitted. "I have thought just the same. For really, is it any great matter for an earl to make up his own mind, regardless of what his dowager mother makes of it? It is one thing for us to be directed by our father, but Lord Baderston is an earl—he has already come into his own."

"Agreed. To my mind, managing the dowager is to be looked upon as an expected minimum," Rosalind said. "I think of his mother as similar to my pickpocket—it is a place to begin. Though, I have been pondering how it all plays out, what shall you do to give him his moment of proving himself to you?"

Lynette had finished buttoning up Viola's dress, a lovely plum silk.

"Cordelia, Juliet, and I did have an idea yesterday and we've spent all day today thinking on it. We thought I'd send a harmless rumor round. Something interesting enough to be bandied about but not truly terrible. Then, Baderston must step forward and defend, or do nothing and prove himself the disappointment of my life. Do you remember my tinker?"

"The little redheaded boy all those years ago?"

"Just the one," Viola said. "I plan on mentioning to someone who might be relied upon to gossip that at one time when I was very young, that tinker proposed that we run off to Gretna Green and that I did consider it, on account of his lovely red hair."

"Oh I see," Rosalind said, looking intrigued. "The story does a double duty. It gives Lord Baderston something to stand by you on, and it also tells him how much you like his own hair."

"Just so," Viola said. "I will send the story round this very night, should I get the opportunity."

"Excellent notion."

Viola glanced at her sister's day dress and said, "You do not attend Lady Hightower's evening?"

"Conbatten felt the other ladies might be intimidated to see me there, after my performance of last year. He says it was much talked of. We do not wish to make anybody nervous, after all."

Viola nodded. "Oh yes, you performed one of your travels through the world of music."

"Exactly. So, instead of attending Lady Hightower this evening, we are having her to our house on the morrow for an intimate dinner, just the three of us. She will give us a full report on how the evening came off."

"What shall you do this evening then?"

Rosalind sprawled on the bed. "I will visit with my sisters for a bit, they already wait for me in the drawing room. Apparently, they are using almonds to try to convince Chester to stop saying murder. Then later tonight, my dear Conbatten and I will have an intimate dinner, just the two of us. Then we will likely take a bath together, at precisely ninety-eight degrees, with chilled champagne."

"He is very romantic, is he not, Rosalind?"

"Very. I positively adore him for it."

"That is just what I would wish for," Viola had said dreamily.

Rosalind had kissed her and run down the stairs, leaving Lynette to finish her work.

Now, Viola found herself and Miss Mayton in Lady Hightower's drawing room and her plan was set to begin.

Lady Clara stood with them, which at first Viola had not been very enthusiastic about. She was the very lady who'd made a visit to Lord Baderston's estate last summer and the very lady Lord Baderston's mother favored.

After thinking on it, though, it seemed that a person like Lady Clara probably made quite a lot of calls around Town. If she was not mistaken, the lady was into her third season—she must know everybody. Certainly, the lady would wish to pass on some little tidbit she'd heard while she made her calls.

Viola gave her aunt a meaningful glance. Miss Mayton, understanding her perfectly, nodded. They would start the gossip on its way around Town.

"Being in London, and it being so new—original sights and sounds, you understand," Viola said, "reminds me of when I almost set off for Gretna Green. Which I expect would have also seemed very new."

"Gretna Green?" Lady Clara asked in alarm. "With…?"

"You see, it was a tinker's son with red hair that asked her," Miss Mayton said.

"A tinker?"

"His son. With red hair," Viola reiterated. "I'm very partial to it."

"Partial to tinkers, or red hair?"

"Red hair, of course," Viola said.

"I see," Lady Clara said coldly.

Viola hesitated just a bit. The idea of putting it about that she'd considered running off with a redhaired person was meant to be a compliment to Lord Baderston. She had not really thought through how Lady Clara would view it. She felt as if Lady Clara did not approve.

Did Lady Clara really have any designs on Lord Baderston? How could it be? If they were meant for one another, then certainly something would have been said when she'd stayed at his house over the summer.

"A tinker," Lady Clara said softly. "Tell me, Lady Viola, what turned you from your purpose?"

"Oh, hmm, well, my father would have viewed it a very unfavorable match and I was far too young, in any case," she said.

"I see," Lady Clara said quietly. "Indeed, yes, I see."

ROLAND WALKED INTO Lady Hightower's house all determination. Though he did not find sitting through piece after piece of music played by nervous young ladies very invigorating, he always attended her soiree. Boring it might be, but he was fond of Lady Hightower and did not like to let her down. However, on this night he would not be at all bored, as one of those young ladies that would play was to be Lady Viola.

He had attended the year before and had witnessed Lady Rosalind's performance, which was much talked of at the time. Now the Duchess of Conbatten, the lady had been the author of a truly bizarre turn at the pianoforte. It had been a mishmash of styles, all run together, that she called a 'travel through the world of music.'

Roland wondered if it was some sort of style that was a tradition in the family and if Lady Viola would provide an equally strange offering. He did not care. In fact, he hoped for it. It could be a thing he defended her on to prove his loyalty. Let people say her playing was odd—he would rail against them! He would argue that Vivaldi and Haydn were mere hacks when compared to Lady Viola.

He strode into the drawing room. There she was. She nearly took his breath away.

She was dressed in the loveliest aubergine gown, her cheeks were blooming, and the various shades of her hair shined in the candlelight.

Lady Viola really did make other ladies seem drab. Her person and her temperament were all color and life!

Miss Mayton was there too, swimming in black bombazine. She was an odd creature. However, she did seem particularly pleased to see him, which fostered some warm feelings toward her.

He was less pleased to see Lady Clara standing with them. He'd not spoken much to her after the exceedingly awkward visit to his estate with her parents, not even when they'd danced at Almack's. He was sure she was not particularly partial to him, but he was not so sure if she was prepared to ignore her parents' bidding.

He supposed he'd always known that some ladies were rather

calculating in their foray into the marriage mart, that they would employ a cool eye and look for the highest rank they could land. But, it had never hit home as hard as it had when his mother had revealed that she'd been just such a creature. It had somehow imbued the idea with more substance and made it more real.

Then, of course, he could never be sure what, if anything, his mother had said to the lady. Whatever it was, he could at least be certain it had been encouraging.

Miss Mayton wildly waved. Where Lady Viola was, he would go. Regardless of Lady Clara's presence. He made his way over.

"Miss Mayton, Lady Viola, Lady Clara," he said, bowing.

"Lord Baderston," Lady Viola said.

She did seem very pleased to see him. That was a relief. He still did not know what his mother had said to Lady Viola at the theatrical evening, but it seemed it had not had any lingering effect.

"Now," Miss Mayton said, "I did so long to show Lady Clara a particularly fascinating item on the sideboard just now, if it would not be too terrible to leave you for a few moments."

"Something fascinating on the sideboard?" Lady Clara asked, as if that were indeed news to her.

"Yes, precisely, come, my dear lady. Prepare to be amazed," Miss Mayton said, taking Lady Clara's arm and rather forcefully steering her away.

Miss Mayton really was a dear to do it! Now he had his moment. There was so much to say.

"Lady Viola," he began, "my mother would not reveal what she might have said to you at Lady Rawley's theatrical evening, but I have told her in no uncertain terms that if it was anything at all unpleasant, I thoroughly denounce it and I threatened to send her packing. As well, I was forced to depart without taking a proper leave of you, as she claimed she was ill."

Lady Viola blushed and Roland could see at once that his worst fears were realized. The words spoken to Lady Viola that night had been unpleasant indeed.

"Might I enquire into what she said?" he asked.

"Well," she said slowly, "for one thing, the dowager said my family was responsible for unpleasant gossip."

"Did she," Roland said in a growly voice. "She fails to realize that I have not a care for anything that might have been said about your sisters or Miss Mayton."

"Things have been said?" she asked, seeming as if that was news to her.

"Only trifles, I assure you," he said. "There has perhaps been mention of Lady Beatrice's wide array of suitors, which I do not even understand the significance of. And then, maybe there was some talk about a kidnapping? Though that was so absurd as to fade away quickly. And I suppose there are some who wonder why Miss Mayton wears widow's weeds? But in my opinion, a person ought to be allowed to wear anything they like, within the bounds of decency."

"Oh, I see," Lady Viola said. "Goodness, I hadn't realized she meant so many different things!"

"I do not care what she meant," Roland said. "She can point to nothing said against *you*. Nothing at all."

"What if she could, though?" Lady Viola said. "What if something *were* said about me? What if some sort of gossip were to travel round and everybody was talking of it?"

"It is a preposterous idea."

"One never knows, though."

"Well then, I would rail against it. I should condemn it left and right, up and down, backward and forward. I should issue the cut direct a hundred times to a hundred people. And, if that were not enough, perhaps I would be pushed to the extreme of arranging certain meetings on certain greens. Very early in the morning, if you understand me."

Lady Viola smiled. "I rather think I do."

Before he could claim he would aim cannonballs at all of London in defense of Lady Viola, Lady Hightower called for everyone to find their seat.

TATTLETON HAD BEEN in and out of the drawing room for various requests from Lady Cordelia and Lady Juliet, along with Lady Rosalind, who was visiting her sisters.

Or rather, he should say Her Grace, the Duchess of Conbatten, née Lady Rosalind Bennington. It felt something of an honor to wait upon the drawing room when one of the occupants was a duchess.

Of course, it was an honor that could run one off one's feet.

First, they wished for a bowl of shelled almonds for the horrible bird. Tattleton had been alarmed to come into the room and note that the creature's cage door was wide open and it was waddling round on the floor.

It had even had the audacity to defecate on the carpet, and then just sashay away as if it had done nothing at all!

From what he could gather from their one-sided conversations with the wretch, the ladies were determined to teach that cursed avian to say nicer words than murder.

He wished them good luck with it.

After that, he'd been called in several times for tea, then a plate of cakes, then fruit.

Naturally, with all the coming and going, he could not help but to overhear some of the conversations that were had between the sisters.

Aside from having an idiot bird shouting about murder, it had all sounded very usual. Lady Cordelia performed just a little bit from her Desdemona death scene. Lady Juliet had recited an ode to Lady Rawley and her doilies, whatever that was supposed to mean.

It was only toward the end of the evening that he overheard something that gave him a deal of pause. A great deal of pause.

As far as he could understand it, Lady Viola had once fancied herself in love with a tinker's boy with red hair.

Of course, he remembered that perfectly well. She'd mooned about for two weeks and said a lot of dramatic things like she was certain she was on the verge of dying from a broken heart or, if she did not die, she would enter a monastery. Fortunately, she got a pony at the end of the second week and that was the end of it.

But there was something they spoke of that he didn't know anything about—they said the boy had suggested they run off to Gretna Green.

It was preposterous. Certainly, if the fellow had said anything of the sort it had been a joke. They had been children, no more than eight years old!

That was odd enough, but what came next sent a shiver down his spine.

Lady Viola was to send a rumor round the *ton* about this tinker's boy. That notion was conceived of to give Lord Baderston ample chances to defend Lady Viola's honor and prove his loyalty.

Of course, he'd already girded his loins to encounter another very bad plan launched by the ladies. But this?

This was madness! One did not start rumors about oneself. One started rumors about other people.

It seemed to him a highly dangerous thing to do. With the help of the queen, one might be able to sweep an arranged kidnapping under the rug, but if a lady was to somehow ruin her own reputation…

What could he do to stop it, though?

As always seemed to happen in these situations, Tattleton felt he ought to go to the earl. However, he could never compose the right explanation without sounding like a madman.

What was he to say this time? 'You see, my lord, Lady Viola is planning to damage her reputation so that a certain Lord Baderston can defend her. This very bad plan has come about because he must prove his loyalty and apparently things have gone along too smoothly to give him his opportunity.'

Had they learned nothing from last year?

Amidst his fretting, he tried very hard to ignore the shouting from the now darkened drawing room. Chester had been returned to his cage and the ladies had retired, which he supposed the bird was not in favor of.

"Murder!" Chester shouted.

"Oh, go murder *yourself*," Tattleton said loudly.

"Bad man," Chester answered.

"If I am, you have driven me to it!"

VIOLA HAD FOUND her conversation with Lord Baderston quite illuminating. Her aunt had been so clever to lead Lady Clara away so that they might have a confidential moment.

She'd had no idea so much talk had gone round about her family. It was encouraging that Lord Baderston thought so little about any of it. But then, none of those things had been about her. She must see that he took the very same approach regarding a thing said about her. She must see that he shook it off as being not worth his notice. She must see that his loyalty overrode all other considerations.

Viola had high hopes that he would do just that. After all, had he not said he'd rail against it? Had he not claimed he would condemn it and issue the cut direct as many times as necessary? Had he not even hinted at a duel?

Lord Baderston, your moment is close at hand, dear sir. Even now, Lady Clara will be passing along the story of the tinker's boy, and then you may set to your work.

Viola had already seated herself in the front row, as she had been directed to by Lady Hightower, as she would be one of the players.

Viola glanced behind her as the lady's guests arranged themselves and determined where to sit.

Lord Baderston had escorted Lady Jancallen to a chair, which was very considerate. The lady was eighty if she was a day and none too steady on her feet.

Darden had told Viola that though she used a cane to assist her, she had somehow never got used to it. She swung it around more than kept it on the ground. Last season, she'd managed to take Lord Gresham down to the floor at a card party after she threw it in frustration because she could not see her cards.

That, and the fact that she used an ear trumpet that must be shouted at if a person wished to communicate with the lady, made her a handful to escort. Viola imagined that there were more than a few gentlemen this evening who avoided the task, and she was proud of Lord Baderston for bravely stepping forward.

Viola was satisfied to see Lady Clara at the very back, whispering to some unknown lady.

It had begun. She was certain it had.

Miss Mayton sat directly behind her. Her aunt leaned forward and said quietly, "I trust you had an enjoyable conversation with Lord Baderston?"

"You were very clever to arrange it, Aunt," she said.

Miss Mayton nodded. "Lady Clara was almost irate though, when she discovered that the fascinating item she was meant to be amazed by was an apple tart. Goodness, it can be difficult to think on one's feet."

Viola giggled, just as Lady Hightower said, "My beloved guests, every year we perform the same dazed and winding minuet round the chairs. Remember, whichever chair you choose is not to be your lifelong destination. There will be other chairs in other rooms in your future."

After that gentle scolding, everyone did settle themselves more quickly.

"Excellent," Lady Hightower said. "Here we are again, poised to welcome a group of new and charming young ladies onto the scene. I am sure you will agree that it is vital for a suitable lady to play proficiently, and I am always so proud that England does not forget it. First, let us hear from Lady Viola Bennington."

Viola rose and was surprised to see most of Lady Hightower's guests had very suddenly leaned forward. Some were even gripping the back of the chair in front of them. Goodness, nobody at home was ever so intently interested when a lady played at a musical evening.

She glanced at Miss Mayton to see if she had noticed.

Miss Mayton nodded knowingly and rose. "My dear gentlemen and ladies," she said, "I think I understand you. However, I am sorry to inform you that it is only Lady Rosalind who performs the travels through the world of music."

Now, Viola understood this seemingly intense interest. They'd had hopes of hearing something similar to Rosalind's wildly unpredictable pieces.

Viola nodded. "I am afraid all I can provide is a rather simple sonata," she said. "I am incapable of the feats of creativity that my sister can provide."

There were disappointed looks all round, except for Lady Hightower, who appeared enormously relieved.

Viola sat down and began to play. She had come into the evening knowing her own skills. She was thoroughly competent, but no master. She was entirely satisfied with it, though.

After all, one person could not be talented in all areas and she did have her skill at an easel to list as an accomplishment.

In any case, the point of the whole evening, for her at least, was not the playing. It was Lord Baderston.

When she had the occasion to glance up, she did note him smiling and looking very approving.

Viola might not be the best musician in the world, but it seemed as if her playing would suit the lord very well.

Of course it would. She and Lord Baderston were like hand and glove. She must just see that her chosen glove stayed steady and stalwart in the face of a rumor about a tinker's boy.

CHAPTER NINE

R OLAND COUNTED THE beginning of Lady Hightower's musical evening a resounding success. The end had been something else entirely.

Miss Mayton was an exceedingly odd creature, but he was growing very fond of the lady. She had been so very helpful in arranging for him and Lady Viola to have some minutes alone.

What a conversation they'd had! He'd been able to declare his very actions, should Lady Viola need to be defended. He'd even hinted at a duel, which he thought had been rather direct in communicating his strong feelings.

Then, Lady Viola played the pianoforte. He'd assured himself that if she presented something bizarre, as her sister had done, he would welcome it. He would take the opportunity to counter all the naysayers and stop their talk. It would be a perfect chance to display his loyalty.

And yet, when it came to it, he'd found himself relieved that she played in a very usual manner.

Watching her so gracefully running her fingers over the keys had led him down all sorts of starry paths. He imagined cold nights, sitting before the fire and listening to her play. He thought of sultry summer afternoons, with the doors to the balconies flung open and her music drifting through them. Mostly, he thought of interrupting her playing to sweep her into his arms.

She would be lovely to interrupt.

After all the ladies had their chance on the pianoforte or the harp, the obligatory circling the room to congratulate them had commenced.

While he would have preferred to stay by Lady Viola's side, the walk round the room with compliments in hand was an absolutely essential activity. It was not so much that the lady who had played would notice if she were not congratulated by each and every person. It was the mamas and chaperones. They had put their young charges on display, like so many items for sale in a shop window, and they would demand to know how it had been received.

Then of course, Lady Hightower had eyes like a hawk and surveyed it all.

Fortunately, Roland had been to so many of these sorts of things over the years, that he had in his pocket several compliments he might throw out.

He ran them through in his head—

"Such was the vivacity of the playing that I would almost think you studied under the great Clementi!"

"It was a positively stirring rendition!"

"If I closed my eyes I would have thought it was the great composer himself at the instrument!"

And, the ever well received—"It was nothing short of a triumph."

He'd done his duty and sprinkled his phrases all over the room. As he'd looked to make his way back to Lady Viola, Lord Thomas had greeted him.

Then had come words he'd never thought to hear spoken.

Lord Thomas had glanced in Lady Viola's direction and said, "I suppose whatever inclination was there is off now."

He'd no idea what the fellow meant.

"Shame really, she is comely and comes with an attractive dowry."

"Lord Thomas, what are you referring to?" Roland had asked warily.

"Oh, I am sorry," Lord Thomas said. "I get ahead of myself sometimes and flatter myself that I am very observant. I had thought I'd detected keen interest for Lady Viola on your part."

"And what if you had?" Roland asked. "Why should such a thing be off now?"

Lord Thomas looked at him quizzically. "My dear fellow, everybody is talking of it. Lady Viola once ran off with a tinker's boy. To Gretna Green, you understand. It didn't come off in the end, but I only say…alone in a carriage and he not even a gentleman."

"That cannot be true," Roland said.

Lord Thomas flushed and said, "Well, I just thought you knew." He hurried away from Roland, clearly wishing he'd not brought the subject up.

But what a subject! How *could* it be true?

He'd wished to rush to Lady Viola, but then he'd paused. What in the world could he say? What could he ask?

She'd smiled at him as she was led out by Miss Mayton.

The two of them seemed so pleased with the evening. Did they not know what was being said?

If Roland had wondered about how *often* it was being said, all he'd had to do was watch the many stares as Lady Viola and Miss Mayton took their leave.

Who invented this pack of lies?

He briefly thought of his mother. But then, he dismissed it. He knew her so very well and while she was capable of sharp words and harsh opinions, she did not invent stories out of the air.

Roland had since got home, his thoughts racing in a hundred different directions. He'd tried to explain the whole thing to Markson, as he must pour it out to somebody.

His valet remained looking perplexed. "So you think she went on some ill-advised trip with a gentleman?"

"Not even a gentleman! A tinker. No, not even a tinker, but the tinker's son!"

"That don't sound promising," Markson said. "Do you think it's true?"

"No, it cannot be true," Roland said. "Lady Viola would never… But then, where did it come from? Why should anybody say such a thing?"

Markson shrugged. "Lords and ladies are notoriously unreliable 'cause they got too much time on their hands."

This was a near constant refrain from his valet. Whenever somebody put a foot out of place, he blamed it on excess time. Roland thought it a rather ironic opinion since, out of all his servants, it was Markson who had the most extra time on his hands.

"On the bright side," Markson continued, "you was waiting for a chance to defend her and this chance has come in like a monsoon to Bombay. I suppose you gave that old scallywag Lord Thomas the what-for over it."

Roland blanched. He had not, in fact, given Lord Thomas the what-for. He'd not said very much of anything. He'd been so bowled over that all his ideas of railing against a thing or issuing the cut direct or arranging a duel had gone up in a puff of smoke.

"Uh, I would not say I delivered the what-for, precisely. The story did hit me as a surprise."

"Well, now you know what's out there. You don't believe it's true and you got a job ahead of you proving you're all in for Lady Viola."

His valet was right. He *was* all in for Lady Viola and now it was time to prove it. He would not ask her to explain the talk going round about her. No, he would put his full faith in Lady Viola. He knew who she was and he would not stoop down to questioning. It was a ridiculous story and there was not a thing true about it.

His mother would attempt to make hay over it. But then, his mother's opposition began to feel like a minnow swimming an ocean. If this story about Lady Viola took flight, he'd be up against circling sharks.

No matter. Let the battle with the *ton* begin.

VIOLA RODE IN the carriage with the earl, Darden and Miss Mayton. They were on their way to Lady Bloomington's masque, and she was quite looking forward to it. She'd not ever been to one and it had been great fun to don a costume.

She was coming as Mary, Queen of the Scots, and wore a lovely tartan gown. Her crown, while not as elaborate, nor heavy, as the real Scottish crown, was edged in pearls and fur as a nod to that item.

Miss Mayton remained dressed as a widow, though she had decided to give it a medieval flavor. She wore a high conical hat with a sharp point from which yards of black chiffon hung down all around her. When she'd come into the drawing room before they'd set off, she'd appeared as a ghostly triangle, a specter that nearly shook the feathers off of poor Chester.

Viola's father and Darden were not half so interesting, as they had come in their usual dominos.

As entertaining as the fun of dressing as a person one was not had turned out to be, Viola was hoping for so much more from this night. She'd sent a rumor going round and of course she could not know how widely it had spread at this early date, but had Lord Baderston heard it? What would he say about it? Would this be the night he proved his loyalty beyond any shadow of doubt?

"Be cautious tonight, Viola," Darden said. "Beatrice might have mentioned Lady Bloomington's style of entertaining."

Viola nodded, as of course Beatrice had told her all about it. Rather than a supper to provide her guests with sustenance, Lady Bloomington sent round trays with glasses of champagne between all the dances. Other footmen would come round with what Lady Bloomington called entremets—bitesize pieces of food speared with a toothpick and handed to guests, accompanied by a linen napkin. Then there were sideboards in every room of the house, laden with all the good things from the lady's kitchens.

Beatrice said one must be cautious in avoiding having too much champagne and that Van Doren had learned that lesson the hard way during her season.

"I find Lady Bloomington's way of doing things very comfortable," the earl said. "Even in the card room there is always somebody bringing me something."

Miss Mayton nodded under her yards of black chiffon. "Indeed, Viola. I am certain that your father and I were able to trounce the Blackwells at whist last year, because Lady Blackwell took every glass coming her way. Lord Blackwell held her up with a sturdy arm when they departed."

"Beatrice said that Lady Bloomington is so generous with her offerings because she has been snubbed by the patronesses," Viola said.

Darden nodded. "Years ago, Lady Bloomington made some comment about Lord Castlereagh, that was the beginning of it. Her champagne and entremets are her answer to Almack's dry cake and sour lemonade. You will never see a patroness there to witness it, but then they will all be forced to hear how entertaining it was in the following days. Lady Bloomington quite enjoys that."

"I shall be very careful of the champagne, Papa," Viola said.

"I have not a doubt of it," the earl said.

The carriage had rolled to a stop and a footman opened the carriage door. "Well now," the earl said jovially, "let us proceed in and discover what Lady Bloomington has on offer."

In the great hall, they found Lady Bloomington dressed as Anne of Denmark, as apparently that queen was also fond of extravagant masques.

The earl introduced Viola and she curtsied low.

"Two queens from different moments in history meet one another," Lady Bloomington said. "I quite like that."

"Goodness, Lady Bloomington," Viola said, "I do not presume to hold myself as an equal."

"Very well said, most charming," Lady Bloomington said. "Earl, Darden, Miss Mayton is that you under there? You are most welcome to my house."

They moved on and found the ballroom alive with wonder. A chimney sweeper, a sultan, more than one Turk, a bishop, a milkmaid, gods and goddesses, soldiers and sailors, flower girls and orange girls. Interspersed with that kaleidoscope of colors, dozens of mysterious black dominos.

Viola gazed over the crowd and hoped Lord Baderston did not come in a domino. She was counting on being able to spot him by his lovely hair and a hood would serve to confound her.

She really should have asked him about his costume!

"Ah," the earl said, "here comes the champagne already."

Viola turned. Then she smiled. The footman holding the tray was Lord Baderston.

"Baderston," Darden said, "what is the game, old fellow?"

"Darden," Lord Baderston said. "Lady Viola, Earl, and…Miss Mayton?"

"Yes, it is indeed me under here, Lord Baderston," Miss Mayton said. "I am a medieval widow."

"Good evening, Lord Baderston," Viola said.

"Might you all take a glass of champagne, so I might dispense with this tray?" Lord Baderston asked. "I thought it amusing to come dressed as one of Lady Bloomington's footmen, but perhaps did not anticipate that I would actually be taken for one. It seems she hires extras for the night and that butler of hers has been ordering me about ever since I got here."

The earl laughed very hard at the idea. "Oh, that is good. I wish I'd thought of it."

Viola suppressed a smile. Had her dear Papa thought of dressing so, it was unlikely he would be taken as one of the footmen. Not unless he was the oldest footman in England.

Miss Mayton seemed to suddenly realize that though Lady

Bloomington's masque was known for providing all sorts of nice things to eat and drink, none of it would penetrate her chiffon drapery. She raised it and threw it over her head, so the shroud trailed down her back and shoulders.

Having handed out champagne all round, Lord Baderston placed the tray on one of the chairs that lined the ballroom.

"May I claim the first dance, Lady Viola?" Lord Baderston asked. "I would request supper, but there is no sit-down supper at Lady Bloomington's masques—only sideboards that are set up even now."

"I would be delighted," Viola said, very gratified by Lord Baderston's explanation regarding his choice of dances. He would send a message by it. "Though," she said, "we were so entranced by the spectacle that I have not yet retrieved my card."

"Consider it my errand, Lady Viola," Lord Baderston said. He bowed and hurried off to fetch it for her.

"He seems very keen," the earl said.

"Is he not marvelous, Papa?" Viola asked.

"Well, my dear, he seems a nice enough fellow."

A real footman came by and exchanged Miss Mayton's glass with another, as she had finished her own. Viola thought they really all should be careful of it. She was halfway through her own when she remembered to pause, as it seemed once a footman noted a glass was empty, another would fly into one's hands.

A second footman stopped at their grouping with a tray of Lady Bloomington's idea of entremets. He gravely announced them to be a bite of seared pineapple wrapped in bacon.

The small morsels artfully surrounded an arrangement of upright greenery and were pierced with a toothpick. Viola was handed a linen napkin and then followed Darden's lead in selecting her own piece from the tray.

She had never tried pineapple, though of course she had heard all about them. Mrs. Pickeward from their own neighborhood was forever talking of how she'd attended her cousin's wedding breakfast and the cake had been decorated with pineapple rings. Beyond that, Viola knew they were near impossible to get, and near impossible to pay for.

The flavor was rather delightful and spoke of sunshine.

Just as soon as she wondered what to do with the remaining toothpick and the napkin, a footman swept round with an empty tray to collect them.

Lady Bloomington had some very interesting ideas!

Lord Baderston returned to them, and Viola could not stop herself from laughing as he carried yet another tray.

"Yes, I have been bullied by that butler again," Lord Baderston said, laughing with her. "I did attempt to clear the confusion, but apparently the fellow has no time for chattering. Miss Mayton, I see you require another."

Lord Baderston handed her aunt a third glass of champagne, though he would have supposed it was only the second. He then collared a passing footman. "Do take this, young fellow. I am not a footman; it is my costume. I am Lord Baderston."

The boy looked confused.

"That butler keeps foisting trays upon me," Lord Baderston said for clarification.

This caused the boy to look a bit terrified. "I'll tell Mr. Brownley of the confusion, my lord."

"Do not bother," Lord Baderston said kindly. "If he attempts to burden me with another tray, I will tell him myself."

The footman looked relieved that he would not be the one to tell Mr. Brownley that he'd been ordering a lord about the place. He hurried away.

"You are a good sport about it, Baderston," Darden said.

"I cannot be offended," Lord Baderston said. "Poor Mr. Brownley appears to be under some stress. He keeps muttering that 'everything must be perfect.'"

Lord Baderston handed Viola her card, and she was pleased that he'd been so ambitious as to mark himself down on it already. He would take the first, as there would be no sit-down supper.

They were then joined by Conbatten and Rosalind, he in a domino and she coming as Elizabeth Woodville. Rosalind's blue silk dress was charmingly decorated with white roses for the House of York, and she wore a coronet of white roses.

The duke might wear a hood as a disguise all he liked, but it was always his height that gave him away. The only other man he might be confused with was Lord Harveston, who was also exceedingly tall.

Viola had hoped that Beatrice might attend too, but Bea had sent a note over in the afternoon that said she and Van Doren would spend a quiet night at home, having husband and wife conversations.

She hoped that meant Beatrice had followed Rosalind's lead and was even now wearing her diamond necklace and drinking champagne with her husband in a tub of water set at precisely ninety-eight degrees. Of course, there was no telling with Van Doren, but if anybody could get him to do it, it was Beatrice.

As they made jolly conversation, Viola noted Rosalind's eyes slightly narrow. Her sister stared over her shoulder, and it was not too long a time before she discovered why.

"Baderston," the Dowager Countess of Baderston said to her son.

Viola shivered. Somehow, the lady's tone was so cold that it chilled the air around her. Her costume was no less prepossessing. She very clearly styled herself as Queen Elizabeth, the stiff ruff round her neck saying it all.

Viola flushed as she realized the ghastly combination—she as Mary, Queen of the Scots, and the dowager coming as Elizabeth, the rival queen who would condemn Mary to her death.

The dowager gave her a little smirk, and so the connection had not been lost on her either.

Conbatten bowed and led Rosalind away without saying any sort of greeting. It was a snub, albeit a quiet one, and the dowager could not have failed to note it.

Viola supposed Rosalind had told her duke of the dowager's unkind words at the theatrical and he would show his disdain for the lady. Heaven help anybody who caused the slightest discomfort to Rosalind, even if it was not anything directly done to her—the duke would not countenance such a person.

"Hello mother," Lord Baderston said. Viola thought his own tone was less than cheerful too.

"I understood you would be attending the theater until my lady's maid spied you leaving the house dressed as a servant," the dowager said with asperity.

"What would have caused you to think I planned on the theater?" Lord Baderston asked. There was something of amusement in his question, though Viola could not identify the cause.

The dowager paled and did not answer his question. Rather, she said, "Lady Clara is here. Just there, as Ophelia. I often wonder if people dress to send a message."

Though it was said enigmatically, Viola could not imagine that anybody within earshot had failed to understand the dowager's meaning. Ophelia went mad and died for lack of love and attention from Hamlet.

Lord Baderston said, "If Ophelia is the message, then it is nonsensical. That Shakespearian lady's dearth of ideas and lack of internal fortitude led to her drowning."

The dowager sniffed at the assessment.

Miss Mayton laughed overloud and said, "Gracious, if every lovesick person is to throw themselves into a river, we should be able to walk across the Thames on all the dead bodies."

This was met with a rather stunned silence and Viola was afraid the champagne had begun to overpower her aunt. Miss Mayton was not much of a drinker to begin, and a footman had just handed her a fourth glass of champagne in a very short amount of time.

"Well then," the earl said, sounding perhaps more cheerful than he felt, "Miss Mayton, perhaps we ought to repair to the card room?"

Dear Papa. He had comprehended Miss Mayton's developing situation and would lead her to the relative safety of the card room.

"Cards? Oh yes, let's trounce the Blackwells at whist again," Miss Mayton said. Leaning conspiratorially toward the dowager, she whispered, "That lady indulges in too much champagne. She loses track of what's been played."

"Does she?" the dowager said coldly.

The earl's eyes widened, and he hurriedly said, "Champagne is always a risk at Lady Bloomington's house; nobody can be faulted for it. Miss Mayton, let us repair to the card room and settle in front of cups of tea."

Miss Mayton nodded. "Very sensible. One must know one's limits!"

With that, she drained her glass and grabbed at a passing footman. Viola imagined she meant to hand over her empty glass, but she caught the fellow by surprise, and she clutched his sleeve perhaps more roughly than she had intended to.

The footman went down to the floor and the tray of glasses went with him. Amidst the ensuing tinkle of broken glass, Miss Mayton wobbled back and forth like a ticking metronome.

Unlike a usual metronome, this one eventually tipped over so far to one side that it did not come back up.

The side she tipped over on was, unfortunately, toward the dowager. It was not a moment longer before Queen Elizabeth and a medieval widow were both collapsed on the floor.

CHAPTER TEN

VIOLA WATCHED FOOTMEN run toward them from every direction, carrying brooms, mops, and piles of napkins. She thought they must have been standing at the ready for such a disaster. With so much champagne flowing freely, and the event held yearly for as long as anybody could remember, it could not have been the first such situation to arise.

The ladies were helped to their feet. The dowager's ruff dripped champagne and her skirt was stained. Miss Mayton said, "Goodness, the floor quite got away from me for a moment. Or came up to meet me!"

The dowager took a napkin from one of the footmen and dabbed at her ruff.

"My apologies, Dowager Countess," the earl said, as footmen efficiently disposed of the glass all round via hand brooms and dustpans.

The dowager did not answer the earl's apology and likely wondered why Miss Mayton did not voice the same.

It was a disaster. Lord Baderston's mother had already made her opinion of Lady Viola Bennington very clear. That opinion could not have been improved by knocking the lady to the floor and dousing her with champagne.

Viola felt rooted to the spot. She felt she ought to do something, but she knew not what. To her left, she could see Darden pressing his lips into a thin line in an attempt not to laugh.

The earl led Miss Mayton away, as she leaned heavily on his arm. Her chiffon shroud, soaked with champagne, left a trail behind her. As it dragged through Lady Bloomington's chalked floors, it rather looked like the sort of track a snail would leave while crossing a pavement.

The dowager's jaw was set and she muttered, "I will take myself to a retiring room to attempt to recover from an encounter with Miss Mayton."

She turned on her heel and stalked off.

Once she was out of hearing, Lord Baderston guffawed with laughter, which set Darden off too.

Viola was at first taken by surprise. She did not know what she had expected. She had thought perhaps Lord Baderston would be angry, or embarrassed.

As she watched the two matrons retreat to their respective corners in their own particular styles, laughter overcame her too. It truly was a ridiculous situation.

Attempting to stop her laughter, she said, "Oh really, we should not be laughing. We really should not."

"Why ever not?" Lord Baderston said. "My mother has long needed a set-down of some sort, though I never imagined the set-down would be actually on the floor."

This sent them all into further peals of laughter.

As they worked to recover themselves, the musicians began to tune. This seemed to prompt the gentlemen in attendance to make the rounds and put themselves on cards if they had not already done so.

Darden was one of those gentlemen and set off with alacrity, seeming to know precisely which ladies he wished to approach.

Lord Baderston did not leave her side, though.

Viola's card was filled with three more dances. This did leave some holes in her evening. She was not quite sure what was to be done during those dances she was not yet engaged for. Did one simply stand at the edges of the room and admire those who were dancing? It seemed an awkward sort of thing.

"You must have arrived very early, Lord Baderston, if you do not need to occupy the next few minutes with securing your spot on other lady's cards," she said.

"I am not on any lady's card but your own," he said. "On those lucky occasions when you, yourself, are not engaged, perhaps we might occupy the time by slowly walking round the room."

Ah, so that was what one did when they were not engaged. What a nice idea.

"That is," Lord Baderston said hurriedly, "if you do not presume it to be too forward. It is not the sort of thing that would be tolerated at Almack's."

"But we are not at Almack's," Viola said.

"No, we are not. It's just that…it might be noticed."

"And talked about, I suppose," Viola said.

"Yes."

"Does gossip frighten you off, Lord Baderston?"

"Certainly not," he said, his chin set resolutely.

Viola could not tell if he perhaps meant to say that any talk he might have heard about a tinker's boy had not put him off. She did not even know if he'd heard it yet.

She would like to ask him but were she to do so she would be practically forcing him, out of good manners, to say that he did not care.

No, she must wait for him to confirm to her that he'd heard it and brushed it off. It must be Lord Baderston who brought the matter to her attention, not her backing him into a corner about it.

"Well, as my aunt has knocked your mother to the floor," Viola said mischievously, "perhaps it is the least I can do."

The first dance was ready to begin and Lord Baderston led her forward. Rosalind maneuvered them into the same set, which was a lovely thing to do.

Dancing with the duke and her sister would be very like she and Lord Baderston were alone in their set, as Conbatten only had eyes for Rosalind, just now acting as his White Queen.

As they began the changes, Viola said, "I do not know if I should ask this, but why did you seem amused that the dowager thought you were at the theater?"

"You may ask anything you like, anytime you like," Lord Baderston said. "My mother is a snooper and she has taken to peeking into my calendar."

"Ah, I see," Viola said, "and you changed your mind about going to the theater and came here instead."

"I was never going to the theater," Lord Baderston said.

"Oh, so she looked at the wrong day?"

"She looked at the wrong calendar," he said. "The real one is locked away and she has been studying one I made for her eyes only."

"You did not," Viola said.

"I most certainly did. I wondered how long it would take her to perceive it, as I did put some ridiculous engagements in there. For next Tuesday, I put down that the queen and I were to ride horses in the park and then sail on the Thames for tea."

Viola could not control a peal of laughter. Lord Baderston really was so clever, he was such a wit. Further, she was gratified to know that he was not overburdened by his mother's opinions. Those opinions had not swayed him in the least.

When the dance concluded, she and Lord Baderston walked casually along the edges of the ballroom. Were anyone to consider what they were doing, it might be thought that they were admiring the room, or the couples who danced.

They were hardly conscious of the room or other couples. Their admiration was for themselves alone.

Naturally, they walked very close together in order to avoid interfering with the dances. Hands may have brushed one another from time to time, but that could not be helped.

Despite her aunt's unfortunate encounter with too much champagne, Viola could think nothing but that it was a glorious, spectacular night.

ROLAND GUIDED TEMPEST through the darkened streets. What a night!

Lady Viola was really a marvel. Her looks could not be equaled, but that was only the beginning of it. Many a pretty lady haunted the ballrooms of London, but was there any other so clever, so genial, so eager to laugh? Really so…her?

He could not think so.

His mother's behavior had been, once again, highly unpleasant. He could not think where she thought to arrive with such behavior. Her power over him had long ebbed—where once she might have directed his actions, he was no longer a pliable boy.

He was a man, with his own preferences. The sooner she took that in, the better.

Perhaps she *had* taken it in when she found herself on the floor at the hands of Miss Mayton.

Roland laughed out loud, his laughter ringing through the quiet streets.

It had been too ridiculous. Miss Mayton was the founding mother of English eccentricity. From her outlandish stories, to her medieval widow's shroud that he was certain was not at all based on any historical fact, the lady danced to her own tune.

That tune had included copious amounts of champagne, broken glasses, and a dowager's ruff ruined on this particular night.

But what was any of that compared to walking the ballroom with Lady Viola?

Oh, he knew people had noticed. They would probably talk about it. Especially when Lord Barnard approached and asked for a dance with Lady Viola and Roland had said she was already engaged in walking with him.

He did not care what anybody had to say about it. Not in the least!

They had strolled and talked and strolled and talked. It had led him to imagine doing the same through his own gardens. He might show her the apple orchards and the hothouse.

It was amusing to think what thoughts he'd brought into the evening with him. He had been sure it would be an uncomfortable sort of night. He'd been certain that the talk he'd heard about the tinker's boy at Lady Hightower's musical evening would have bloomed and spread like ivy up the side of a house.

It had not though. Nobody had said anything about it. Nobody had stared unduly or whispered behind their fan.

Was it possible that it had gone no further? That it had just died out?

Perhaps the talkers were afraid of Conbatten. That could be the case.

But then, Lady Viola had asked him if he was afraid of gossip. He'd answered that he was not, in the strongest manner possible. Had she been referring to that story?

No matter. This evening could not have gone any better.

As he approached his house, the groom he'd made arrangements with slipped out of the shadows and walked Tempest quietly back to the stables.

Roland himself slipped down the narrow mews and entered the house through the servants' entrance.

It was too glorious a moment to encounter his mother in a champagne-soaked ruff and a temper.

Viola had risen very late. It was one of those delicious mornings when she'd awoke far too early, it was just a bit chilly in the room and so rolled over. She thought of it as a "second sleep" and found it a delightful thing to do.

She supposed she had dreamed of Lord Baderston, though she could not recall where her mind had wandered in her slumbers.

The carriage ride home from Lady Bloomington's had found a rather sobered Miss Mayton. The earl had served her cup of tea after cup of tea in the card room.

"I'm sure I do not understand how the champagne got away from me," she'd said.

The earl, always so kind, had said, "Many a person has wondered that very same thing after one of Lady Bloomington's masques. It is indeed hard to keep track when the footmen are so quick to hand out another glass."

"I do hope Lord Baderston was not too put out about the mishap?" her aunt asked her.

Viola smiled. Her aunt had now several times referred to knocking the dowager to the floor as "the mishap," as if it had little to do with her.

"Not at all," Viola said, happy to put her aunt's mind at ease. "He thought very little about it."

This seemed to put the earl's mind at ease too and so they happily continued on to Portland Place. Miss Mayton, being rather tired from her adventures, had retired at once.

Viola found her sisters asleep in her bed. She crawled in with them and woke them up to whisper to them the happenings of the evening. She told them of the lovely times with Lord Baderston and the fate of the dowager's ruff at the hands of their aunt, assisted by four glasses of champagne.

They all fell asleep as Juliet worked to compose an ode to a wet dowager.

Now, the sun had risen in the sky and she'd entirely missed breakfast. Lynette, always so practical, had arranged for a tray to be sent into the drawing room. Viola hurried down the stairs to find her sisters there.

"Murder, murder, murder!" Chester said, by way of greeting.

"Good morning to you, too, Chester," Viola said.

Cordelia and Juliet were at the windows, looking across the street. "Viola, do come and see," Juliet said.

Viola hurried to her sister's side. Both of Van Doren's carriages were stopped in front of his house, and the viscount himself was out there directing footmen running in every direction.

"What do you suppose he's doing?" Viola asked.

"We do not know," Cordelia said, "but it is very odd. We've just watched a vast number of pillows being stuffed into one of the carriages. We think he is preparing to transport something very delicate—an old oil painting, or a porcelain figurine, perhaps."

"Though we cannot think why he'd need two carriages to do it or where he would be taking it."

"You do not think he's taking things to auction?" Viola asked. "Beatrice has not said a thing about money troubles."

"Van Doren? Money troubles?" Juliet said, laughing. "He's far too sensible about his estate for that. Beatrice says he is out with his steward nearly every day and he visits his tenants more than they probably appreciate. I know I would not like seeing him forever at my door."

"Oh, look there, Jules," Cordelia said, "the footmen are putting luggage into the second carriage. They must be going somewhere!"

"Beatrice never said they were going anywhere," Viola said.

Miss Mayton came into the room, and it must be said that she looked rather bleary-eyed. "There you are, girls. Goodness, what a head I have this morning. What is it we're doing?"

"It is not what *we* are doing, but what is Van Doren doing?" Viola said.

Miss Mayton peered out the window. "Goodness," she said, "let us walk over and find out."

This was, quite naturally, hailed as an excellent plan. As it was mild weather at that moment, they did not even stop for their cloaks.

Walking across the road at a clip, they reached the other side just as Van Doren was coming out of the house again.

"That carriage must be fully padded against any jostling," he shouted to his butler.

"My lord," Genroy said, "we must still leave room for two people."

"Yes, of course, people!" Van Doren said, running a hand through his hair.

"Van Doren," Juliet said, "what on earth are you doing?"

The viscount spun around, seeming to have no idea where they'd come from.

"What am I *doing*? I have no time to explain what I'm doing!"

Beatrice walked out of the house and laid a hand on her husband's arm. "You really must calm yourself, my darling." To her sisters and Miss Mayton, she said, "I have told him the news."

"Are you going back to Somerset, then?" Viola asked.

Beatrice nodded. "I'm afraid my lord does not believe in the efficacy of London air," she said laughing.

Juliet peered at the pillows in the carriage. "But what is all this? Are you planning on sleeping all the way there?"

Van Doren stared at her as if she'd lost her wits. "My God, does nobody have any sense around here? It's for the jostling. Lady Van Doren must not be jostled."

"It's a baby, not a porcelain cup," Cordelia said.

"Very true," Viola said. "Mrs. Ranford rode her horse right up to her confinement."

"Then Mrs. Ranford is a madwoman," Van Doren said.

"You ought to talk to Mrs. Ranford about her experience with madness, then," Juliet said, "maybe she can give you some tips now that you are slipping into your own lunacy."

"I am a busy man, Juliet!"

Beatrice patted her husband's arm and said, "Genroy, please take Lord Van Doren inside while the other carriage is being packed. Give him a cup of tea…or a brandy if that seems better."

"But you will be all right out here? In the out of doors?" Van Doren asked Beatrice. "Is there a chill? I am so distracted that I cannot even tell."

"I will be quite fine and must say goodbye to my sisters. You know perfectly well that would only aggravate you further. Juliet might call you scoldy-breeches or recite you an ode."

Van Doren narrowed his eyes at Juliet. "Wouldn't she just."

Genroy led the very shaken viscount back into the house.

Beatrice turned back to her sisters and Miss Mayton. "Goodness, I knew he would be a bit cautious upon being apprised of my condition, but I hadn't thought I'd be riding on pillows all the way home."

"Must you really go though, Bea?" Viola asked.

"I'm afraid so. You see what sort of state he's in, and that's the calm *after* I agreed to return home. No matter though, for all his blustering, he is right. I find my mood has changed and I am very much looking forward to doing a bit of nesting."

"Making things all cozy in the nursery," Juliet said.

"Precisely," Beatrice said. "One of the lures he used to convince me we ought to go home is that there is no limit on what I might spend to make the nursery everything I wish for. Well, once I got to thinking about it, there are no end of things I would wish to change. He will no doubt live to regret that offer."

"I'll write an ode about nesting in the nursery," Juliet said.

"Oh please do write me something, Juliet, and send it to me. You must all write to me. I must know how the rest of the season unfolds for Viola."

"I do wish you were staying, Bea," Viola said. "We've just launched a plan to provide Lord Baderston with his opportunity to prove himself."

"Oh that is interesting! What have you done?"

"Well, at Lady Hightower's musical evening—"

Before Viola got further, Van Doren was storming out of the house again, the butler chasing him with a glass of brandy.

"That's it!" he shouted. "Daylight waits for nobody—we must set off at once!"

Beatrice bit her lip and kissed her sisters and her aunt. "Write me the news," she said to Viola. Then, she was very carefully helped into a carriage full of pillows.

They waved her off, Beatrice leaning back on pillows and laughing, while Van Doren only looked crazed.

As they'd been talking with Beatrice, Viola had seen three different footmen arrive to her father's house with invitations left in Tattleton's hands.

Goodness, there were so many parties when one came to London, it was impossible to keep up with it all.

She must, though. She must make her best guesses as to where Lord Baderston would be found in the coming days.

At least this night was assured. She, Miss Mayton, and her father would go to the theater and Lord Baderston had already told her he would be there. He had a box, as they did too. When they'd compared notes on the location of those boxes, it seemed very likely that they would be able to see one other.

They waved forlornly as Beatrice's carriage wheeled round the corner and then went back into the house.

"We ought to write Beatrice every day," Juliet said. "Just think, she'll be on her own in the countryside, stuck with her lunatic husband."

"His lunacy is rather endearing though," Miss Mayton said. "I think it's nice that he loses his faculties over care of Beatrice."

"That is very true," Cordelia said. "I fully expect my own husband to rant and rave when he's worried over my health. It's just that it's so odd because it's Van Doren."

They had got back to the house and Tattleton brought the recently delivered invitations to Viola in the drawing room.

"Heavens, what are these and how will I squeeze them onto my calendar?"

She opened the first.

My dear Lady Viola and Miss Mayton,

You were very gracious to accept my invitation to a night of cards for the 21st. I am sorry to say we currently have an uneven amount for whist and know you will gracefully bow out as you must have so many other worthy hostesses eager to secure your attendance. I hope we may see you next season.

Very best regards,
Lady Margaret Hardwick

"How odd, Aunt," Viola said. "It appears that we have been disinvited to Lady Margaret's card party due to an uneven number of people. Have you heard of such a thing?"

"No, I never have," Miss Mayton said, wrinkling her brow.

"What shall she do if someone she thought was coming does not turn up?" Viola asked. "Then she will be uneven again. I do not understand the sense in it."

"Nor I," Miss Mayton said. "Oh dear, I wonder…"

"You wonder…oh. But you do not think…" Viola said, the gravity of a horrible idea sinking into her thoughts.

"I do not know," Miss Mayton said. "The story of the tinker's boy is really very innocent. I would not have thought…but then Lady Margaret is such a stickler, perhaps she heard it and took offense to it somehow? Perhaps she thinks you should have never allowed the tinker's boy to speak to you?"

"Why should she though?" Lady Viola said. "The story is a tinker's boy asked me to run off to Gretna Green, I admired his red hair and declined. What could be more proper than that? A lady can hardly stop people from saying odd things."

"Open the other two letters," Cordelia said.

"Yes, do," Juliet said. "I will guess it is only Lady Margaret being strange."

"I am almost afraid to open this one," Viola said. "It is from Lady Rumsgartner. She is such a stickler that she makes Lady Margaret seem almost wild and carefree."

Miss Mayton nodded. "She is the one that never hosts any sort of frivolity. It is all for a charitable cause. We were meant to go to her…what was it? Some sort of lottery, I think."

"For the Pauper's Society," Viola said. "The money is to go for supplies, fabrics and threads, so that disadvantaged girls might be trained as seamstresses."

She cautiously opened the letter. After reading it, she dropped it in her lap.

CHAPTER ELEVEN

VIOLA'S SISTERS READ the letter from Lady Rumsgartner. She had no need to reread it herself—its message was burned into her thoughts.

Lady Viola Bennington—

An alarming report has reached my ears—it is an unfortunately reliable report that I have heard from several reliable people. It is said that you ran off with some sort of traveling tinker, did not go through with a wedding, and returned to your father's house. You may be free to bring such shame to your father's house, but I am offended that you would have imagined you might bring it into MY house. You are stricken from my guest lists this season and forevermore.

Also, that chaperone of yours, Miss Mayton, must be included in the shame as I will suppose she did not keep a very close eye on you if you were at liberty to set off for Scotland.

Lady Penelope Rumsgartner, Marchioness of Medham

Viola felt a cold chill seep into her body. What had she done? That was not the story that was meant to go round. How could the lady believe she'd actually *gone* to Gretna Green? It was a preposterous idea.

But how stupid that she had not considered that the story might be embellished.

No. One could not even call it embellishment. It was an outright fabrication.

Had Lady Clara done it? Or had it been someone else who'd heard it and decided it was not scandalous enough?

Whoever had done it, Viola recognized that she had nobody but herself to blame. She should have seen that playing with gossip was too risky. She had been so desperate to give Lord Baderston his moment to prove himself that she had been rash and foolhardy.

Her sisters and Miss Mayton had pored over the letter with several gasps. Chester, seeming to sense the upset all around him, groomed himself and muttered, "Murder, murder, murder."

Before anybody but Chester could say a word, Darden burst into the room.

"Viola! I have just heard the most terrible report!"

ROLAND HAD BEEN looking very much forward to Lady Margaret's card party. The lady was long known, she provided an excellent sideboard, and she always had an interesting selection of guests. He had every year been invited, not because he was himself so very interesting, but because Lady Margaret was a cousin to his father and had always been a great friend to him.

He had been delighted to hear that Lady Viola had been invited too, and of course it made perfect sense. Lady Margaret was very friendly with Conbatten and was said to be charmed by his new duchess. Those genial feelings had very naturally extended to include the duchess' younger sister, Lady Viola.

Though Lady Margaret was a relation, Roland was in no danger of encountering his mother there. For one thing, those two ladies had never cared for one another. Roland did not know the whole story, but there had been some sort of rift created. He had the feeling that Lady Margaret had not rejoiced when his father had announced his engagement. So, while his mother had no trouble at all barging into a party without an invitation, she would never think to barge into Lady Margaret's house.

The other guarantee that he would not be plagued by the dowager is that he knew from Barnard that his mother had been snooping into his calendar again. As it was not his *real* calendar, but the false one he had set up to stymie her, she would get nowhere with it.

Despite him having entered some ridiculous notations in it, and despite discovering he'd not gone to the theater the night before, she would continue with the idea.

He had managed to avoid her since her encounter with Miss Mayton at Lady Bloomington's masque. He simply was not interested in her endless complaints and he was certain she would have no end of them to add in regards to Miss Mayton.

If she were intent on tracking him down on this particular night, she'd find herself on her way to a rout at Mrs. Persweiler's house. Upon arrival, she'd discover that house dark, as he understood Mrs. Persweiler to be in York just now. Wherever Mrs. Persweiler actually was, she was definitely not hosting a rout anywhere but from the inside of his false calendar.

"Lady Margaret," he said, as she approached with a smile. Roland scanned the room over her shoulder. He spotted Conbatten and his duchess. There were several others he knew, including Lady Clara's brother, who he was not anxious to see. That particular viscount considered himself a Corinthian of the first order, though Roland just found him a rather surly fellow with rough manners.

There was no sign of who he really looked for—Lady Viola. At least, not yet.

"My dear Lord Baderston," Lady Margaret said. "I am pleased that you attend my little card party. One of my advanced age is well aware of how many invitations a young man is in receipt of."

"Nonsense to the idea that your age is advanced," Roland said. "I was delighted to receive the invitation. I say, I wonder if in the pairing up, you might consider matching me with Lady Viola

Bennington for piquet. We've spoken about the game and she is keen on it."

Of course, he and Lady Viola had not spoken of piquet. He did not even know if the lady preferred to play it. He almost wondered how they hadn't, as they had seemed to talk about everything in the world at the masque.

But that was no matter. It would give them an excellent and extended time to talk even further.

Roland was puzzled by the look on Lady Margaret's face. Should he not have asked? He did not perceive anything shocking in it.

"Lady Margaret?" he said.

"Oh, well, I am sorry," she stuttered, "I do not believe Lady Viola attends this evening."

"Really? We did discuss it. She did say she would come."

"Perhaps some other amusement presented itself?"

Could that be true? Could it be that some other invitation was received that was thought to be more attractive when she knew he would be here?

He did not flatter himself, but he did not think so.

"I find that hard to believe, Lady Margaret," he said. "Did she in fact send you her regrets?"

Now Lady Margaret looked almost panicked. She took his arm and pulled him to the side. "Lord Baderston, I have been put in a most difficult position!"

"What position?" he asked, a feeling of dread creeping over him.

Lady Margaret sighed. "I am sure you are aware of the current rumors circulating about Lady Viola. Now, I do not tend to pay any attention to that sort of thing, as I was once the victim of an untrue falsehood myself."

Roland stared at her, willing her to go on.

"But you see," she said, "there was pressure from all sides! Lady Rumsgartner threatened to throw me off her committee for raising up the paupers, and Lady Jellicoe said she would wonder if her son were really suitable for my daughter if I were not careful of the company I keep. There is to be a match there! And then, of course, Lady Clara's family has been quite vocal about it. I was quite overwhelmed."

Lady Margaret may have felt overwhelmed, but Roland was positively stunned. He had grown certain that the rumor had not taken flight. Nobody at Lady Bloomington's had seemed to know it.

He supposed it had been too soon. He supposed that today, as calls were being made, the story had wended its way through the town.

That understood, it was one thing for people to talk, and even for Lady Rumsgartner to snub a person. That lady had snubbed so many people in the past and was so generally unpleasant that there were those that claimed they *wished* to be snubbed by her so they could be done with her. But for her or anybody else to attempt to influence another hostess in her invitations…it was outrageous.

"I hardly knew what to do," Lady Margaret said, stealing a glance at Conbatten and his wife. "I was being forced to disinvite the duke's sister-in-law."

"But you did disinvite the lady?" Roland said, anger seething through him.

"I had no choice," she said, "but I did it in the politest terms possible. I said we had an uneven number of couples and that I was certain she was drowning in invitations and would be happy to hear it."

Before Lady Margaret could go further, Viscount Setterdown, Lady Clara's brother, interrupted.

"What ho, Baderston," he said in his usual coarse style. "I'll suppose you don't dare challenge me to a game of piquet. I'm known at my club to be quite the sharp."

Roland stared at him. Who did he think cared if his friends at Boodle's thought he was a good card player? It was probably a lie anyway.

The scoundrel's family had been part of the cabal putting pressure on Lady Margaret. He was one of the reasons Lady Viola was not here.

Roland could not fault Lady Margaret too very much. Her daughter's engagement had been held hostage over it. But this buffoon…

"Hahaha," Setterdown said, "I can see it on your face, you're afraid to try it."

"Viscount," Lady Margaret said weakly, "I hardly think the earl—"

"Do not distress yourself, Lady Margaret," Roland said. He was so enraged he felt as if his head might blow off his shoulders. "Return to your guests while Setterdown and I have a private word in your hall."

Lady Margaret looked all but panicked but did as she was asked.

"Setterdown?" Roland said through clenched teeth. "Step out a moment."

Setterdown grinned, as if there were some big joke in the offing. He was about to discover otherwise.

In the great hall, Roland sent the lone footman away.

Setterdown sneered and said, "Gad, Baderston, if you don't want to play piquet, just say so."

"I have a few things to say to you, none of them about piquet," Roland said. "It has come to my attention that you and your family members are responsible for pressuring Lady Margaret to snub an innocent lady."

"Lady Viola?" Setterdown said. "She is hardly innocent. My God, man, she ran off with a tinker."

"She did no such thing. Lady Viola is a lady of the first order and anybody acquainted with her must know it. The story that has gone round has been authored by a meanspirited and low person."

Setterdown got very red in the face. "My own sister was told the tale by Lady Viola herself. Do you say that she embellished it?"

Lady Clara. He should have known.

He would not for a moment believe that Lady Viola had told such a tale about herself because he would not for a moment believe the truth of it.

"Embellished it?" Roland asked. "I say she has invented it."

"You are walking on dangerous ground, Baderston. Retract that at once."

Roland folded his arms. "I will not."

"You have insulted my sister," Setterdown said. "I will have my answer for it."

"Oh, you want to meet me on a green, do you?" Roland said. "The great Corinthian would like to show his skill with a pistol?"

"You leave me no choice."

Just then, Conbatten came into the hall. "Lady Margaret is concerned that there might be some trouble here?" he asked.

"There is no trouble, Your Grace," Roland said. Daringly, he said, "I would be grateful if you would condescend to act as my second in this matter, as it concerns the honor of your in-laws."

"He has called my sister a liar," Setterdown said.

"As she most certainly is," Roland said. To Conbatten, he said, "Lady Clara is the individual who sent the tale on its rounds about Lady Viola."

Conbatten sighed, rather like he was disgusted. "I am certain that if that is the case, Lady Clara was only mistaken or misheard. There is certainly no need to duel over it."

"I insist," Setterdown said.

"Then I insist, too," Roland said. He was beginning to think Conbatten was right. There might be better ways to untangle whatever had happened. However, he would not for the world back down to a fellow like Setterdown.

"Wonderful," Conbatten said drily. "Setterdown, send your second to me in the morning—we will agree on the details. Both of you go home now. I will not have you interrupting Lady Margaret's card party. Speak to nobody about this. If I hear it mentioned anywhere, I will flog you both. Do not wait for your cloaks or your horse, I will have them sent on."

Roland nodded. "You will say nothing to your duchess? I would not wish Lady Viola to know of it."

Conbatten nodded. "I do not wish *anybody* to know of it. Both of you go home and reflect on what this actually means and hopefully you'll have the good sense to call it off."

Roland nodded, though it would have to be Setterdown to call it off. He turned on his heel and left.

It was a rather long walk home, so he decided to stop at the YBC. The walk there gave him time to reflect on what he had engaged himself to. He had never thought he'd find himself a party to a duel. In truth, he'd always viewed them as particularly stupid. But what was he to do?

Lady Clara may have sent the untrue story around, but at the end of the day, it was his fault. If Lady Clara had not been led to believe there was an engagement to him in the offing, she would not be so vindictive now.

She was vindictive to Lady Viola because she'd noted his interest in her. Lady Viola was being punished on his account and, therefore, he must avenge her.

In any case, if he were absolutely forced to shoot somebody, he did not mind that it was Setterdown.

TATTLETON FELT DOOM settle on his shoulders like a cold blanket. As a butler, he was often not privy to all the details of a thing. He heard this and that, in dribs and drabs, and then must piece the bits together to make some sort of whole.

He very much wished he'd not pieced anything together at this particular moment.

Lady Viola was being disinvited by people in society. She had fallen out with the *ton*.

Lady Viola! Disinvited! It was inconceivable—she was an earl's daughter.

The reason she was being shunned was not entirely clear, though he gathered it was something along the lines of a story about the redhaired tinker's boy that Lady Viola had admired when she'd been very young.

Why was anybody talking about that tinker's boy? Why could they possibly care that she'd mooned over the little fellow when she'd been a young child?

He had, of course, been previously aware that the young ladies had formed the very bad plan of inventing a rumor and sending it round so that the red-haired fellow of today could defend Lady Viola in the face of it.

Tattleton presumed the tale of a tinker's boy had been it, though he could not fathom why they'd chosen that story or why the *ton* seemed to take such offense to it.

An eight-year-old boy who'd winked and an eight-year-old girl who'd taken it to heart—where was the shame in that? There must be earls all over England who were in possession of dramatic daughters who swore they would pine away in heartbreak at the age of eight.

Did the *ton* question Lady Viola's taste on account of it? Would it have made a difference if the boy in question had been higher placed? Society's rules were often mysterious, but this was the most mysterious thing he'd yet encountered.

Whatever trouble was brewing, it was Miss Mayton's doing, he was sure of it. Never was there a woman so unqualified to guide young ladies.

Of course, the earl would not think so. Not when Lady Beatrice and Lady Rosalind were so satisfactorily married. But he, Horace J. Tattleton, had eyes in his head! Watching Miss Mayton lead the young ladies forward was akin to viewing them all stagger through a moonless night on the Cliffs of Dover, hoping they did not accidentally go over the side and plummet into the sea. Sooner or later, though, the disastrous plunge would occur.

Perhaps it had. Perhaps this was it.

Just now, though he was in the hall, he heard Lord Darden practically shout, "But everybody is saying you actually traveled to Gretna Green, not that he asked and you declined."

What was this? Gretna Green?

Miss Mayton's quiet voice, if he could understand her properly, was explaining that was not the story they'd told.

Of course it would not be the story they told. Did they not understand the nature of gossip at all? One plus one equals two, until in the blink of an eye it equals five or six or seven. A fish caught begins the size of a man's hand until it becomes the size of his arm. Stories always grow, they never shrink.

What would the earl say? The poor lord had been shielded from other of Miss Mayton's terrible ideas, but they could not hide this one. The earl would go somewhere in the town, and somebody would say something about it.

Then, an icicle of fear stabbed at Tattleton's heart. There were other letters that had arrived to the house for both Darden and the earl. They were sitting on the silver tray, waiting to be collected.

Perhaps the earl and Lord Darden were being disinvited too.

Tattleton staggered and sat down heavily on a chair in the great hall.

Could it be true? Was the entire family in disgrace?

Was he to be known as the butler to a disgraced family? Only days ago, he'd been happily contemplating that he was the butler to a family now related by marriage to a duke.

"Murder!" Chester shouted in the drawing room.

Tattleton sighed, long and heavy. He was the butler to a disgraced family that owned a bird that shouted about murder.

Where had it all gone wrong?

THOUGH IT WAS growing late, Roland had gone to the Young Bucks Club thinking he could ascertain just how far this rumor about Lady Viola running off to Gretna Green with a tinker had spread. He also hoped he could gather a series of allies to counter it, if it had taken flight as far as he was afraid it had. After all, her own brother was the founder of the club. There would be nobody against her there.

He'd not found Darden in the rooms. He had not found much of anybody. He had, unfortunately, found Chelderberry. That fellow was as new to the club as he was, and Roland had not liked him from the first. He was an unseasoned fellow just out of school who was a cousin to Harveston.

Harveston was a good friend; Roland had known him since they first started school together. Harveston was something of a scholar and would often explain a thing in a way that was understandable when he found Roland was on the verge of hitting his head against a wall in frustration.

Harveston's young cousin Chelderberry was not, unfortunately, as fine a fellow. He had a boyish immaturity about him. An annoying boy, at that.

As far as Roland could tell, Chelderberry considered himself quite the wit. He was forever making some cutting comment and Roland thought he'd made a few quiet enemies in the process. It was all well and good for Mr. Brummel to throw round insulting bon mots, but Chelderberry was not Mr. Brummel. He did not have the standing and he did not have the quickness or the cleverness or the facility of language.

As Chelderberry was the only gentleman in the coffee room, Roland asked him if he knew where Lord Darden could be found.

Chelderberry smirked. "Poor Darden," he said. "He's rushed off home to make sure his sister is not even now jumping into a carriage and heading to Scotland with a grocer."

"What?" Roland said, feeling a rage course through him like a wave coming in hard at the shore.

"Well, Gretna Green and all that," Chelderberry said with a

snort.

Seeing that Roland did not seem to appreciate his words, Chelderberry rose. "It was only a joke," he said.

"No, it was not. Furthermore, it never is. You spend all your time posing as some sort of wit, when in fact you are an immature and spiteful idiot."

"I say, now!" Chelderberry sputtered.

"We all *wish* you would cease saying anything," Roland said. "And, if I hear Lady Viola's name on your lips ever again, you will regret it."

"Will I?" Chelderberry asked, his face tinging pink. "What precisely do you mean to do about it? Get me kicked from the club because *you* cannot take a joke?"

It would have behooved Roland to walk away at that moment, especially since not an hour ago he'd engaged himself to a duel. He'd got himself in enough trouble for one evening. Chelderberry was not worth his time.

"It's not my fault that a lady decided to run to Scotland and then change her mind," Chelderberry said sulkily. "A woman spends days alone in a carriage with some ruffian and we're all supposed to pretend we didn't hear it?"

Roland felt himself going blind with rage. He'd never experienced anything like it. He felt as an animal with no reason or judgment.

Then he boxed Chelderberry in the face.

CHAPTER TWELVE

CHELDERBERRY WAS FELLED by the surprise of Roland's punch and collapsed to the floor. He did not stay there though, and before Roland knew it, they were locked in a battle.

They rolled round the floor, both landing punches when they could. Somewhere far in the distance, Roland heard Harveston shout, "Ho! Stop this instant! Blakeley, give me a hand here."

Lord Blakeley pulled Roland in one direction and Lord Harveston pulled his cousin in another, separating them.

"He threw the first punch," Chelderberry said, rubbing his jaw.

"It was well-earned," Roland said, already feeling the skin round his right eye begin to swell. "He has been insulting regarding Lady Viola and I will not stand for it."

Chelderberry threw his chin up. "It must be difficult to see your lady love has disgraced herself."

Roland once more felt the blindness of rage come over him. He attempted to lunge at Chelderberry, intending to kill him.

Blakeley held him back.

Harveston smacked his cousin on the head. "You are going right back to the country. I told your mother you were too childish to come to Town this year and she should have listened to me."

"You can't send me back!" Chelderberry cried.

"I can and I will," Harveston said. "Your mother holds the

purse strings and I will insist on it. In any case, what would be the point of staying? I can assure you that you are out of the YBC."

"You cannot do that either!" Chelderberry said. "You don't run the club."

Harveston looked at his cousin as if he were a halfwit. Roland was beginning to think that was not far off. For a wit, he was rather dense.

"Lord Darden runs the club," Harveston said, "and you have disrespected his sister. Of course you are out. The rest of us are astute enough to realize that whatever the real story is, it has been blown out of proportion. According to my investigations, Lady Clara is at the bottom of it. She's taken some innocent statement and turned it to something shameful. We at the YBC will stand by Lady Viola."

"How was I to know the story was made up?" Chelderberry said petulantly.

"What you were to know," Harveston said, "is that there is never a bad time to keep your mouth closed and your thoughts to yourself. You will go home and read some books. It will do you good, as I have found your education lacking and your judgment nonexistent."

Harveston turned to Roland. "We are friends and I would like to keep it that way. I apologize for my cousin. He will not bother you further."

Roland nodded, as he had no wish to take the thing any further than it had already gone. He hadn't swung a fist at anybody since he and Markson had a ruthless fight when they were seven.

In any case, the idea that the YBC stood firmly behind Lady Viola had soothed him a little and Chelderberry would shortly be in a carriage heading out of Town. He could not think of one person who would miss the rotter. Not even his own cousin.

On the morrow, he must see Lady Viola. He must call on her. It would not be a particularly ideal time, as his right eye had swollen to an alarming degree and he was certain it looked hideous. But he must see her. He must tell her that he did not countenance the rumor going round and would box any man having the nerve to repeat it.

Arriving home, he jogged up the stairs at a fast pace. There were candles still lit in the drawing room and he supposed the dowager lay in wait there, like a tiger behind a tree in an Indian forest. He slipped into his bedchamber before his mother could spring at him. She might stalk him through the house, but she would always be stopped at his door.

Not even the dowager would dare cross into a gentleman's sanctuary.

Markson emerged from Roland's dressing room.

"What ho!" he said, staring at his eye.

"Chelderberry," he said.

"Ah, the annoying one," Markson said, nodding.

"He spoke ill of Lady Viola and I put a stop to it."

"Right. I'll send for some ice from the icehouse and then a comfrey salve. Though, all the remedies in the world won't make the damage disappear anytime soon. A blackened eye heals on its own time."

Roland had been afraid that would be the case. It was no matter though—let anybody ask him what happened and he would tell them. He would tell them that Chelderberry had dared to affront him on the subject of Lady Viola and been sent packing.

"Also," Roland said slowly, "there has been one other little matter that has come up," Roland said. "I have engaged myself to a duel with Setterdown."

Markson sank into a chair, which must indicate his shock as he had never sat down in Roland's bedchamber. At least, not while he was in it.

"Lady Clara's brother?" his valet asked. "My God, does the dowager know?"

"Yes, it is Lady Clara's brother and no, my mother does not know. Nor does she need to."

"No, of course not," Markson said. "Not unless you turn up dead! Then she will need to know, won't she?"

Markson had begun fanning himself with a handkerchief. "You'll be dead and that awful cousin of yours will turn up and throw us to the road. I was really counting on you having a son to prevent that disaster!"

"I am very sorry that contemplating my death is such an inconvenience to you," Roland said drily. "Though, I have no intention of dying."

"When is it to be?" Markson asked.

"I do not yet know. Conbatten is acting as my second."

"Conbatten," Markson said thoughtfully. "Well that is something, at least."

"I'm glad you approve."

"Do you still go to the theater tomorrow evening?" Markson asked, looking dubious over the idea.

"Yes, I will certainly go. The YBC will be there in full force to show our support for Lady Viola."

Markson nodded. "Just don't take no more swings at anybody. If you bruise the other eye, you'll be staggerin' round like a blind man. You won't do very well at a duel if you can't see!"

Roland lifted his chin. "I am an earl. I will not seek out a fight, but if a fight comes to me, I will fight it."

VIOLA HAD BEEN so startled when Darden had come crashing into the drawing room. Of course, as soon as he'd said he'd heard a terrible report, she'd known what it was.

They'd had a lengthy and painful discussion about her father. It had always been settled between all his children that he ought not be troubled over anything. They had done surprisingly well with the effort—her father had not been vexed since Cordelia had last accidentally set the house on fire.

This circumstance, though, could not be concealed. It was far too public to be hidden. The only thing worse they could conceive of, aside from telling him themselves, was that he heard it from an outsider.

The earl had gone out to play cards at his club and so they'd decided between them that they would see him after breakfast on the morrow.

That breakfast had been a solemn affair, with nobody very cheerful. The earl had not seemed to notice—he was, as usual, buried in his newspapers.

Now, and with heavy hearts, Viola, Darden, and Miss Mayton went to the library to find her father. Before going in, Viola asked Tattleton to see they were not disturbed and, while he nodded his acquiescence, he also looked as if he might faint.

Their poor butler was so high-strung these days. She really did not know the cause of it and supposed it was some personal problem they were not privy to.

Darden knocked and they entered the room.

Viola's heart nearly broke upon observing how happy her father looked to see them.

"Gracious," the earl said, "what is the occasion for this happy visit? You've not gone off and got yourself engaged already, Viola?"

"She has not," Darden said, "and I am afraid this visit is not a happy one."

The earl leapt to his feet. "Is somebody ill? Is it Beatrice? She is with child, you know. Oh, I do fret about that."

"Everyone is in good health, father," Viola said. "I am afraid I have made a mistake. A mistake in society which I imagine you will hear of soon enough."

The earl sat down slowly. Viola placed herself in the chair in front of the desk.

"I really view it as more of a mix-up than a mistake," Miss Mayton said.

"What is this mix-up or mistake," the earl said gravely.

"Well, you see," Viola said, "my sisters and I have spent years discussing what would be most important to us in a husband."

"Yes, I have heard quite a bit of it."

"Of course you have, and you've been very patient with us all. I have always felt that, for me, it must be loyalty. Papa, I just could not bear to find I'd wed a fickle man whose feelings might change over time, or who might resent me for doing something wrong. I'm bound to do something wrong sooner or later, am I not?"

"Sooner has arrived, I'm afraid," Darden muttered.

The earl's brows furrowed. "Child, I do not see anything mistaken in wishing for a loyal husband."

"It's the proving of it that's brought on the difficulty," Miss Mayton said, as if that clarification would answer all questions.

"The proving of it?" the earl asked.

"Lord Baderston has indicated his admiration for me so I thought," Viola said, "that he must prove that he would always be loyal to me."

"Is that the fellow with the red hair?"

"Copper-colored, really," Viola said.

"Well? Has he?"

"We do not know yet," Viola said. "But I fear I have made it impossible."

"I do not see where any of this is going," the earl said. "What is the mix-up or mistake in all of this?"

Darden, no doubt seeing that it would take Viola all day long to actually communicate the facts, said, "Viola put about a story to see if Baderston would stick by her. It was all very innocent, but you know what happens to stories when they travel round."

"People can be terrible gossips," Miss Mayton said, shaking her head sadly.

"Out with it, Darden," the earl said. "The whole thing."

Viola shuddered.

Darden nodded and cleared his throat. "The story put about was that, long ago, a red-haired tinker's boy asked Viola to elope to Gretna Green and she was flattered, but declined. Somehow, the story that travels round now is that Viola actually *went* to

Gretna Green and then changed her mind and returned to her father's house."

There. It was said. The whole horrible thing was said.

Viola gripped the sides of her chair. She had never seen her father appear so grave. She had never before feared that she had disappointed him. Shamed him, even.

"Well," the earl said slowly, "that is a tale indeed. And you think it's known widely?"

"Widely enough for Viola to have received notices from a few matrons that her invitations are rescinded," Darden said.

The earl was silent for what seemed an age. Thoughts raced through Viola's mind—she would be sent home in disgrace, she would become a spinster or be forced to marry some local man who did not care what was said about her. She'd held onto a shred of hope that Lord Baderston could be counted on, but that hope had fled upon seeing her own father's reaction to the news.

How could Lord Baderston stand up against it when all of society believed she'd run off with a tinker? His mother's dislike was one thing, she might be managed. But all of society believing such a shameful thing about Viola? It was impossible that he should go forward with any ideas he might have had. Loyalty was one thing, but absolute shame and disgrace were another. Who would wish to be loyal to a lady who was capable of such a thing?

Lord Baderston would consider it such a betrayal that he'd not been told of it directly from her, even though there was nothing to tell!

"Viola," the earl said, "what you have done in starting this gossip is akin to setting alight a pile of brush in a dry wood. You meant it as a small thing, but it speedily burned out of control."

He sighed and continued. "As anybody might have guessed it would. It was not wise to do it, but I believe you are paying an unjust price for what was really only girlish foolishness."

Girlish and foolish. Yes, that is what she had been. Really, she'd probably been worse than that, but her father was always very kind in his assessment of things.

"Miss Mayton," the earl said, "though I know it seems the girls are all grown, I am afraid you'll need to enact some closer supervision."

Viola stared at her father wide-eyed; her aunt fanned herself. Darden quietly snorted.

"I suppose you'll wish me to pack my things and return home," Viola said.

For one, she thought it likely she would be sent home and would wish to know her fate at once. For another, she would not care for her father to spend any amount of time wondering about her aunt's role in this disaster.

"Return home? Quite the opposite," the earl said. "Running away would only serve as a confirmation in people's minds. This must be faced down."

"That's what I thought, Father," Darden said. "I can assure you that the YBC is prepared to back Viola vigorously. I will call on Rosalind too. With the duke behind us, we cannot fail to make some inroads into the idea that the story is not true."

"Yes," the earl said, "do all of that. The duke can rally some powerful people, not the least of which are the queen and Lady Hightower. I will speak to my friends who are in Town. Meanwhile, we are meant to go to the theater this evening and we will go, heads held high."

"Oh, Papa, I am so sorry that I have brought this much trouble to you," Viola said.

"Do not destroy yourself over it, my dear. If every person ever talked about by the *ton* fell into despair, London would not be half so crowded. I will be interested to see what your copper-haired fellow makes of things."

Viola brushed a tear from her eye. "I am afraid this might be too much for anybody. Even Lord Baderston. And it is all my own fault—has any woman managed to ruin her own happiness so stupidly?"

"Well, it seems I've done it a few times," Miss Mayton said sympathetically. "Remember poor Gregorio? My Italian count dealt himself a deadly blow because I arrived minutes too late. I did very stupidly linger over my breakfast that morning. One less piece of toast might have made all the difference! Alas, one never really knows how things will turn out."

"I should have known though," Viola said. "Everything was going so well, I should have left it going the way it was. I should have trusted without needing proof."

"Do not think the worst of Baderston," Darden said. "He may yet come through."

"Would *you*?" Viola asked her brother. "Would you stick by if you believed the lady you had admired had run off to Gretna Green with another? That the lady you thought you understood had been so flighty and unprincipled? That she had allowed you to admire her without informing you of circumstances that would become known?"

Darden looked away. That was answer enough for Viola.

There was a sharp rap on the door and Tattleton entered. "I am sorry," he said, "I was instructed not to disturb but find that I must. Lord Baderston is in the drawing room. I informed him that Lady Viola and Lord Darden were in conference with you, my lord, but he pushed by me and said he knew all about it. Also, it appears he has been in some sort of brawl. At least, from what I can gather from the state of his face."

Viola felt her heart nearly stop. He was here. He had come.

Why was he here? What brawl?

"You'd best find out what Lord Baderston does here, Viola," her father said. Then very kindly, he said, "Whatever it is, always remember that you have your family. We will always be the bedrock to your foundation—never wavering, never failing, never shifting beneath your feet."

Viola nodded. Her father was such a dear man. Then she looked to Darden. "You will come, Brother?"

"Oh yes," Darden said, "I will be interested to hear what Baderston has to say and even more interested to hear who he has been brawling with."

"It's bound to all come out right, is it not?" Miss Mayton said hopefully.

If Miss Mayton was at all cognizant of the puzzled glances from everybody else in the room, she did not say so.

CHAPTER THIRTEEN

ROLAND HAD EXPERIENCED a very startling morning. Markson had brought him up a tray with two letters on it. One was from Conbatten. The duke had tried to negotiate an apology with Setterdown's second, but it was refused. That was just as well—he would never have apologized to the rogue. The duel was set for Wednesday dawn in a remote spot in Hyde Park.

Seeing it in writing made it very real. More real than it had been. It had been very stupid to engage himself to a duel, but he'd done it and there was no going back now. Setterdown had earned himself a set down.

The second letter was a deal more surprising. It was from Chelderberry, demanding satisfaction. Since there had been blows exchanged, there could be no apology. As Chelderberry was being very unfairly sent home and set to depart Thursday, he demanded a duel on Wednesday. Roland's seconds were to determine the location and inform his own. All further communication should be made to his friend, Mr. Hammish.

Roland presumed that since Harveston was not mentioned, he did not know anything about it.

Should he inform him of it?

How could he possibly be engaged for another duel? What was he getting himself into? Further, it was to be on the same morning as the other one!

There was nothing for it, a gentleman could not with honor

turn from a duel that arose from fisticuffs. Nor could they run to a cousin to tattle about it.

If it were to be the same morning, he'd best make it the same location. He could not be in two places at once. As for his own second, he thought he would not tell Conbatten of it. At least, not yet. After all, the duke would already be there for the duel with Setterdown, he did not suppose it was too much of a burden to stay for a second go round.

He wrote Mr. Hammish the details and then was determined to drive it from his mind. It was two days away and he had other matters to attend to.

Since then, he'd pushed his way into Lady Viola's drawing room, determined to see her.

The butler had informed him that neither she nor Lord Darden were available, as they were in conference with the earl. He'd been certain he could guess the topic of conversation and told the butler he already knew all about it. He only hoped Lady Viola was not being persecuted by her father over this unfortunate circumstance.

Or worse, sent away.

Once inside the drawing room, he became acquainted with several things. The ladies Cordelia and Juliet, Lady Viola's younger sisters, had taken him in hand, introduced themselves, and then interrogated him.

"Lord Baderston," Lady Juliet said, "I cannot help but notice that you have a blackened eye."

"Is it black already?" he asked.

"More of a purple color," Lady Cordelia said. "Were you in a boxing ring recently?"

"Of a sort," he said, having no intention of laying out the facts to these two young ladies.

"One would like to think you've boxed a fellow right into the ground over my sister," Lady Cordelia said.

"Pounded into dust over Viola," Lady Juliet said nodding. "It's a lovely thought, is it not?"

A parrot in a cage near the window screamed, "Murder!"

Roland jumped. Seeing his alarm, Lady Juliet said, "That is Chester. Unfortunately, he's picked up that word from Cordelia's acting out of Desdemona's death from *Othello*. You really should see her perform it, it's terribly heartbreaking."

"Now, Jules," Lady Cordelia said, "you are putting a bushel over your own light." To Roland she said, "Our Juliet is a poetess. Just now she's completed a new ode in under a quarter of an hour. I expect you'd want to hear it?"

"Ah, of course," Roland said, not entirely certain of what was soon to come in his direction. A parrot cried murder, one sister seemingly routinely acted as Desdemona dying, and the other one wrote an ode in fifteen minutes?

He must assume this was one of the very short odes that Lady Viola had mentioned as being superior to Wordsworth.

Lady Juliet stood. "Ode to Beatrice."

The news on the road was perfectly wild
Our sister Beatrice is now with child.
Van Doren has very predictably lost his mind
That is the truth and therefore not unkind.

Both sisters looked to him for his reaction. His real reaction was, *What on God's green earth was that?* Instead, he said, "Brava, Lady Juliet."

They nodded at him approvingly. Lady Juliet said, "Now, you are in for an even bigger treat. Follow us."

He did as he was told and followed them to the far end of the drawing room to an easel and canvas.

What he beheld there was…he did not know what it was. It was a multi-colored oval of…something.

"You see?" Lady Cordelia said. "It is Chester! Viola took up painting last year and well, you can judge for yourself how it's going."

He certainly could judge *something*, though the idea that it was going anywhere was bizarre.

Roland had a sudden remembrance of something Lady Viola had told him—the great portrait painter, Thomas Lawrence, had viewed one of her works.

Well, it could not have been as bad as this one. Perhaps she was a deal more skilled at capturing the likenesses of people, rather than parrots.

"One might even imagine having a lady take up a permanent residence in one's house and that lady might paint portraits that could be hung in the great hall," Lady Juliet said.

"Did you ever imagine anything like that, Lord Baderston?" Lady Cordelia asked.

Quite naturally, he had not ever imagined having such a canvas hung in his great hall. However, seeing how keen the sisters were, and guessing they were hinting that the lady painter was Lady Viola, he nodded and said, "It is a thing to contemplate and look forward to."

The drawing room doors were thrown open. "Lord Baderston," Lady Viola said.

There she was, and looking particularly smashing in a simple muslin. She was not alone, as Darden and Miss Mayton were on her heels.

Roland bowed. "Lady Viola, Lord Darden, Miss Mayton."

"I've asked for a tea tray to be sent in," Lady Viola said. She hesitated, then said quietly, "If you can stay, of course."

"I'd be delighted," Roland answered.

This seemed to be met with approval from everybody. Except for the parrot, who screamed, "Murder!"

"Baderston," Lord Darden said. He then turned to the younger sisters and said, "Cordy, Jules, Miss Mayton will take you above stairs."

"What?" Lady Juliet said, clearly outraged over the suggestion.

"Come, now," Lord Darden said. "This is important. You so rarely follow any of my orders, but I beg you to do so now."

Lady Juliet's face fell. Lady Cordelia said, "Very well, we will humor you this time, Darden. Our aunt can read to us from *The Harrowing Homecoming of Harrowbridge Hall.*" She turned to Roland and said, "It's getting very exciting. There are two dukes, and one of them is not real. Who will the gentle governess choose?"

As Roland did not have a firm answer to that, he just said, "The right one, I hope?"

"I know what to do," Miss Mayton said, "let us take the book into the library and read to your father. He does not like to miss a chapter and he could use some cheering up and…distraction."

The sisters seemed very approving of the idea and made their curtsies. They left the room with their aunt, just as the butler and footmen came in with a tea tray.

"Murder?" the bird shouted.

"Oh dear, he means almonds," Lady Viola said. She hurried to the tray as it was set down and took a small bowl of the nuts to the cage.

The arrival of the almonds seemed to capture the bird's entire attention and Roland hoped there would be no more mention of murder.

The butler and footmen retreated. Roland said, "If I may speak plainly, Lady Viola. Lord Darden."

"Please do," Lady Viola said quietly. She looked rather shaken. That was to be expected, of course, considering what she was going through.

Roland had thought long about what he would reveal. He'd decided that he absolutely could not reveal the two duels he was engaged for on Wednesday. It would put Lady Viola, and Darden for that matter, in a terrible position.

He would relay the facts to Lady Viola afterward. Assuming he was alive.

On the other hand, he had also decided that he absolutely *could* tell her of boxing Chelderberry.

"Lord Darden, it is my duty to inform you that I have boxed

Chelderberry in your coffee room. The encounter occurred last night. I know that sort of behavior is anathema to everything the YBC stands for, however, what Chelderberry had to say for himself could *not* be stood for."

Lord Darden nodded. "It looks like he boxed you back."

Roland raised his chin in what he hoped was a very stalwart manner. "There was a minor scuffle."

"I presume he had something to say about my sister?" Lord Darden said.

"He did, and I shut his mouth permanently on the subject. Harveston is sending his young cousin back to the countryside and we shall hear no more about it."

"I trust you and Harveston have not had a falling out over it?" Darden said. "I know you have been longstanding friends."

"We remain so," Roland said.

Lord Darden said, "I cannot say I am sorry to see Chelderberry go. We accepted him as a courtesy to Harveston, but I got the feeling the club members never really liked him. I get the feeling that even Harveston doesn't like him."

"You boxed this Chelderberry on my account?" Lady Viola asked, looking rather pleased to hear it.

"I did," Roland said. "Most violently."

Here, this moment, was his opportunity to prove his loyalty.

"I will not countenance any man," he continued, "who dares to repeat this ridiculous story making the rounds. I know it to be untrue and will not stand for it."

"Good man," Darden said, looking pleased as Punch.

"*How* do you know, Lord Baderston?" Viola asked. "How are you so sure it is not true?"

"I know because you are a lady of the highest caliber. Nobody will ever convince me otherwise. There is nothing I could ever hear that would have the slightest effect upon me." He paused, then said, "I am right, though? Am I not? It is not true."

"Of course it is not true," Viola said. "I told a very innocent story to Lady Clara, about a tinker's boy who once asked me to run off with him. I most certainly did not actually go anywhere. I should probably have clarified that I was only eight-years-old at the time, as was he.”

Roland felt struck once again that the author of this disaster had been Lady Clara.

It was his fault this had happened. If his mother had not been forever pushing a match…if he had not ignored the dowager’s plans for so long…none of this would have happened.

He did not believe Lady Clara was in the least interested in him. He guessed that she was offended, and feeling vindictive, that *he* was not interested in her either. She had sought to strike out at someone, and she had struck at Lady Viola.

“Lord Darden,” he said, “I vow I will make every effort to ensure that all of society knows this tale to be false.”

Lord Darden nodded. “The YBC will be out in full force and I will visit my sister and the duke for their backing. We will go to the theater this night and I plan for club members to be there and acknowledge Viola. That will send a message.”

“You can count on me. I will be sure to attend,” Roland said.

“But, Lord Baderston,” Lady Viola said, “do you think you will be able to see the play. With your eye…”

As Roland could no longer see out of his right eye, he very well knew it had swollen shut.

“A small inconvenience,” he said stoically.

“I am sorry that Chelderberry got a shot in,” Lord Darden said.

“He was only lucky,” Roland said with a sniff. “I can assure you that he got the worst of it. So will the next gentleman who tries it.”

⤜⤜⤜❋⤛⤛⤛

VIOLA THREW HERSELF onto the sofa after Lord Baderston had left.

“Darden,” she said dreamily, “he’s done it. He’s proved his

loyalty beyond any shadow of a doubt."

"So he has."

Viola sighed. "Just an hour ago, I felt as if I had destroyed my whole life. And now look! Everything is roses."

"Not quite roses," Darden said. "We have a road ahead of us. You must prepare yourself for this evening, Viola. We will be stared at, and it will be all too evident that we are talked about."

"What care I about this town's opinions?" Viola said.

"I care, and father cares," Darden said. "If Cordy and Jules had a lick of sense between them, they'd care too. Do not forget that your sisters will follow you for their own turns in society. We must ensure that they are not tainted by what has happened."

Viola sat up. She had not even thought of such a thing. "Oh Darden! I had not thought…"

"Do not upset yourself unduly. We must only stand firm together and bring in everybody we can. And please promise— start no more rumors about yourself!"

"No more stories," Viola said. It was an easy promise—there was nothing left for Lord Baderston to prove.

The door opened and Rosalind very unexpectedly flew through it. "My dearest Viola, what mischief has been stirred up!"

"I see the story has traveled to your door?" Darden asked his sister.

"Indeed, it has. Now, I do not know how such a ridiculous thing is being at all believed. Clearly anybody with sense must see that it has been blown up and embellished. But do not worry, I have told my duke all about the truth of the tinker's boy and he is ready to assist. I believe you go to the theater tonight? We will abandon our box and sit in yours."

"That will send a strong message, I think," Darden said.

Rosalind nodded. "My darling of a husband says he will stare down anybody looking our way. You know how grim he can be when he has a mind."

"He is a dear to do it," Viola said. "Now Rosalind, do sit and have a cup of tea. Lord Baderston has boxed a person named

Chelderberry right in the face and said some lovely things."

"Goodness, I want to hear it all," Rosalind said.

Darden rose. "As I have already heard it, I will depart. I will go to the club and rally the members."

"You are a stalwart brother, Darden," Rosalind said.

"Yes, I know," Darden said, no doubt remembering the stalwartness that had been required of him *last* season.

After Darden had left, Viola told her sister all about how Lord Baderston was the best man living and had a black eye.

ROLAND HAD HOPED he might slip in the house unnoticed, but that was not to be. He'd gone in through the front doors, assuming she would be out somewhere, as she usually was during the day.

As it happened, the dowager had been cruising the great hall like an enemy warship guarding a harbor.

She followed him into the library.

"What has happened to your face?" she asked.

"A minor scuffle not worth reviewing," he said, not at all wishing to discuss it.

The dowager sniffed. "Perhaps Miss Mayton has claimed another victim."

Roland did not answer, and she continued on, "Never mind, I will not be turned from my purpose. I have heard alarming reports. Alarming reports, Baderston."

"Yes, alarming reports seem to be the fashion these days," he said drily.

"Lady Rumsgartner paid a visit this morning," the dowager went on. "Guess what she told me?"

Roland suppressed a sigh. He had no need to guess. "That old bat told you that Lady Viola once ran off with a tinker's son to Gretna Green, then changed her mind and went home."

The dowager staggered and sat herself in a chair. "What?"

"What?" Roland asked back, entirely nonplussed. If Lady Rumsgartner had not told that story, what *had* she told?

"Lady Rumsgartner informed me that she has written to Lady Viola and told her not to attend her soiree. She informed me that everybody has seen that you are partial to Lady Viola, but the girl is not what she appears to be. What is this about a run to Gretna Green?"

Roland really did not feel like explaining things to his mother, and he really *did* feel like hitting Lady Rumsgartner over the head with one of her own ridiculous bonnets. How dare she shun Lady Viola?

Of course, if Lady Rumsgartner had turned her back on Lady Viola, just as Lady Margaret had, there were probably others. Lady Viola was so brave in the face of it all!

"From your silence, I will presume that tale is what Lady Rumsgartner meant when she came to warn us away from Lady Viola. As if I needed any warning. I've said right from the start that countenancing that person was a mistake. Really, Baderston, at this point it is difficult to even style her as a lady. My own opinion—"

"Stop where you are, Dowager," Roland said.

The dowager did stop, likely from surprise. She was not accustomed to being interrupted and certainly not accustomed to her son calling her dowager.

"The story going round is entirely untrue," Roland said, "and it was your protégé, Lady Clara, who sent it round. The real story, if you must know it, is that a tinker's boy asked her to run off when she was *eight years old*. Obviously, she did not go anywhere."

"Well, regardless of what the truth of it is—"

"No! Not 'regardless of what the truth is.' What a ridiculous thing to say. Lady Clara has caused a deal of trouble, and all because you have encouraged her to think there will be a match, which there will never be. You will stop your meddling or you will be out of this house. This is your last warning. Furthermore, you can tell Lady Rumsgartner that she is a sour old thing and I would sooner she jump off a cliff than give me her opinion. That is my final word."

He left his mother looking rather pale and jogged up the stairs and into his bedchamber.

CHAPTER FOURTEEN

VIOLA HELD HER head up high as she entered the theater box. Miss Mayton had been very clever in counseling her on what dress she ought to wear. They had chosen a white silk edged in yellow daisies. The white would signal that she was not in hiding, she was not afraid to be seen in the dim light of a theater, and the daisies communicated her innocence.

As further ammunition, Rosalind and Conbatten had brought their carriage to Portland Place and then followed them to Drury Lane so that they might be noted walking in together.

Conbatten held his arm out for her, while the earl took Miss Mayton and Darden took Rosalind.

The duke certainly knew what he was about. The stares and whispers were noticeable.

She was seated next to her father and Miss Mayton, with Conbatten, Rosalind, and Darden behind her. Amidst all the stares, there was one that did not weigh upon her—Lord Baderston was in his box and had just very publicly bowed to her.

Viola nodded in acknowledgement. From the distance, she could perceive that his eye did not seem much improved. She was both thrilled at the idea that he'd boxed Chelderberry on her behalf, and worried that it looked even worse than it had when he'd visited the house.

Rosalind leaned forward and said, "It seems Lord Baderston only has eyes for you, Viola. He is using his one good eye very forcefully."

Viola turned her head and said, "I do think he will ask the momentous question—I only hope it will be soon."

"We all hope it will be soon," the duke said drily.

"Ah, look at that," Darden said from Rosalind's other side. "The YBC has turned up in force in the pit."

Viola gazed down upon the pit and one gentleman after another made a very obvious bow in her direction.

She smiled to indicate her appreciation and then looked away to indicate her modesty.

In the looking away, her eyes fell upon a box she'd rather not have noticed. Lady Clara sat with her parents, staring in her direction.

"I find her very bold," Rosalind said.

"No, my darling," the duke said to his wife. "*You* are bold, she is simply an annoyance."

The acrobats finished to applause, though Viola had hardly been cognizant that they were there. The play they were to see was called *Hear both Sides*, which Viola thought was ironic, since the *ton* never did pause to hear both sides. Lady Clara had spread a false story and it had been devoured unquestioned.

Viola had felt a bit shaken in the carriage, as the day had brought more letters from matrons who no longer wished to know her. What had once been a very full calendar had significantly dwindled. As well, her aunt had speculated that there might be hostesses who did not write, but just hoped she would not turn up.

She had wondered what she would walk into when she entered the theater. Would anybody make their disdain for her publicly known?

As the acrobats left the stage and it was prepared for the play, the theater was filled with the general chatter of people talking.

Then, one lone voice shouted from the pit.

"Has anybody seen where the tinker's boy got off to?"

Conbatten and Darden both leapt to their feet. The earl, in a calm and controlled voice, said, "Sit down, if you please."

They did both reluctantly sit down. The earl was right, there was no point in leaping into any sort of action. The members of the YBC were already down there and looking everywhere about themselves.

It was impossible to tell where the shout had come from.

Movement caught Viola's eye and she saw that Lord Baderston had leapt up and pointed.

What was he doing?

"He's seen the culprit," Darden said. "Good, he will tell me on the morrow and the entire club will snub the villain."

"I believe the young lord has more in mind than a snub, if I know him sufficiently," Conbatten said with a disgusted sigh.

The duke was right. Lord Baderston had just raced out of his box.

"Good for Lord Baderston," Rosalind said approvingly.

The earl said quietly, "It would be better to leave it ignored."

"He cannot help it, Papa," Rosalind said. "He is a young man in love, what else can he do?"

"That is very true," Miss Mayton said. "Goodness, I suppose Count Tulerstein would have fought anybody for my love. If anybody had turned up that needed fighting."

"Before he fell off the cliff?" Conbatten said, with what Viola was certain was a snort of laughter.

"He threw himself off, Your Grace," Miss Mayton said. "He very determinedly flung himself."

Viola leaned forward to watch Lord Baderston enter the pit. It seemed she was not alone in noticing that he'd gone there to confront the shouter. Others were leaning over their boxes and watching him too.

Lord Baderston pushed through the crowd, seeming to know precisely where he was going.

Just then, a fellow seemed particularly struck to see Lord Baderston heading in his direction. The man turned on his heel and began to push through the other people to get away.

"Do not dare run from me, you rogue!" Lord Baderston shouted.

Viola sighed. He was magnificent.

ROLAND HAD BEEN scanning the crowd, looking for anyone who might cause trouble. He'd already shamed one young gentleman who had been glancing at Lady Viola's box and whispering to a friend.

When that fool had looked about, Roland had very determinedly caught his eye and given him a deadly stare. The fellow had pinked and turned away.

Everyone was to know—the Benningtons were not without friends.

Between threatening stares, he found time to look over at Lady Viola's box. Conbatten and his duchess were there, and the duke was looking suitably grim.

Squinting and using his good eye, Roland was able to satisfy himself that no other lady in the theater, or in all of England, could hold a candle to Lady Viola.

She sat very regal, with her head held high. She wore a white silk dress with delicate yellow daisies round the neckline and the message was not lost on him. Daisies for innocence.

Well done, Lady Viola.

He forced himself to look elsewhere as to not be unseemly about it. Then, his eyes settled on Mr. Berger. Roland did not like Mr. Berger. Mr. Berger was the son of a baron and formed along the same lines as Chelderberry. Too unseasoned, lacking in correct instincts, thinking himself a wit, and somehow very crass.

He watched Mr. Berger talk to his companion, smirking and looking up at Lady Viola's box. Then he ribbed his friend and shouted, "Does anybody know where the tinker's boy has got to?"

Roland was out of his box like a shot. He raced down the stairs and into the pit. He pushed his way through the crowd.

Mr. Berger saw him coming, and no doubt noted his rage. He turned and attempted to escape.

There would be no escape for Mr. Berger.

Roland was vaguely aware that the chase was becoming a spectacle, as people were shouting to him about which way Mr. Berger went.

He was not enthusiastic about garnering so much attention, but there was no turning back now.

If the crowd were to be relied upon, Mr. Berger was heading out of the theater. The coward.

Roland redoubled his efforts. He was helped along by those in the pit who would be amused to see him catch up with Mr. Berger.

That fellow had just burst out the doors and into the saloon, no doubt headed for the street.

Roland followed him just as fast.

⟫⟩✕⟨⟪

Viola had just watched Lord Baderston chase through the pit after a gentleman she did not know. That fellow had been the horrible shouter—how ghastly that someone who did not even know her made public comment on their opinion of her.

She was all but certain that Lord Baderston was just now in another boxing match. When she'd thought of him proving his loyalty, she had not considered the toll it might take on his physical person.

"Young men these days," the earl said, shaking his head.

"Oh Papa," Rosalind said, "you cannot mean anything by it. What would we have thought of Lord Baderston if he'd not answered the insult?"

"He could not ignore it, Papa," Viola said. "Though I take full responsibility for putting him in the situation."

"And what a situation it is," Conbatten said behind her.

"I find Baderston is shaping up to be a fine fellow," Darden said.

The play had started and Viola turned her head toward the stage, though her eyes were elsewhere.

Were anyone to apply a lorgnette to discover what she was doing, they would note that while her head seemed to look one way, her eyes were looking at Lord Baderston's box.

Would he return to it? It was hard to know. If he'd ended up boxing that rude fellow he'd chased out, his clothes might be rumpled and torn.

She did so long to see his face, even as it was now—marred by a rather gruesome swollen and purple eye.

The play proceeded, but Viola could not have explained to anybody what it was about. Her thoughts were all taken up by Lord Baderston. If he would ask her the momentous question, they might marry in all haste and leave London. They need not linger to hear what people would say about her. Or what his mother would say about her.

They would go on a wedding trip somewhere. Rosalind had done her best to convince all her sisters to never set foot on a boat after her harrowing trip to the continent, but Viola did not think she would mind it. She imagined floating up and down on the waves and thought it might be very soothing. In any case, wherever they went they would go together and that was the important thing.

Her thoughts took her here and there, all with Lord Baderston. Finally, sometime into the second act, the lord did return to his box.

Viola instantly realized that she'd not been the only person wondering if he would come back. Heads turned in waves as if the king himself had taken his box.

This gave Viola just enough of a moment unobserved to apply her lorgnette without being spotted.

Lord Baderston sat, very straight and stoic, looking at the stage as if he were intrigued by the play.

His poor dear face, though. Could he even *see* the play? His other eye was swollen now too, and his lower lip cut.

He must have had a terrible fisticuffs with that rude fellow.

"Hard to tell who got the worst of it," Darden said.

"I cannot quite imagine worse than what I am seeing," Conbatten said. "He'd best be careful he does not find himself spending his mornings on lonely greens."

"You may be right," Darden said to the duke. "Chelderberry is being sent out of Town, but too many more of these fights and he just might receive a challenge."

A duel? Viola's heart felt as if it had turned to ice. Before she'd come to London, when she'd only dreamed of gentlemen in fine clothes who were desperately in love with her, imagining a duel had sounded highly romantic. It had sounded like some sort of game for a gentleman to risk his life for love of her.

It did not sound romantic now. It did not feel like a game. She could not bear it if something were to happen to Lord Baderston.

"Duke, you do not think…"

Behind her, the duke said gravely, "Many a hot-tempered fellow has found himself in that ridiculous situation."

There was something in the duke's tone that she did not like. It was almost as if he *did* think Lord Baderston would end up in a duel.

It could not be! She could not allow it.

But how was she to know of it or stop it if she did know? Duels were never spoken of else they be interfered with by a magistrate. Sometimes they were widely known, but that was only afterward if there had been a serious injury that could not be concealed. Or worse, a death.

Viola's ideas about love were changing so rapidly she could hardly keep up with them. Where once she would have thrilled over a dawn meeting to defend her honor, now she only wished that she and Lord Baderston could go on to live a quiet and peaceful life.

That was how it must be. She must find a way to stop Lord Baderston from boxing people who caused her offence. She would have once demanded his fury. She would have expected it and approved of it. Now she wished for quite the opposite.

WHEN ROLAND WOKE up, he found his eyes had swollen to such a degree that he could only see through two narrow slits.

It was like looking at the world through window shutters. It was not ideal, but at least he had not allowed the insult to Lady Viola to pass by unanswered.

Markson knocked and then brought in his breakfast tray. When his valet had first caught sight of him last evening, Roland had worried that he might have some sort of fit.

His valet had then blathered on about how when one went to the theater, one ought to watch the play—not chase after fellows and roll around the street with them.

Roland had pointed out that a lady's honor had been at stake. Markson had said any lady *he* might associate with could find herself insulted down to her shoes with nary a shrug from him. Women were not the delicate creatures they were made out to be and could fight their battles on their own. His evidence for this theory was the two washerwomen who had apparently done just that not a week ago when he was out for a stroll.

Had Roland been not quite so bruised up, he might have scolded his valet for placing Lady Viola in the same category as two bad-tempered washerwomen.

At least this morning his valet had seemed to have regained his composure. "There's a letter on the tray, just delivered," Markson said.

Roland nodded, though it hurt his head to do so. "I see you intend to mock me, as I cannot possibly read anything just this minute."

"Gerald is fetching some ice from the icehouse," Markson said. "Shall I read it to you?"

"Yes, go ahead," Roland said. He was fairly certain Markson made himself free with reading various letters he left around anyway.

Markson opened the letter and scanned its single page. He dropped it on the carpet.

Roland sat up straighter. "What is it? Who is it from? What does it say? Why are you looking as if you've seen a ghost?"

"I ain't seen a ghost this very morning," Markson said. "But I expect to see one soon and he'll be driftin' round in *your* clothes."

"What are you talking about? Clarify yourself."

"This here is from a Mr. Berger and he says considering the actions taken last night at the theater, he must demand satisfaction. He inquires about who your second might be."

Roland leaned back into his pillows. Another duel? That was three!

"Turn it down," Markson said, "tell 'em you already got a duel scheduled so your calendar is full."

"Two."

"Two what?" Markson asked.

"Two duels," Roland said quietly. "Chelderberry wrote yesterday."

"But," Markson said, sputtering, "this would make three! A fellow is lucky enough to come out of one duel alive—how is he to come out of three of them?"

"I do not know," Roland said in a tone of resolve, "but I have scheduled the other two for the same morning. I might as well throw this one in there too. Get a sheet of paper and I will write back."

Roland paused, then said, "No, I will dictate and you will write. I can barely see and do not wish for my handwriting to give away any weakness."

"Your *handwriting* to give you away? It's your face that will give away the weakness!"

"My eyes should be a deal better by the morrow," Roland said, hoping that was indeed the case. "In fact, get me a second sheet of paper too. I would not like Lady Viola to see me in my current condition—it might put her off—but I must reassure her of my continuing devotion."

"I see. You'll write a love letter to the lady," Markson said. "Or, rather, I'll write a love letter to the lady."

"Do not be ridiculous," Roland said. "I cannot write anything over-personal until I've spoken to her father, and I cannot declare myself until I have come out the other side of these duels."

"*If* you come out the other side. But wait, if it's not a love letter, what is it you're sending then?"

"A ham," Roland said. "That will say more than my words ever could. The note will simply read: To Lady Viola, from an admirer. Tell the footman who delivers it to wear his own coat—no livery. It would not be seemly to be able to so easily identify the admirer."

"A ham," Markson said quietly.

"She adores ham," Roland said. "What could be more obvious?"

There was a soft knock on the door and Markson went to answer it. It was young Gerald with a bucket of ice.

Markson took it from him and said, "Tell cook to put aside a ham. He's to wrap it all attractive-like."

"A ham?" Gerald asked.

"That's right, a ham," Markson said. "I'll tell ya where to take it and you're to wear your own coat. Don't go questioning it, it'll just give you a headache."

After Markson closed the door, he said, "And what am I to write to this fella who wishes to blow your brains out?"

"Tell Mr. Berger that I will meet him at dawn on Wednesday, up Constitution Hill to the Field of Blood. Write that Conbatten will be there as my second, but he is a busy man and need not be bothered by any further communications."

"The Field of Blood?" Markson cried.

"It is just the name for a convenient spot to duel, he will know where it is. Anyway, that's where the other two will be."

"What does Conbatten say to this? Is he comfortable acting as your second for all these duels in one morning?"

Roland shifted. "The duke will be informed of the...extra gentlemen...on the green that morning. There is no reason to disturb him beforehand—one or three, what matter, really? Now, do put ice in a cloth for my eyes and fetch the writing paper. I want that ham delivered this morning."

CHAPTER FIFTEEN

TATTLETON FELT IT would be a very fine thing if he went deaf and heard nothing else coming in through his ears that traveled on to disturb his mind. These days, it seemed that all the snippets and ideas that came into his ears as he went in and out of the drawing room were in some ghastly competition with each other to see which of them could stop his heart first.

The latest, from what he could gather, was that Lady Viola's copper-haired gentleman had been in two different physical altercations. The sisters and Miss Mayton were mulling over how to keep the fellow out of a duel.

A duel.

Tattleton had a great respect for the *ton* and all its habits and idiosyncrasies. He had always liked being one who was elevated enough to be in the know about them. It gratified him that, unlike the majority of people living in England, he knew the difference between an oyster fork and an olive fork. He took pride in the precise measurements of his place settings and his vast knowledge of fine wines. He appreciated the elegant rules of a high-placed house.

However, he could never, hard as he tried, make any sense out of a duel.

What right-thinking gentleman looks about him and notices he is as rich as Croesus and has a title granting him entry into all the fine houses and then thinks, "I should fight a duel and leave this earth unnecessarily early. I should have a drunken argument over anything at all and demand satisfaction. I will, for some reason, be satisfied that I am dead."

Even now, the papers were full of the *Newfoundland Dog Duel*. Two idiots fought over their two idiot dogs and now one was dead and the other being tried for murder. As far as Tattleton knew it, the dogs themselves were perfectly sanguine about this turn of events and could care less.

Now, there was a concern for Lady Viola's gentleman engaging himself in that madness?

What sort of uproar would overtake the house if he were maimed or crippled or killed?

And even more bone-chilling to contemplate, what sort of plan would the ladies come up with to stop the young lord? Their remedies were almost always worse than the initial complaint they were meant to cure!

One of the footmen raced down the hall to him. "A visitor for Lady Viola, Mr. Tattleton," he said.

"Let me hazard a guess," the butler said. "He has red hair and looks as if he has boxed with Gentleman Jackson."

The footman squinted. "No, Mr. Tattleton, it's Lady Hightower to see Lady Viola."

VIOLA HAD SPENT the morning with Juliet, Cordelia, and her aunt, discussing the idea that they must not allow Lord Baderston to somehow get lured into a duel.

At first, Miss Mayton had not entirely understood the reason for Viola's concern. Certainly, she thought, a duel must convey the strongest of sentiments and she was in no doubt that all of her many loves on the continent would have been enthusiastic at the prospect of proving himself on a green.

But then, Viola had pointed out that it might not go their

way, Lord Baderston might end up being killed. Miss Mayton had thought that over and then confirmed that having to say a final goodbye to a would-be husband was in fact dreadful.

Once they were agreed on what must be done, the further problem of how it was to be accomplished had been wrestled with.

Viola could not simply request that Lord Baderston refuse any and all offers of duels, nor attempt to ban him from issuing any challenges. No gentleman would countenance such a thing and she did not even have the standing to ask it.

His mother might, but that lady had not proved herself very helpful and Viola trembled at the thought of going to her. What was she to say? She was currently a nobody to the dowager. A not approved of nobody. In fact, her standing would have sunk even lower than it had been with the lady. The dowager would have heard the rumor by now.

"Perhaps we do nothing at all," Miss Mayton said. "After all, I am certain that the talk will dwindle and disappear once you are married. You will be a countess and the elevation of it will tamp it down. A countess whose sister is a duchess—who would dare slander you then?"

Her aunt was probably right. But, he had not yet asked! When would he ask?

"That's it, then," Juliet said. "I don't know what he's waiting for, but you've just got to hurry him up."

"I agree," Cordelia said.

"But how to hurry him?" Viola said. "I believe he knows my inclinations, what else can I do?"

"Perhaps you will need to be direct," Miss Mayton said. "As we've seen in past seasons, gentlemen are not the sharpest needles in the sewing box. Subtlety appears to be lost on them— we need a proverbial hammer to the head."

"Hammer to the head?" Juliet asked. "I like that idea—I will write an ode about it."

Tattleton opened the drawing room doors. "Lady Hightower,

my lady."

Viola leapt to her feet, as did her sisters and Miss Mayton. Lady Hightower was about the last person she expected to visit. She did not know the lady over-well—she had only met her at Almack's and then played at her musical evening. Of course, she did know that the lady was a great friend of Conbatten's.

Viola felt herself deflating just a little bit, when she contemplated that Lady Hightower may have come to express her displeasure. Her musical evening had come and gone, but perhaps she wished to say that if she had known about the talk going round, she would not have invited Lady Viola Bennington.

"Lady Viola, Miss Mayton, I hope I do not intrude," Lady Hightower said.

"Goodness no, we are very pleased to see you," Viola said.

"And these must be your younger sisters? I remember them from the park last season. During the pickpocket incident." With a barely suppressed smile, she said, "Your sister's *darkest hour*, if I recall correctly."

Viola certainly remembered Rosalind writing of her darkest hour to Lady Hightower afterwards. She just did not know why it seemed Lady Hightower thought the sentiment was amusing. She clearly did, as this was the second time she'd referred to it.

Viola's sisters had curtsied low. Viola said, "Indeed yes, these are my youngest sisters—that is Lady Juliet and this is Lady Cordelia. Tattleton, do send in a tea tray."

"It is already being prepared, my lady."

The butler closed the doors in his most elevated and grave style.

"I will be direct, Lady Viola, as I do not have the first idea how so many people stumble through life being indirect."

Viola nodded, though she was rather frightened of what direct thing she was about to hear.

"I will allow your younger sisters to stay and listen. They will have their own seasons and perhaps they will learn something from what has transpired recently."

Cordelia and Juliet did not look quite as eager as they usually would when not being sent off.

"Murder!" Chester shouted from his cage.

Lady Hightower jumped and clutched her fichu.

"I am sorry, Lady Hightower," Viola said hurriedly. "Chester does not mean anything by it. He heard me mention a tea tray and now he will expect almonds."

Tattleton once more opened the doors and let in two of the footmen with the trays.

"Murder, murder, murder!" Chester shouted enthusiastically, hopping from one claw to the other.

Tattleton swiftly took a bowl of almonds from one of the trays and threw its contents into the cage.

"Bad man," Chester whispered.

"There now," Miss Mayton said, "he will quiet for a time."

"That is a badly-trained parrot, Lady Viola," Lady Hightower pointed out. "If one wishes one's parrot to request almonds, one ought to teach it to say almonds."

Viola, Cordelia, and Juliet all nodded sadly. Miss Mayton just shrugged.

"We acquired him only recently from a certain Mr. Ladle," Viola said. "Chester was his wife's dear bird and when she died Mr. Ladle was trying to sell poor Chester at an inn. Upon becoming acquainted with Mr. Ladle, we fear poor Mrs. Ladle did not have a happy life."

"And so you purchased the bird," Lady Hightower said, seeming a bit softened toward Chester.

"We paid nothing, Lady Hightower," Juliet said. "We told Mr. Ladle that it was certain that Mrs. Ladle and God were watching his shameful behavior from heaven and were disgusted."

Viola wondered if Juliet ought to have been so bold, but not for long.

Lady Hightower roared with laughter. "Oh, that is good. Mr. Ladle is no doubt creeping through life now, eyes darting everywhere."

Cordelia nodded gravely. "We hope so, Lady Hightower," she said.

The lady recovered herself and said, "Well, you Bennington girls do keep one on one's toes. Though, Lady Viola, perhaps the *ton* is a little too much on its toes regarding you just now."

"The rumor that's gone round," Viola said. "It is not true, though. A tinker's boy asked me to run off to Gretna Green and I declined."

She paused. Then she said, "Even *that* is not true, though it was the story I told. The real truth was he winked at me as he passed by and I thought myself very much in love. I did have some idea that were he to ask me, I would marry him."

"I advise that you do not send that clarification round," Lady Hightower said.

"Viola," Cordelia said, "you keep leaving out the most important point. You were only eight years old, and he was just as young."

"Eight?" Lady Hightower said, seeming taken aback. "You were a young child? Gracious, that makes all the difference in the world. Who of us has not had some fantastical romantic idea at that age? I used to make eyes at a poor footman and even swore to my father I would run off with him when I was of age."

"Was he very handsome, then, Lady Hightower?" Miss Mayton asked.

Lady Hightower seemed surprised by the question. "I hardly remember, Miss Mayton, as my father sent the poor fellow to work for a cousin. I would also say that is neither here nor there. The point is, we must send the real facts of the case round the *ton*, chasing this ridiculous story that is currently on wagging tongues."

"Can that be done?" Viola asked.

"Anything can be done, my dear, when one puts one's mind to it."

"I wonder who will even listen to me," Viola said. "I suppose you are not aware—more than a few of my invitations have been rescinded."

"I guessed that would be the case. Hostesses in this town are a bunch of jumpy rabbits afraid of their own shadows. No, Lady Viola, I do not expect anybody to listen to *you*. I expect them to listen to the oldest bat in the rafters."

"Who is the oldest bat in the rafter?" Cordelia asked, eyes wide.

"I am."

"What shall you say?" Juliet said, leaning forward, chin in hand.

Before Lady Hightower could expound on what the oldest bat in the rafters planned to say to the jumpy rabbit hostesses, Tattleton opened the door once more.

"Please excuse the interruption, Lady Viola. Lady Hightower, my apologies. A footman who refuses to say where he is from has come with a package he insists must be handed to Lady Viola directly. I have threatened to fetch a magistrate, but he is quite obstinate. I thought I'd better check before forcibly throwing him to the road, in case there was something in it I did not understand."

Viola was entirely perplexed. Why would a footman turn up and refuse to say where he'd come from? What did he bring?

"You are Mr…" Lady Hightower said, looking enquiringly at Tattleton.

"Mr. Tattleton, my lady," the butler said, appearing very honored to be asked.

"Excellent. Mr. Tattleton, show this young man in." To Viola, she said, "If this is some sort of jest or meanspirited delivery, I will beat the name of his employer out of him."

She rapped her cane on the carpet and Viola presumed they were all to know that would be her preferred weapon if it came to a beating.

Tattleton appeared very approving of the sentiment. He motioned behind him and one of the earl's footmen led the visitor in.

Viola had supposed that the boy's livery would give him away, if not to her, then to Lady Hightower, who knew absolutely everybody. Rather, he wore a drab blue coat with no hint at all of where he'd come from.

"I see you slink in here disguised, young man," Lady Hightower said, observing his lack of livery.

The boy threw his chin up and said, "Beg pardon, ma'am, I ain't never slinked in my life. I just do as I'm told to do."

"Hmm. Do you know what it is you carry into this house?" Lady Hightower said, staring at the box in his arms.

"I been informed," the lad said.

"I see," Lady Hightower said. "And were you planning on relaying that information to me? I can assure you, I have a sturdy cane and you will know it."

"It's a ham, ma'am."

Lady Hightower stood up. "A ham? A ham, you say?"

"The finest one in the kitchens, wrapped up all nice-like for Lady Viola. It ain't my place to inquire why and so I don't know it."

Lady Hightower turned to Viola. "What can be the meaning of this? Have I missed something of the story? Is it speculated that the tinker's boy lured you away with a ham?"

Viola smiled at the boy. "You are from Lord Baderston, I know you are. He can be the only gentleman so well acquainted with my fondness for ham."

The boy gave himself away with a smile, then quickly wiped it off his face. "I am bound to secrecy, my lady. I am only tasked to say—For Lady Viola, from an admirer."

Viola said, "Tattleton, escort this young man to the kitchens where he can deliver the ham to Cook, then give him refreshment before setting him on his way. When he returns to his house, he may say that the ham was very well-received. Very well, indeed."

Tattleton nodded, though he did not look particularly enthused. He led the boy out and the door was shut behind them.

"Lord Baderston has sent you a ham?" Lady Hightower asked.

"Oh yes, I am certain it is from him," Viola said.

"They have that in common," Miss Mayton said. "They both have an unusual interest in ham."

"Yes, that is a bit unusual," Lady Hightower said. "Tell me, Lady Viola, is there something serious between you and Lord Baderston? I have, of course, heard of his behavior at the theater. Everybody is talking of how he chased after Mr. Berger. But I had supposed his actions were prompted by his membership in the YBC and his loyalty to Lord Darden."

"We think he is in love with Viola," Cordelia said.

"He has not said anything, though," Viola said.

"I believe the sending of ham is quite a direct statement," Miss Mayton said.

"This complicates things," Lady Hightower said thoughtfully.

Viola and her sisters stayed silent, as it was clear that Lady Hightower was mulling something over, though less clear what it could be.

Finally, she said, "Heaven help us."

"Why do you say so, Lady Hightower?" Viola asked, beginning to be alarmed.

"Child," she said, "it is bad enough that we have this mess to clean up regarding the gossip being passed on about you. But now, we add in a love interest complicating things. If it is true that Lord Baderston holds a special regard for you, and I suppose it must be as no other person but a lovesick lunatic would send a person a ham, then we have the further danger of what he might get himself into. He will wish to rush hither and thither, fending off all those who dared speak ill of you."

"Indeed, I believe he has already done so," Viola said. "He boxed Lord Chelderberry."

"And chased Mr. Berger, who I imagine he also boxed," Lady Hightower said, "if reports of his subsequent battered appearance are to be believed. Gracious, it's to be the Meldover affair all over again."

"The Meldover affair?" Viola asked. She did not know what that was, but from Lady Hightower's tone, it was not anything good.

Lady Hightower nodded. "Back in 1788, a story began going round that Miss Felicia Broadbent had accepted Lord Hynesley, and then broke it off with him when she received a better offer from Lord Jacinda. Hynesley was a new-minted baron, you see, and Jacinda was an earl. There was no truth to it—Hynesley had tried it out with Miss Broadbent and got nowhere. But, he was desperate for Miss Broadbent's dowry and sought to ruin her engagement to Jacinda. I suppose he thought a shamed woman would have nowhere to turn but to him."

Lady Hightower sighed. "It is so often the case that a new-minted title comes with less than the necessary funds, causing the new-minted gentleman to become desperate."

"Was she forced to it?" Viola asked. "Did Lord Jacinda fail to stand by her?"

Lady Hightower laughed. "She was not forced to it and of course Lord Jacinda stood by her. There was not the least chance that he would not. Never have I seen a man so smitten. Therein lay the problem though. He did as I am afraid your Lord Baderston will do—challenged anybody who even looked wrong at his lady-love. Duels were lined up for every day of the week."

"Gosh," Juliet said, "was he killed, then?"

"No, not in the end," Lady Hightower said, "but it was a close thing. They live in Yorkshire now, happily married by all reports, but never coming to Town."

"But how was disaster avoided?" Viola asked, thinking she might employ whatever Miss Broadbent had done. She wished for just the same outcome—she and Lord Baderston going to live quietly in Dorset.

"Not in any way *you* might employ," Lady Hightower said. "Miss Broadbent was a very rash young lady. She paid a man to act as coachman, stole her father's carriage, and turned up to Lord Jacinda's residence early on the morning the first duel was scheduled for. She informed him that his challenger had been killed in a carriage accident, which was not at all true, and then she urged him to take her to Gretna Green. He wrote out letters informing the rest of his would-be challengers on when they might expect his return to London, but fortunately they all gave it up after hearing of the couple's romantic departure from Town."

Viola and her sisters all glanced at one another.

Miss Mayton nodded and said, "So it all worked out in the end. Things often do. I have not been so lucky, but I've noticed that other people generally are."

"Have you?" Lady Hightower asked, looking skeptical.

"But what can *I* do?" Viola asked Lady Hightower. "I do not wish for Lord Baderston to engage himself in a duel, but how can I intervene?"

While she asked it, her mind was furiously racing ahead of her. What if she and Lord Baderston *were* to set off for Gretna Green? After all, she was already accused of doing it once. Why not actually do it?

It was not a thing she'd ever thought she would consider—her father would not like it. But she did understand why Miss Broadbent had taken such a drastic measure. Miss Broadbent had been desperate to remove Lord Jacinda from danger and Viola was beginning to feel equally desperate to remove Lord Baderston from the same.

She'd seen how quickly he'd reacted at the theater. How long would it be before some gentleman demanded satisfaction?

"All that comes to mind at this moment," Lady Hightower said, "is to tamp down the talk. If Lord Baderston pays a call on you, please cajole him into swearing he will not get himself into anymore fisticuffs."

Viola had nodded, but considering what she'd witnessed at the theater, she did not believe Lord Baderston would heed the warning. He might well promise, but in the heat of the moment…

Lady Hightower rose. "I will leave you now, and I will do my bit, as will Conbatten."

Viola, her sisters, and Miss Mayton rose as well and curtsied deeply, while Viola rang the bell for Tattleton.

Viola said, "I thank you, Lady Hightower, for your consideration. I realize you had no need to so kindly call on us."

"Nonsense," Lady Hightower said. "Your family is now connected to Conbatten, and so you have now become my concern. In any case, I cannot be entirely opposed to a group of sisters who have so bravely rescued a parrot from the clutches of Mr. Ladle."

Tattleton hurried into the room.

Lady Hightower said, "Mr. Tattleton, I take my leave if you would be so good as to escort me to my carriage. I trust you will forge on as dignified as I see you now, regardless of any unpleasantness that has come upon the house. These things do pass, you know. I have taken an interest in this matter, so you can be assured of it."

Tattleton appeared delighted with Lady Hightower. As for Viola, her thoughts ran in one direction only—and that was north to Scotland.

Should she do it? It did not feel right, but when weighed against the idea that Lord Baderston might find himself on a green some morning, it sounded more than right.

What did she care for the *ton's* penchant for talking? She only cared for Lord Baderston.

CHAPTER SIXTEEN

CONBATTEN HAD COME and gone and Roland had been glad to get him out of the house. First, the duke had looked at his two swollen eyes and shook his head as if he were disappointed in them. Then he'd posed paying a visit to Lord Setterdown's father, in the hopes that his father might pressure Setterdown into accepting an apology and dropping the idea of a duel.

The duke pointed out that they were both only sons with no younger for the title to fall to and it was irresponsible to allow an estate to drift to a cousin over such a small matter. Then he'd pointed out that he did not understand how Roland was to be a very good shot when he looked like he couldn't see a thing.

The duke was not far wrong regarding his eyesight at this very moment in time. Roland had only managed to not trip over furniture in his drawing room because he knew where it all was. But certainly, the swelling would have gone down by morning.

Roland had not agreed to Conbatten approaching Chelderberry's father and argued that a gentleman must not have his father brought into such a thing. Really, though, there was no point in it—he'd have to turn up for the other two duels on the morrow. Then of course, he'd been offended to hear the rift with Chelderberry spoken of as a "small matter," though he knew Conbatten was just doing his duty as a second.

Further, he did not wish to keep Conbatten in conversation as he had not mentioned there would be two other gentlemen turning up at dawn on the morrow.

It had been hard enough to convince the duke that he must bring three sets of Roland's pistols. He'd claimed that it was prudent to bring all three, just in case a set or two appeared to be in less than good order on the day.

He was all but certain that Conbatten had chalked that up to nerves.

That was fine with Roland. As long as the duke had not chalked it up to three different duels to be had. It had seemed such a practical way of doing things—all the duels together. Now, however, it was beginning to feel like an awful lot to do in one morning. It was also beginning to feel like Conbatten would be more than a little put out about it.

The duke had left with his usual mien of disgust and Roland was certain he viewed duels as the stupidest thing in the world.

Roland had thought the very same thing until he was forced to engage himself.

He'd had no choice though. Lady Viola's honor was at stake. He would not let her down.

Barnard came into the library and said, "Gerald has returned from delivering the ham, my lord."

"Send him in," Roland said. He did not know what the young footman would say for himself or whether the idea that the package must be delivered to Lady Viola directly had even worked, but he would know how it was.

Gerald came in looking remarkably cheerful.

"Well?" Roland asked. "Tell me everything that happened. Did you see Lady Viola or were you forced to hand over the ham to the butler?"

"I seen her, my lord. Mind you, that old grim-face did his best to wrestle it off me, but I was all stalwart-like and wouldn't be moved. Not even when he threatened me with a magistrate."

"Good lad. What did she say? How did she seem?"

Gerald, looking very pleased to be able to relay the story, said, "T'was like this, I get took into the drawing room and there

I find a whole gaggle of ladies. One was your Lady Viola, then there was two younger, and two older."

Roland nodded. "The younger were the sisters and one of the older was Miss Mayton. I do not know who the other older lady might have been."

"Nor me neither," Gerald said. "But I can tell ya this—she was mighty stern and she had a cane and hinted she weren't afraid to use it on my head."

This set Roland back just a little bit. Who was the lady?

No matter, it was Lady Viola's impressions he was interested in. He said, "So you repeated the message you were given?"

Gerald nodded. "I said, clear as day, that t'was for Lady Viola, from an admirer. Well, the old one with the cane seemed irate about it but Lady Viola was all smiles and she said she knew it was from you. I said I wouldn't admit to nothin'. Then she said…"

There was a long pause and Roland thought it was done for dramatic effect.

"She said?" he urged.

"She said, you may tell Lord Baderston that the ham is very well received."

Well received. *Very* well received. That's what she'd said.

Excellent.

What were a couple of duels when a gentleman's ham had been well received?

AFTER LADY HIGHTOWER had left, Viola, Miss Mayton, Cordelia, and Juliet hurried above stairs. Viola had given them all a particular look as Tattleton had cleared the tea trays and they all understood that something exceedingly confidential must be discussed.

"What an extraordinary visit by Lady Hightower," Miss Mayton said. "While she says we are of interest to her because of our connection by marriage to Conbatten, I wonder if she does not feel a particular kinship toward me. Widows do have a certain camaraderie, you know."

Viola nodded, but privately thought that Lady Hightower had not seemed very struck by her aunt.

"Well?" Juliet said. "What is going through your mind, Viola?"

"I cannot stop thinking of the Meldover affair that Lady Hightower mentioned. I cannot stop thinking of how Miss Broadbent acted boldly to save her one true love."

"That did sound romantic, did it not?" Miss Mayton said. "Off to Gretna Green, just like that."

"I was wondering if I ought to consider the same?" Viola asked. "Oh, Juliet, Cordelia, if you could have seen him at the theater! He did not hesitate for a moment! Lady Hightower counsels that I should make Lord Baderston swear he will not engage in a duel, and I am sure he would promise it to please me. But then, if I were insulted again, he would just race off and forget all about his promise. Sooner or later, somebody would demand satisfaction."

"I suppose Papa would not like it if you were to run off," Cordelia said.

"No, I do not suppose he would," Viola said. "But then, would he like it better to know that my only true love was killed on a green and it was all my fault?"

"He shouldn't like that at all," Juliet said.

"I see what you say, Viola," Miss Mayton said. "Running off to Gretna Green would be the lesser of two evils. Gracious, you girls are always so clever."

"But how to do it, Vi?" Juliet asked. "Lord Baderston has not even proposed, and even if he had, what carriage would you use? If it were his idea, then of course he would come with his carriage, but if you are to go to him…"

Viola tapped her chin. "Sandren would never agree to it."

"No," Cordelia said, "especially not since last season when we disguised Miss Mayton to challenge the duke—he remains suspicious about that, I'm sure."

"He definitely does," Juliet said. "Do you notice how he frowns and seems to be thinking about it whenever he is taking us somewhere, but then his brow is perfectly clear when Papa is with us? He's known us too long, I'm afraid."

"We dare not hire anyone," Miss Mayton said. "We saw how that can go awry with Rosalind's kidnapping."

"We would somehow have to arrange it so poor Sandren did not suspect anything," Viola said.

"How would it be possible though?" Juliet asked. "How is he not to notice something is amiss when he is driving you and Lord Baderston all the way to Scotland? If I know Sandren, he'd refused to budge once Lord Baderston got in the carriage."

"Sandren need not take us to Scotland," Viola said, suddenly having an idea. "He must only get me to Lord Baderston and then we can take Lord Baderston's carriage. The key will be to make it all a rush so that neither he nor Tattleton has time to think about it."

"It must be very early in the morning, then," Miss Mayton said. "Before the breakfast sideboard is set up. Mr. Tattleton never comes above stairs until seven."

"Yes," Viola said, "we could rush down the stairs unexpectedly and order one of the footmen to alert Sandren that we must be off to…off to…"

"See a sick friend," Miss Mayton said. "I could accompany you and we could leave a note for your father that it was simply the lesser of two evils. Yes, I really must go with you—remember your father said I ought to keep a closer eye on things."

"Goodness, I wish we all could go, Vi," Juliet said.

"As do I," Viola said. "But never mind, I will tell you every detail when I return a married lady."

"But Viola," Cordelia said, "even though we know Lord Baderston to be hopelessly in love with you, he still has not asked."

Viola nodded, as that was indeed a sticking point. But then, he must ask soon, must he not?

ROLAND HAD NOT had any intention of visiting Lady Viola until after he'd dispensed with the three duels on the morrow, but upon hearing of the ham very well received…well, what else was there to do?

Though Conbatten had advised him to stay at home and speak to nobody, he sent for his horse shortly after the duke departed.

The trip had not been an easy one—the sun practically blinded what eyesight he had through the swollen slits that were currently his eyes. It was fortunate that Tempest had the good sense to move out of the way of oncoming carriages, else he'd have been shortly rolling under the wheels of one of them.

Somehow, and with great determination and a few wrong turns, he located Lady Viola's house.

Now, Tattleton had escorted him directly to the ladies in the drawing room.

Roland had held out some sort of slim hope that he might find Lady Viola alone. Or perhaps Miss Mayton would be there and take herself off to the other side of the room.

As it was, he found Lady Viola and Miss Mayton keeping company with the two younger sisters—Lady Cordelia and Lady Juliet.

"Gracious," one of the sisters said, though he was not entirely clear who as she was a bit blurry.

"Oh dear," Miss Mayton said.

"Never mind it, Lord Baderston," Lady Viola said. "It is only the initial surprise of…the state of your eyes. But these things do not last forever. I am certain you will find yourself healed in no time at all."

"Of course that must be right," Miss Mayton said encouragingly.

Roland was well aware he looked dreadful, but he supposed he had not taken in the full effect of his mangled appearance on a lady.

"Murder!" Chester shouted.

"Juliet, do give poor Chester something off the tray," Lady Viola said. "Lord Baderston, we have made an error regarding training Chester, I'm afraid. He is now quite set on the idea that almonds are called murder. It is entirely our fault, of course."

"There is no harm in it, I suppose," Roland said, squinting at the parrot.

As Lady Viola poured the tea, she said, "I know you will not admit to sending the ham, but I thank you anyway, Lord Baderston. It was very thoughtful."

"I admit to nothing," Roland said gallantly, "though if I *had* sent a ham, it would be gratifying to know that it had been well received."

Lady Viola nodded prettily and all was understood between them.

She handed him his cup, which he at first missed, as his depth perception was not currently what it ought to be. He finally grabbed hold of it and set it down with a clatter on the table. He'd probably spilled some of it, but it was hard to see on the dark wood of the table.

"Lord Baderston," Lady Juliet said, "what are your views on Scotland?"

"Scotland?" Roland asked. He was not entirely certain how that ought to be answered. Though he had, in getting to know the family, noticed that when they mentioned a thing, they generally held positive views on it.

"I suppose I like Scotland very much," he said. "I have a small fishing lodge there, gifted me by an old bachelor uncle. It is small but charming, I like it very well."

The sisters all glanced at one another and nodded knowingly, so he supposed he'd guessed right on his views on Scotland.

"Now Lord Baderston," Lady Viola said, "I did wish to communicate a particular opinion on a matter."

"Please do," he said, feeling the smallest bit of trepidation. If a lady set out to bring up a particular opinion, he supposed there must be some strong feeling behind it.

"I find myself very against dueling, Lord Baderston. Very against it."

"Very against it?" Roland said. Lord, had she heard of any of these duels that were to take place on the morrow?

"Very," Lady Viola said. "So I wondered, if it would not be too bold to ask, and considering your recent encounters with both Lord Chelderberry and that person at the theater, if you would vow not to engage yourself to a duel."

"To not engage myself?" Roland said slowly.

"Now mind," Juliet said, "it is only a care for your person. We should not like to hear you were shot some morning."

No, he would not like to hear that either. But then, he was engaged three times over on the morrow. What was to be done about it?

Nothing was to be done about it. A gentleman could not back out of an arranged meeting.

"I only say, Lord Baderston," Lady Viola continued, "that I really would not prefer it."

"Lady Viola," he said, "I do not think there is anybody that prefers it. But what is a gentleman to do if he is engaged in a matter of honor?"

"Perhaps avoid the situation altogether?" Lady Viola said. "Perhaps it is best to avoid those sort of disagreements right from the start?"

Roland nodded. "I believe I have come to agree with you on that particular view," he said. "One ought not be too rash."

"Precisely."

"Well, lesson learned," Roland said, leaping up. "I really must go…someone expects me…somewhere. The hour grows late, I'm afraid."

He bowed and hurried from the room without waiting for a footman to be called. At least, he attempted to hurry from the room and would have done so had an ottoman not been placed in his way. He went over it and hit the floor with a thump.

Two footmen raced into the room upon hearing the crash. While Roland could not see their faces perfectly clearly, he was certain they were perplexed.

As the two young men helped him to his feet, the ladies assured Roland that people were always tripping over that piece of furniture.

That seemed highly unlikely, though he appreciated their attempts at painting the situation as commonplace.

Once back on his feet, he asked for his horse, and then went outside to wait for it.

As he waited, he had the uncomfortable feeling of eyes upon him. He slowly turned and found four blurry faces at the window. They speedily disappeared.

Lady Viola must wonder at his abrupt and rather clumsy departure, but what else could he do? Why had she thought to bring up dueling and her opinions against it, just when he had three set up for the following morning?

A groom brought his horse round, at least he presumed it was Tempest as it had the right size and shape. He mounted and did his best to appear confident in the saddle as he set off in what he hoped was the right direction.

He would see what the morrow would bring. At least, he hoped he could see it. Whatever it was, he must just live through it and then all would be well.

VIOLA HAD WATCHED Lord Baderston depart the house. His eyes

really were in rather terrible shape, but that was the least of her concerns just at the moment.

"Well," Juliet said, "you did as Lady Hightower asked you to—you made Lord Baderston promise he would not get himself into a duel."

"Have I, though?" Viola asked with a sinking feeling.

"I thought so," Cordelia said.

"As did I," Miss Mayton said.

"But what he said," Viola said quietly, "about avoiding those situations that inevitably lead to a duel. He said, 'lesson learned.'"

"You do not think…"

"I *do* think," Viola said. She was all but certain that Lord Baderston had been overly vague and made a comment on lesson learned because he had already engaged himself. That was why he'd leapt up and tried to get out of the house so fast. He did not wish to outright lie, which meant she was too late in asking for the promise not to engage himself.

"Goodness," Miss Mayton said, "and you being so very much against it in case he ends up dead."

"I could not bear it," Viola said.

"I wonder if it is Lord Chelderberry, or that fellow from the theater?" Juliet said.

"Chelderberry is being sent home," Viola said, "and so certainly that might anger him enough to demand a meeting. And then, the theater fellow was chased so publicly…"

"What shall you do?" Cordelia asked.

"I fear I must get Lord Baderston out of London forthwith," Viola said.

"But then we circle back round to the same old problem—he has not declared himself yet." Juliet sighed and said, "I had hoped he would do it just now, right in front of us. Instead, he just got very strange and tripped over the ottoman."

"He only became strange when I mentioned my opinion of duels," Viola said, "which is more confirmation than not."

"Let us hope he gets around to proposing before he sets off to some lonely field or other to get shot at," Miss Mayton said.

"No, I cannot take the chance of that happening," Viola said.

"What other choice do you have?" Cordelia asked. "Until he declares himself, you can do nothing."

"Nonsense," Viola said, feeling a surety of purpose filling her breast. "If Lord Baderston is just now a bit slow to the mark, then I will help him along. *I* will declare *myself*. First thing on the morrow, so he has no chance of getting killed."

"Can you do that?" Juliet asked. "Can you propose, instead of waiting for him to do it?"

"I can, and I will."

TATTLETON SAT CONTENTEDLY at the servants' table with Mrs. Huffson, a generous glass of brandy by his side. All the house was abed and even the diabolical parrot had quieted.

He could not remember when he had last felt so content—it had recently felt as if he would live his entire life on the edge of nervous exhaustion.

He was, perhaps, not particularly proud of how his contentment had been arrived at. He'd been compelled to listen at the drawing room door during Lady Hightower's visit.

He could not feel too terrible about it, though. Was it not his duty to ensure all in the house were well?

A terrible thing had befallen them, and he'd not known what ought to be done about it. Lady Viola had sent a rumor round about herself, it had grown and blossomed to such a degree that she'd been shunned by several hostesses and it had been necessary that the earl be told. It seemed as if nothing would ever be right again for the Benningtons.

Then, Lady Hightower had arrived, and he'd taken great comfort in her visit.

What a lady! Forceful, direct, and courageous. He must consider Lady Hightower as made in the mold of Queen Boudica herself. A veritable warrior in silks.

Quite the change from the likes of Miss Mayton. Lady Hightower was a discerning hawk and Miss Mayton was a baffled titmouse.

No, that was not even it. Lady Hightower was a Phoenix prepared to rise them up from the ashes. Miss Mayton was akin to Chester the deranged parrot, talking nonsense, causing trouble, and accomplishing nothing.

And then, what had Lady Hightower said, addressing him directly? 'I trust you will forge on as dignified as I see you now, regardless of any unpleasantness that has come upon the house.'

Lady Hightower was astute enough to perceive his dignity and fortitude just by looking at him.

"You seem a deal more at ease than you have been, Mr. Tattleton," Mrs. Huffson said.

"Indeed I am, Mrs. Huffson. The Bennington household has come under the protection of a powerful figure. A powerful figure, indeed."

"The duke," Mrs. Huffson said.

She said it with almost a sigh. Tattleton was aware that she was pleased for Lady Rosalind, but that she was not over impressed by a ducal title. It was one of the few areas of temperament and understanding where they differed.

"I speak of Lady Hightower," Tattleton said. "The duke has the utmost standing, I'll not argue that point. But Lady Hightower has an elevated standing and a certain sort of vigor. She will not be brooked! She was not afraid to bring her cane down upon the head of that footman who turned up with a ham and he knew the truth of it."

Mrs. Huffson nodded. "I suppose a matron of the *ton* is well able to shake the knees of a young footman."

"That is not all," Tattleton continued. "She has decided that the Benningtons are of concern to her and she is prepared to venture out into society and set it straight regarding Lady Viola."

"That is very kindly done," Mrs. Huffson said.

"Kind, and necessary. I am certain all this gossip going round is riding in the convenient vehicle of lady's calls. Who else better to stop it than a lady for whom every door will be open?"

"Mr. Tattleton!" Mrs. Huffson said, peering at him in some surprise. "You do not imply that women are more prone to gossip than men are? As far as I can tell, all they do at Lord Darden's club is tell stories to one another."

"Perhaps, Mrs. Huffson. But the stories told at the YBC are of an elevated nature and comprised of sporting events and such."

"Elevated nature? You do not really believe that."

"I wish to believe it, Mrs. Huffson. I wish to believe I understand how we have come to such a pass in this house. Understanding is the only way to hold on to my sanity. Furthermore, I put my full faith in Lady Hightower and find myself soothed that a solution has been found. Do not work to take that from me."

"Ah well, if it soothes you, I'll leave it alone."

Tattleton meant what he said—he would hold on tight to his belief in the powers of Lady Hightower. What else was there to hold on to?

CHAPTER SEVENTEEN

ROLAND WAS IN his dressing gown and dining in his bedchamber to escape a dinner with his mother. So far, he'd managed to dodge her for two days running and she'd not even seen that he'd progressed from one black eye to two.

He'd taken to slipping in via the servants' entrance and while it appeared to frighten the kitchen maids, the dowager had not yet figured it out.

"I'd even be willing," his valet said, "to emigrate to America. I hear it's a rough place, but we could be some of those pioneer settlers. You know, those people who wander out to the wilderness and pick a spot and build something. Who knows— one of these days the Americans might even set up their own notions of nobility and you'd have a leg up there. You could explain how it's done."

Roland had been listening to his valet posit various wild ideas for the past half hour, all centered on one thought—Roland should not turn up for the three duels on the morrow.

"I see," he said. "So we will wander round the wilderness, then build something in a likely spot. Then what? You will venture into the forest and club some sort of animal for dinner? Then you will bring it back to whatever Godforsaken thing we hammered together and the dowager will cook it?"

"Well, when you put it like that, it don't sound so attractive," Markson said. "What about saying you was suddenly taken with the consumption and we was sending you to the country to die?"

Roland glanced down at his well-muscled chest and said, "I'm hardly in advanced stages, am I?"

"You could say the dowager is on her death bed."

"And then lock her up in the house so nobody notices her out and about and making calls while she's supposed to be in the final throes?"

"All I'm sayin' is, your chances of surviving three duels is zero. Let's say the first duel is fifty-fifty and you come out of it. Now you're down to fifty and you survive the next and there you are at twenty-five. Then here comes the third and you're down to zero."

"Your grasp of maths is tenuous indeed."

"You understand my point, though."

Roland sighed. "I do. The difficulty is, you do not understand *my* point. A gentleman cannot run away from a duel of honor. Not to America, not from consumption, not for a dying mother, not for any reason. It just cannot be done. The rest of my life would be no life at all."

"I knew there was a downside to bein' a lord, and now here it is."

Roland could not argue with that, at least. Honor was everything and without it a lord was a titled buffoon, a shame upon his name. He would never consider it.

Markson sighed. "Very well. I'll not trouble you further on it then. I'll turn my efforts toward getting you prepared. Your green coat—it's not your best, but it's got a bit of room in the shoulders, so you're not constrained when you go to fire. You got to be well-rested, too. I'll send up a brandy with a drop of laudanum in it."

Roland nodded. It was not a bad idea—otherwise he should not sleep a wink.

For all his talk of honor and his wish to defend Lady Viola's honor, he was not an idiot. Coming out of three duels unscathed would take a miracle.

⟩⟩⟩✳⟨⟨⟨

NOW THAT VIOLA had made her decision, the dawn could not arrive soon enough. It was bold, what she planned to do, but she could not risk Lord Baderston dying on a green on her behalf. Whatever the *ton* chose to comment on, and they certainly would have plenty to say about an elopement, she did not care.

Though she would wish to have retired directly after dinner, she dared not stir up any suspicion. It was to be a family night in, mostly because nobody had anywhere to go. Her father was not at all downcast over it, as Miss Mayton was preparing to read more from *The Harrowing Homecoming at Harrowbridge Hall*.

They had gathered in the drawing room directly after dinner, as the earl and Darden brought their glasses of port in with them rather than tarry at table.

"Now," Miss Mayton said, "as we know, the poor gentle governess has had her thoughts all awhirl. Both of the would-be dukes are exceedingly handsome, but she knows one of them is a scoundrel and impostor. Unfortunately, she does not know which one. The two dukes have had a rousing competition between them to see who could do things the way a duke would do them. You will recall the exciting moment when they demonstrated who could fire the butler in the most duke-like fashion. This has given our gentle governess no clarity and, unfortunately, the butler is now convinced he is fired and keeps trying to pack and leave. Thank heavens his eyesight is so bad he has not been able to find his luggage."

"I worry for our gentle governess," the earl said, "I really do."

"She will be all right, Papa," Juliet said, "they always are."

"We shall see," Miss Mayton said. "One never knows if the romances in these sorts of books will end happily. So far they all have, but we never know. All right, here we go, onto chapter three."

"Well?" Duke One said, leering at the gentle governess.

"Yes, well?" Duke Two said, crossing his arms and staring at the gentle governess.

The gentle governess clutched at her fichu and staggered to a chair. Sinking down in it she cried, "I do not know who fired the butler like a duke! I've never seen a duke fire a butler before."

Duke Two turned to Duke One. "I know what we should do," he said, "we'll both demonstrate how we would greet the queen."

"Very well!" Duke One said. "Gentle governess, stand in for the queen!"

The gentle governess staggered to her feet, very unsure of how she was to judge such a contest. She had never herself been in the queen's presence and did not know how it was to be done.

Duke One jogged to the far end of the room, turned, and made a gallant approach. He bowed low and said, "Your Grace."

Duke Two leapt to his feet. "Aha! You have revealed yourself, you scoundrel! The queen is to be addressed as Her Majesty, as any real duke would know!"

"Rubbish!" Duke One shouted. "I had the honor of becoming acquainted with the lady before she was queen. All her intimates addressed her as Your Grace. It was a term of endearment."

"Double rubbish!" Duke Two shouted. "Before she was the queen, she was a princess! Therefore, it would have been Your Royal Highness!"

The gentle governess sank back into her chair. She had not spent much time in her life thinking about the queen. Princess did sound right, though.

"You have insulted my honor!" Duke One shouted. "I demand satisfaction!"

"Oh, you would, wouldn't you?" Duke Two said. "You'd really like to shoot me to get me out of the way and take over my life!"

"Aha!" Duke One said. "No real duke attempts to wiggle out of a duel of honor. You have revealed yourself!"

"I have not and will shoot you full of holes!"

"I will shoot YOU full of holes!"

"Dawn tomorrow!"

The gentle governess fanned herself. It appeared that she was to have two dukes full of holes lying on the lawn on the morrow.

Miss Mayton closed the book. "So now we see there is to be a final denouement. We can only pray that the real villain dies and the real duke lives on to wed his gentle governess."

"A duel!" the earl said. "I did not see that coming. Gracious, I'm on the edge of my seat."

Viola sighed. She was, of course, deeply concerned for the gentle governess, but just now her thoughts were too taken up by Lord Baderston and she could not worry herself over the duel between Duke One and Duke Two.

Rather, she prayed Lord Baderston would not be too shocked at her unexpected arrival, and even more unexpected proposal, on the morrow. She prayed he would joyously accept. With any luck, they would be off in his carriage before the dowager realized what was happening.

Viola had packed a small valise and she and Miss Mayton would fly down the stairs just before the sun came up and overwhelm the poor footman on duty with the speed with which the carriage must be called. With any luck, they'd do the same to Sandren.

She must just get to Lord Baderston's house before he ventured out to any duels. She was certain one had been scheduled, but she could not know for what day.

Nothing was likely to occur on the morrow, else he would not have been out making calls today. At least, she did not think so. She imagined that a gentleman faced with the prospect of his own mortality would spend the day in quiet reflection. Lord Baderston had been doing quite the opposite. He'd been sending her a ham and coming for a call.

Though his life would not be in danger at the next dawn, she was sure a duel was engaged for some day soon. She would get him away from Town before it happened.

The gentle governess of Harrowbridge Hall might be drowning in duke problems, but Viola Bennington was prepared to take in hand her own earl problem.

ROLAND HAD SLEPT soundly the night before. Surprisingly soundly. What was even more surprising was waking up to Conbatten shaking him on the shoulder.

It was still dark in his bedchamber, a lone candle illuminating the duke's face.

Why was he here? He could not think of a time when he'd woke to find the duke shaking him.

"What is wrong with him?" the duke said.

"Wrong with who?" Roland asked.

Then he heard Markson say, "I'm afraid I might'a dosed his brandy a little too liberally last night, Your Grace. Laudanum. I thought it would help him get some rest."

"Blast it!" the duke shouted. "He can barely see and now he's drugged too?"

"Who is?" Roland asked.

"You are," the duke said, pulling him into a sitting position. "Your wonder of a valet has filled you up to your eyes with Laudanum and those eyes were not operating very well to begin, considering they're nearly swollen shut."

An idea of what was happening began to slowly seep into Roland's thoughts.

"Ah, now I remember why you're here!" he said. "All the duels."

"*The* duel," the duke corrected.

"Oh no, there is more than one," Roland said sleepily. "I'll fight them all," he said, waving his fists around.

The duke shook him and said, "What do you mean, there is more than one?"

Roland laughed. "You know, all the scoundrels."

The duke turned to his valet. "Talk," he said sternly.

Markson looked a little abashed, which Roland thought was interesting. His valet was never abashed. He wondered what had affected him so.

"Well, Your Grace," the valet said slowly, "as you know, there is Setterdown. And then there was an unfortunate encounter with Chelderberry."

"Chelderberry?"

"Yes, Chelderberry. There was an awkward moment at the club that led to fisticuffs."

"You are telling me that there are *two* gentlemen turning up this morning?" the duke asked.

"I'd like to tell ya that, but not exactly," Markson said. "I believe you were at the theater when Mr. Berger was so bold as to affront Lady Viola?"

"He has engaged himself to Berger too?"

"That's about the size of it," Markson said sadly.

"He's engaged all three! On the same morning?"

"Do not thank me, duke," Roland said sleepily. "The fact is, I respect your time. I thought to myself, let's make them all on the same morning so the duke doesn't have to get up early three days in a row."

"Very thoughtful," the duke said in a tone so dry it could burn down all London.

"You are extremely welcome!" Roland said, rolling over on his side and propping his head on his hand. The duke was really a genial fellow when it came to it. He would have thought Conbatten would be very put out about the whole thing, but instead the great man had commended his thoughtfulness.

The duke turned to his valet. "Strong coffee and a bucket of cold water."

"Yes, Your Grace," Markson said, hurrying off.

"Now you've gone and arranged for my coffee too," Roland said, laying back against his pillows. "I don't understand why people say you are so standoffish. You are rather jolly, Conbatten."

"Am I?"

"Do not deny it!" Roland said, thinking the duke was also

very modest. "I have a mind to tell everybody that very thing. I'll say, the real Conbatten is very jolly and will come to your house, wake you up, and order you a coffee."

"Tell them anything you like, if you live to tell anything at all," the duke said.

For some reason, Roland found this exceedingly funny. "You are a wit, on top of it all! Say Duke, what do you think about joining the YBC? We worried that you might accept an invitation and then what would we talk to you about? That's over now! Conbatten is jolly!"

Roland's valet came back into his bedchamber carrying a bucket. "The coffee will be up in a tick, Your Grace."

Conbatten took the bucket from Markson and promptly heaved it in Roland's direction.

The shock of the cold water left him speechless.

➤➤➤❰❰❰

VIOLA AND MISS Mayton had slipped down the stairs just before dawn with good wishes from Juliet and Cordelia.

Though they had never been downstairs so early, they had thought a footman would be about. All they found was a housemaid dusting the drawing room with a lone candle to assist her in her work.

That, it turned out, worked to their advantage. The housemaid was near terrified to see them and when they sent her to the stables, she raced out in that direction as if her hair was on fire. There was no skepticism in her looks, as Viola thought they might face from a footman.

Sandren had been told of a distant relative of Miss Mayton's that was suddenly taken very ill. They told him the woman's lady's maid had been sent to rouse them as her mistress demanded it and likely did not have much time left in the world.

The coachman was perhaps not as easy to convince as the

lady's maid, but he set off. What else could he do when Miss Mayton directed him, as she was chaperone to Viola?

Viola leaned forward in her seat. She had expected the coach to stop at any moment and Sandren to confront them with questions.

They were here now, though. They would take a gamble and send him on his way. If they could successfully get him to take the carriage home without waiting, it would give them extra time to get going to Scotland before the alarm was raised.

As there was no groom accompanying them, Sandren jumped down and helped them down to the pavement.

"Thank you Sandren," Viola said, "there is no need to wait, we will likely be here for some time."

Sandren narrowed his eyes.

"We will send word when we require you to return for us," Miss Mayton said.

"I do not mind waiting, Miss Mayton," Sandren said.

"It will be ages, I think," Viola said. "And then, you know Papa will wish to go to his club. He shouldn't like it if you are not there to take him."

Sandren seemed to be considering that idea. The earl went to his club most mid-mornings to catch up on the latest news and play some cards.

"Very well. I'll see that you are admitted into the house, at the least."

Viola nodded, but she also realized she had not thought through that particular step in the plan. For some reason, she'd had a vague idea of Lord Baderston just appearing at the door when she arrived.

Goodness, he was likely still asleep.

"Come Viola," Miss Mayton said. "Sandren, I warn you that we might be knocking for some time, as my cousin keeps a very slim staff in her dotage."

They hurried toward the doors, Viola not knowing what in the world to expect when they knocked. However, they had made it this far—there was no turning back.

Viola knocked sharply on the door, hoping to be let in by a housemaid as pliable as their own who would agree to fetch Lord Baderston without questioning why two ladies had turned up so early in the morning.

She glanced back at Sandren, who stood staring with his arms folded.

"Try again, dear," Miss Mayton said.

Viola used the knocker with force, rapping three times.

The door flew open as a gentleman cried, "Back already?"

"What?" Viola asked.

The man appeared taken by surprise to see her there, as she supposed he might. But what was he talking about?

"Oh? Nothing, nothing at all," the man said. "So sorry, I am Markson, the earl's valet. I was expecting a coat delivered from the earl's tailor and I do get rather high-strung about those things. How can I help you?"

He was expecting a coat? Who would expect a coat delivered before the sun was even up in the sky?

No matter. She had little time to solve a valet's problems. She said, "I must speak to Lord Baderston at once."

"At once?"

"It is very urgent," Miss Mayton said. "Do let us in so our coachman does not fall victim to the apoplexy. He is very high-strung too."

Markson stepped aside and they hurried into the house.

Viola turned. "Now, do be so kind as to bring Lord Baderston downstairs. We really are in a terrible hurry."

"Well…I…well, you see, I don't like to wake him. He wouldn't like it. Maybe you could come back in a few hours?"

Viola took a deep breath. She must overcome this fellow somehow. "We really cannot come back in a few hours. I must speak to him this instant and I am prepared to go above stairs and find him myself if you will not help me."

The valet looked very stricken by the idea, as was Viola herself. She did not think she could really climb the stairs and begin opening doors.

"Lady Viola!" a voice from the top of the stairs bellowed.

Viola looked up to see the dowager countess in a dressing gown, hands on hips.

"Goodness," Miss Mayton said quietly, "she is precisely who we did not wish to be up and about at such an early hour."

The dowager stormed down the stairs. "What on earth do you do here at this time of day? Or any time of day, for that matter. Explain yourself this instant!"

Had it been any other moment, Viola would have quaked in the face of the enraged matron. This was not any other moment, though.

She threw her chin up and said, "I demand to speak to Lord Baderston at once."

"You demand it, do you?" the dowager asked. "Perhaps I should inquire of Miss Mayton what a young lady does at a gentleman's house before dawn."

Miss Mayton appeared to be closely examining a portrait on the wall and pretended she'd not heard her name spoken.

"I can speak for myself and my business here is no concern of yours," Viola said stubbornly.

Why would she not go away? The dowager must go away!

"It is no business of mine? We will see about that. Markson," the dowager said, "bring Baderston down here at once. I will have this whole shameful situation explained to me before these people are escorted out of this house for the first and last time."

"Well," Markson said slowly, "you know how my lord hates to wake early, Countess."

"I do not care about my son's sleeping habits, do as you are directed," the dowager said in a steely tone.

This seemed to somehow break the valet's spirit. He covered his face with his hands and cried, "I can't! He's not here!"

"Not here?" Viola said. "Where is he? I must know where he is at once."

"Excuse me," the dowager said, "it is *I* who must know where Baderston is. At once."

"I can't say," the valet answered.

Viola felt the blood drain from her face. "It is a duel, is it not? Lord Baderston has gone to a duel."

As Markson did not deny it, Viola knew the truth. She was too late. Lord Baderston had gone to an engagement on a green somewhere.

"Do not be ridiculous," the dowager said. "Baderston does not duel. He is not such a fool as that. Stop this nonsense, Markson."

"It is not nonsense, I'm afraid. He left with the duke acting as his second not a half hour ago."

"What?" the dowager said. "Conbatten? But…who is my son dueling?"

Markson counted off on his fingers. "Setterdown, Chelderberry, and Berger."

"Oh dear," Miss Mayton said.

"Three?" Viola said, tears springing to her eyes. "Where? Where are they? Tell me at once or I will…I will hit you over the head with that vase."

"Hyde Park, up Constitution Hill to the Field of Blood," Markson whispered.

The dowager staggered and clutched her robe. "Duels. The Field of Blood. He is my only son, he is the only heir."

"Markson," Viola said, determined not to collapse in a panic, "call a carriage. This must be stopped!"

Markson nodded and raced off. Viola opened the front doors and much to her surprise, Sandren was still there with the carriage.

"Never mind the carriage! My own is still here. Let us go."

The dowager stood stock still, as if she'd turned into a statue.

"Dowager," Viola said, "you will come?"

The dowager nodded her head. "Come? Yes, do not be absurd." She staggered toward a closet and pulled out a cloak. The dowager struggled into it and Viola rushed to her side to steady her.

They approached Sandren, who seemed very surprised to note their approach. He said, "Is this the lady who is doing poorly?"

"What mother would not do poorly under these circumstances?" the dowager said, staring at him.

"Sandren," Viola said, "this is the Dowager Countess of Baderston. We are in all haste. Take us to Hyde Park, Constitution Hill, we're to look for a green. Lord Baderston is in terrible trouble! We must get there before it's too late!"

The coachman did not seem as if he understood much of what was happening, but he did at least comprehend the urgency of the situation.

"I know where it is," he said.

He helped them into the carriage and set off in good time.

As the carriage barreled through the quiet streets and the sun began its rise, Viola felt as if this one moment in time would direct the course of her life. She was racing toward misery or joy, and she knew not which.

"My son," the dowager said quietly.

"It's all bound to come out right," Miss Mayton said, trying at cheerfulness.

The dowager looked at her in such a fashion that Viola was rather glad that the lady did not have a pistol in her hand.

Her aunt smiled weakly at the lady, but she said nothing more.

Viola clasped her hands together and prayed. They must just get there. They must get there in time. She would stand in the middle of the green and dare them all to shoot through her. Let them try it.

CHAPTER EIGHTEEN

TATTLETON HAD RARELY felt the sort of fear creeping through his breast that he did at this moment. He imagined a soldier might feel something similar when faced with the enemy on a battlefield. It was cold and leaden arms pressing on his chest that prevented him from taking full breaths, his fingers and toes had gone numb, his heart was beating too fast.

Standing by the sideboard, he felt a little dizzy.

He could not faint. He would not allow it. There could be nothing more undignified than the butler of the house fainting in the breakfast room.

What a situation he'd found in the kitchens this morning. One of the housemaids was all aflutter and in tears. He had, at first, presumed she'd broken a vase or spilled something on the carpet.

Daisy was a nervous sort of creature and had broken no end of things, especially since the parrot had arrived. Tattleton could not convince the girl that when the bird screamed "murder," he really meant almonds. Daisy was convinced that if that avian devil ever got out of its cage, it would chase her down and claw her to death.

But no. Daisy had not dropped anything. That was not it. Once he'd heard what *was* it, he began to pine for news that a vase had been shattered.

Daisy reported that Miss Mayton and Lady Viola had come

downstairs before dawn with some ludicrous story about a sick relative.

Not once in all the years that Miss Mayton had been terrorizing the house had she ever mentioned this nameless and now deathly-ill cousin who lived in London.

It was all a lie! He knew it!

Where had they really gone? What were they up to? It could not be anything sensible. For one, the time of day they set off did not bode well for anything sensible. For another, Miss Mayton was involved, and she was never sensible.

Just the day before, he had found himself very sanguine. Lady Hightower had taken an interest in the family and was going to stamp out the talk going round about Lady Viola. Invitations would flow freely once more.

Now, he stood by a very quiet breakfast table. Lady Cordelia and Lady Juliet were silent, stealing glances at the empty chairs across from them.

The earl laid down his newspaper. "Gracious, Miss Mayton and Viola are not down yet? What keeps them, I wonder."

The ladies Cordelia and Juliet paled.

Tattleton cleared his throat. Now was the moment when he must speak. Now was the moment when he must deliver some very unwelcome news.

He said, "My lord, early this morning, Miss Mayton informed one of the housemaids that she and Lady Viola were rushing off to the bedside of Miss Mayton's cousin. It was communicated that the lady was very ill."

Tattleton waited for the earl to leap to his feet and demand answers from the two daughters who *hadn't* left the house in the early hours of the morning.

"Really?" the earl said, once more picking up his newspaper. "I had no idea Miss Mayton had any close relations in Town. Well, I do hope the cousin comes through it. Perhaps we ought to have her to dinner after she makes her recovery."

Tattleton gripped the edge of the sideboard. That was it?

They should have this phantom cousin to dine?

He did not know what to do. What should he do?

He could not follow his own inclinations in this matter. His inclination at this moment was to shout, 'There is no cousin! I do not know where they have gone, but I can assure you they are even this moment knee-deep in one of their bad plans!'

⋙✷⋘

ROLAND HAD BEEN brought to his senses after being doused with cold water and having hot coffee poured down his throat.

At least, he felt he'd been brought to his right mind, though Conbatten remained dubious about it.

His eyes, on the other hand, were a little bit of a different matter. The duke had been forced to lead him by the arm to his carriage.

Roland had nursed hopes that the swelling would have come down overnight, but that had not occurred.

The duke pointed out that the swelling was always going to be worse in the morning, after lying down all night.

Roland had not, it must be admitted, taken that into consideration.

He could just see through the slits of his eyelids and so he knew they had entered the park.

Conbatten rapped on the roof and the carriage slowed to a stop.

This was it. Somehow, he must survive three duels.

Conbatten leapt out of the coach. Roland stumbled after him.

The green was crowded with three challengers, three men acting as seconds, three doctors, three grooms, and the twelve horses that had carried them there.

Setterdown stepped forward. "Your Grace, can you explain the meaning of this? Both Chelderberry and Berger claim they were engaged for this day and time. I have assured them that my arrangements were made directly with you and that circumstance is an impossibility."

"I am not mistaken on the day," Chelderberry said.

"Nor I," Berger said.

"None of you are mistaken!" Roland said. "I had three duels lined up and thought to dispatch them all on the same morning. You do not imagine that I would trouble the duke with three different early mornings, do you?"

Setterdown, Chelderberry, and Berger all looked at one another as if they did not know what the protocol would be if a duke acted as a second and there was more than one duel engaged.

Conbatten said, "Nobody knows what ought to be done in such a case because there has never been such a case. There has never been such a case because the situation is absurd. Do you not see the ludicrous nature of this meeting? How are you to arrange yourselves? Who is to be numbers one, two, and three? Is Baderston really to be shot at three times in one morning? The fellow is practically blind, and his valet has overdosed him with laudanum."

"Your Grace, I engaged all three," Roland said, "and so must be shot at by all three."

Conbatten folded his arms. "Please do no further advocating for yourself. I am trying to keep you alive. At the moment, you are a shell of a man. No decent gentleman would agree to go forward."

"Now, I say, Your Grace," Setterdown said. "If you imply that I would act less than a gentleman—"

Conbatten ignored him. "If there are any of you determined to carry on with this foolishness, then know this—you will *not* have acted as a gentleman. To fire upon a man who can barely see and who has been drugged with laudanum could not be defended and I would be sure to make all of society know it. The most you can do this morning is arrange for a later date.

"If you refuse these terms, I will make it my life's work to make you miserable. I will denounce you, very publicly cut you, I will speak to the queen about you, I will shut every club door against you, and I will ground your marital prospects so far into the dust that you will be forced to take a bride from Philadelphia."

"Philadelphia?" Chelderberry muttered. He shook his head at his second. "I'm very set on a lady from my own neighborhood."

"My father will never accept an American!" Setterdown said.

"The clubs, though…what would I do all day if not for my clubs?" Mr. Berger fretted.

Roland stepped forward. "His Grace, as my second, is doing his duty in trying to delay my duels. However, I am prepared to fight all three of you this instant!"

Behind him, he heard the rumble of a carriage and briefly searched his mind. Was there a fourth fellow he'd forgotten about?

"Lord Baderston!"

It was Lady Viola. What was she doing here? As it was entirely likely he should be shot very shortly, she really should not be here.

Roland turned. He squinted his already squinty eyes. Good Lord, the dowager was with her.

"Baderston," the dowager said, striding toward him, "what on earth are you doing here?"

"I'm going to shoot at these three fellows," he said.

"Preferably not," the duke said.

"I have to do it," Roland said stubbornly. "They have all three insulted Lady Viola's honor. I will not stand for it."

Lady Viola herself pushed past the dowager and said, "Lord Baderston, I was very afraid this would happen. I've come to take you off to Gretna Green and I do not care what those three beastly fellows think about it."

"Have you?" Roland said.

"Oh yes, she has," Miss Mayton said.

"No, she has not!" the dowager cried.

"I most certainly have, Countess," Lady Viola said to the dowager. "And I am surprised at you, I must say. Do you really wish for your only son and heir to be killed on this fine morning?"

"No, but—"

"There is no but to it," Lady Viola said. She marched over to where Chelderberry, Setterdown, and Berger stood, all looking entirely perplexed.

"You three," she said, in a marvelously scathing tone. "I'll have you know that when that tinker's boy asked me to run off, I was eight years old, as was he. We certainly did not go any-where."

She pointed at Setterdown. "I told the story to Lady Clara and she embellished it. She has sore feelings and lashed out."

"As she might well have," Setterdown said, sounding affront-ed. "There was supposed to be a match!"

"The match was all in the dowager's head," Lady Viola said, "and not in Lord Baderston's heart. He and your sister are not at all suited and the dowager did Lady Clara an egregious disservice in convincing her otherwise."

"How dare—" the dowager sputtered.

Lady Viola ignored the dowager's outrage. "And you," Lady Viola said, turning to Chelderberry, "I do not know what brings you here, but you are very foolish to have engaged yourself in such a manner."

"My cousin is making me go home on account of it," Chelderberry said sullenly.

"Excellent. We will see you next season in a better frame of mind," Lady Viola said. Finally, she turned to Mr. Berger. "Naturally, I know why *you* are here. Calling out an insult in the theater was very bad form. I dearly hope you were not ever planning on attempting to join the YBC. That behavior from a gentleman would never be tolerated."

Mr. Berger shrugged. "It was only a joke."

"Then you are not the wit you imagine yourself to be," Lady Viola said.

Gad, she really was marvelous! What fortitude! One might expect the daughter of an earl to be in the carriage fanning herself, if she were anywhere near a duel at all.

A sudden thought occurred to Roland. She had given them all a terrific dressing down, but there were more important questions hanging in the air. "Lady Viola," he said, "Gretna Green. Let's get back to that conversation."

Lady Viola turned to him and touched his face with her soft hand. "Look at you. Your poor eyes. And to think, all of this trouble was for me."

"Well, what could I do? I have loved you since the first moment I saw you in the park last year."

"No you haven't!" the dowager shouted.

"I have felt just the same," Lady Viola said. "I thought about you all summer long."

"As did I think about you!" Roland said. "I even began eating an immense amount of ham…so I could mention it when we met again."

"Did you?" Lady Viola asked, looking very pleased.

"Stop talking about ham!" the dowager said, her tone all irritation.

"I haunted the doors of Almack's so I could be first on your card."

"My sisters and I imagined it would be so and then there you were."

"So we are off to Gretna Green?"

"We can be, assuming you…"

Assuming he? Assuming he what?

Then it came to him.

"Blast, that got away from me," Roland said. "Lady Viola Bennington, I will love you and be loyal to you all my life if you will consent to be my adorable and treasured wife."

Roland heard his mother groan. Lady Viola said, "Most happily."

"Excellent," Roland said. "I must only dispense with…this

particular matter."

"All of you," Conbatten said to Setterdown, Chelderberry, and Berger, "either fire into the air and settle this thing or send your seconds to me to request a reappointment when Baderston has his eyesight back."

The men shuffled and complained and talked amongst themselves. Berger and Chelderberry reluctantly fired in the air. Setterdown threw his chin up. "I am afraid I cannot allow the matter to drop, as it pertains to my sister."

Conbatten straightened his cuffs. "Very well," he said. "Keep in mind though, when you do re-engage Baderston, the matter will pertain to his *wife*."

"Curse it," Setterdown said. He took a pistol from his second and fired into the air.

"The matter is settled," Conbatten said. "God help the man who ever drags me into another such situation. I will not be nearly as good humored about it."

Viola threw herself into Roland's arms. "And we, my love, are off to Gretna Green."

Roland picked her up and carried her toward her carriage. "Let us be off this minute."

The earl's coachman stood there with folded arms. "You could not torture me or put a pistol to my head to take you to Scotland, Lady Viola. I will drive you home and nowhere else."

Of course, he should have thought—the earl's coachman would hardly drive the earl's daughter to an elopement.

"Never mind," Roland said, "we'll take Conbatten's coach."

"You'll do no such thing," the duke said. "You will very sensibly approach Lady Viola's father and state your intentions. If he's willing to overlook your current appearance and the events of this morning, I daresay he will consent to the marriage."

Lord Baderston set Viola down. He looked into her eyes and she instantly perceived that he asked for her opinion on Conbatten's words. She nodded.

"Consent to it?" the dowager cried. "After the outrageous

behavior of that girl, the earl ought to beg for it."

Lady Viola kissed Lord Baderston's cheek and walked to the lady. She hooked her arm through the dowager's. "The problem with you, Countess, is that you are very stubborn. I love your darling son to the ends of the earth and back and come with a respectable dowry. Certainly you cannot wish for more than that?"

"Of course I can," the dowager said. "Lady Clara was pliable and easily guided. That is what was wished for. I could have molded her into a proper mistress for Trewellian Hall."

"Oh, I see," Lady Viola said, laughing. "You wished to have your own way. Well, I will give it to you as much as I can."

"Let us go at once to your father," Roland said. "Mother, you can acquiesce or not, you can rejoice or not, you can adapt or not. It matters little, as I am determined to marry Lady Viola and if her father refuses, we *will* run off to Scotland."

Roland paused. "We will, is that right?"

"I am sure he will agree," Lady Viola said. "Of course, if he did not, we would certainly run off. We will not be stopped in this matter. Not by anybody."

"There you have it," Roland said. "We will not be stopped. Return to the house and if you find you remain disagreeable, return to the dower house in Dorset."

The dowager sniffed, but she did not reply.

Roland looked down at his lovely fiancée. "Gad, this morning turned out far better than I thought it would."

VIOLA SIGHED HAPPILY in her dear Lord Baderston's arms. They were in the carriage, with Conbatten and Miss Mayton as ersatz chaperones, on their way to Portland Place.

The duke and her aunt were doing a wonderful job of not paying attention, which was well, as their behavior was rather shocking. Once they arrived home, they would acquaint the earl with the remarkable events of the morning.

Lord Baderston kissed her long and deep. What a marvel it was.

Viola realized that all the imagination in the world could not approach what it really was. She was a little startled to realize that she had just started to imagine Lord Baderston with his clothes off.

"We ought to marry soon," Viola said.

Lord Baderston nuzzled her neck and said, "Very soon."

"Perhaps we ought to run off to Gretna Green even if my father gives us leave to marry. He shouldn't mind, I do not think."

"Whatever you wish."

Conbatten sighed and said, "I expect he *will* mind."

Neither of them answered the duke, as before she knew it, her bonnet was off and pins were coming out of her hair. "Lady Viola's beautiful hair," Lord Baderston said, twisting a ringlet round his finger.

"It is your own hair that first struck me," Viola said, touching it.

All this time, she'd been admiring its charming copper color, now she could touch it. She could touch it whenever she liked. The head that housed it belonged to her now.

The carriage rattled to a stop and Viola had no idea how they'd got there so fast. In Lord Baderston's arms, time seemed to fly ahead faster than it ought.

Suddenly, from across the carriage, Conbatten said, "For the love of heaven. Miss Mayton, do pin up Lady Viola's hair before we go in."

"I do not even know how that happened," Lord Baderston said.

"Nor I," Viola said laughing and picking up pins from the seat.

Miss Mayton pinned up her hair as best she could. Viola

thought she and Lord Baderston must look very original just at that moment—she with her hair disheveled, and he with two black eyes.

Sandren opened the carriage door, his expression communicating that he did not at all approve of the morning's activities.

"Come," she said, taking Lord Baderston's hand.

They raced up the steps and found Tattleton at the door. He did not look any more approving than the coachman.

"Where is my father?" Viola asked.

"In the library," Tattleton said. Looking over Viola's shoulder, he said, "I am certain he will be grateful for news on your cousin's illness, Miss Mayton, as he has mentioned having that lady to dine when she is fully recovered."

Viola did not stop to hear what Miss Mayton would say to *that* idea. She held Lord Baderston's hand and pulled him down the corridor to the library doors. Viola threw them open.

"Papa!" she said.

"My dear," the earl said, "how did you get on with Miss Mayton's cousin? I pray she is in recovery from whatever ails her."

The earl then took on a look of confusion to see Lord Baderston by her side.

"Oh, Papa," Viola said, "I am sorry, but that was only a ruse. I had to rush off to make sure Lord Baderston did not kill himself on my account."

Lord Westmont stood. "Lord Baderston, were you considering doing a violence to yourself? Really, that is never the answer."

"No, Lord Westmont," Lord Baderston said, "Well, what I mean is, I met three fellows on a green this morning. You see, I challenged all three of them to defend Lady Viola's honor."

The earl sank back down to his chair. "Three gentlemen challenged? Over the story of the tinker's boy?"

"Just so," Lord Baderston said.

"Then…as I see you are still standing, I must presume at least one other is not. Will you make a run to the continent to avoid a prosecution?"

"Goodness, no," Viola said. "They all gave it up and fired into the air. How could they go forward when I had come to steal Lord Baderston away to Gretna Green?"

"Gretna Green!" the earl said.

"The fact is, Earl," Lord Baderston said, "I am hopelessly in love with Lady Viola and have been since last year. With your permission, we will wed. I can assure you I am from a respectable family and have the means to support her in a fashion befitting her."

The earl waved his hands. "As to that, Darden has already marked you as respectable. A Trewellian, I believe. Viola, is this the fellow you want? Truly?"

"A thousand times over," Viola said.

"Well, I can have nothing against it. I am not certain I understand what occurred this morning, though I can hardly fault a gentleman for risking his life in defense of my daughter. But what's this about Gretna Green?"

"Papa, we really do wish to run off to Gretna Green. Just think, to plan a wedding takes so long, even with a special license, and who would we even invite to a wedding breakfast? It would be a rather small affair, at least until the rumors about me are cleared up."

"I see your points, of course," the earl said tenting his fingers. "But a father cannot simply sanction an elopement. It would be most untoward. I am liberal, I think, but that would be a step too far. As well, it would only cause further talk and we have our hands full on that front as it is."

"I care nothing for what is said," Lord Baderston declared gallantly.

"Nor I," Viola said.

"I do care," the earl said. "I have two more daughters to launch and will not have them tainted by such talk."

"Oh dear, that is true," Viola said. "Darden has mentioned the same idea."

"What if we were to all go together?" Lord Baderston asked.

"All the family might make the trip. Miss Mayton could continue as chaperone until we are properly wed. There can be nothing shocking in that."

"Would your dowager agree to such an idea?" the earl asked skeptically.

"That would be her choice, of course," Lord Baderston said. "Realistically, she is not very agreeable in general, so it makes little difference what plan is posed to her."

The doors to the library suddenly burst open and Cordelia and Juliet ran through them.

"We could not help but listen at the door. Do say yes, Papa," Cordelia said.

"Please do, Papa," Juliet said. "You know we are such very good travelers and just think of what new scenery we might view. The odes would practically pour out of me."

"I do like new scenery," the earl said thoughtfully. "And I haven't been up to Scotland in an age. I have a cousin up there, Halford, who's got a rather comfortable fishing lodge."

"And there would be nothing disreputable about it," Viola said. "It would not be an elopement. It would be the Benningtons deciding to conduct the ceremony in Scotland."

"That is true. However, before we can make any decision, the marriage contract must be settled. If we are to say it is not an elopement, that must be done first."

"My lord, if your solicitor will draw something up, we might settle it in a day," Lord Baderston said. "I am prepared to sign anything and have no intention of haggling."

"He is a dear, is he not?" Viola said.

"Yes, I suppose," the earl said. "But Baderston, should you not wish to recover from, well, what has happened to your eyes, before you make your vows?"

"Not if Lady Viola will have me as I am."

"I will have him, Papa, just as he is."

"Hooray!" Juliet cried. "We are going to Scotland!"

"Not so fast, Juliet," the earl said. "I will agree to the trip if the following conditions are met. One, a marriage contract is signed. Two, Lord Baderston's mother agrees to go on the trip as well. I cannot be comfortable leaving that lady behind to miss her son's wedding. No, I cannot be comfortable with that at all."

Viola sighed. The dowager would never agree to it.

"I will speak to her forthwith," Lord Baderston said. "Nothing shall stop us, least of all my mother."

The earl sighed. "I admire your confidence, but I do not think the dowager is particularly fond of me."

"She is not," Lord Baderston said, "though I do not understand why."

"I cannot say conclusively why," the earl said, "and even if I could, I would not presume to speak for the lady. I imagine it was something she had a particular view on long ago."

"No matter," Lord Baderston said. "Every obstacle must be overcome. Every obstacle *will* be overcome."

The door swung open and Darden entered the library.

"Guess what, Darden?" Juliet said.

Lord Darden took in the scene and it was no surprise that he could not possibly make a guess at what had transpired.

"We're going to Scotland as soon as Lord Baderston convinces his mother to come along," Viola said.

Lord Darden blinked. "As usual, I am entirely lost."

AFTER VIOLA HAD said a very long goodbye and good luck to Lord Baderston at the front doors, Conbatten drove him home to speak to the dowager.

Viola joined her family in the drawing room, where Lord Darden was apprised of the goings-on of the day.

"So it is to be a family elopement?" he asked.

"Of sorts," the earl said. "I've sent a note to my solicitor so we might draw up the papers for the marriage contract."

"It all hangs on Lord Baderston's mother though," Viola said. "He must convince her to accompany us."

"Well," Lord Darden said, "he strikes me as a determined sort of chap."

⟫⟫⟩✕⟨⟨⟨

ROLAND FOUND HIS mother sitting in the drawing room. It was odd to see her so, as she was generally on the move—going somewhere or directing the servants about something. If she were sitting, she worked on her sewing or played the pianoforte. Just now, though, she was entirely unoccupied and had her hands folded in her lap.

"I suppose you will send me off to Dorset to live quite alone after I have expressed my displeasure with your recent actions," the dowager said. "You can hardly want me scowling at the wedding breakfast."

"Actually, I want you take a trip, but not to Dorset."

The dowager laughed bitterly. "Oh I see, now I am even thrown from the dower house? Where am I to be shipped off to? My cousin Ada's cottage in Brighton, I suppose? I know you can make her take me in, as you pay all her debts."

"I have no intention of shipping you off anywhere. I want you to come to the wedding, which will be in Scotland. All the Benningtons are going, and there are quite a lot of them. I wish you to represent our side."

"Scotland?"

"Yes, Scotland. We wish to set off as soon as possible, but Lord Westmont says the idea is off if you do not consent to come."

"Does he say that?" the dowager said skeptically.

"He does, and he knows you do not like him. Though, he said he would not presume to speak for you. I would know the cause of your dislike."

The dowager sighed and much to Roland's surprise, she looked a little defeated. "Very well, if you must know it and I will thank you to never repeat it. I have told you of the earl that I preferred and that he married another."

"It was the Earl of Westmont," Roland said. He should have known. He had briefly wondered about it when she'd told him that his father was second choice, but he'd dismissed it.

"It was he. There, now you know it. I suppose that now he is a widow, that Miss Mayton will get her claws into him."

"Miss Mayton?" Roland said, laughing. "I rather think not. That lady has been on the premises for nearly seventeen years. If the earl had a preference for her, I think he would have mentioned it by now."

"Seventeen, you say?"

"Indeed. She's been there since the countess died in childbirth."

"I did not realize it had been so long."

"I really do not think it would matter if she'd only been there for an hour," Roland said. "She is a remarkably flighty woman."

"Yes, she is, is she not?"

"I cannot imagine they would be at all suited."

"No, the earl is certainly not flighty himself."

"You will come, then?" Roland asked. "I think your feelings against the earl might undergo a thawing and I think you will learn to love Lady Viola. She will not be as pliable as you might prefer, but she could be a friend and she has been rather undaunted by your treatment of her."

The dowager tapped her chin. "Lady Viola has been stalwart, I am willing to give up that small point."

"Very stalwart," Roland said. "It is not any lady who will march onto a green to put a stop to a duel."

"True," the dowager said. "Of course, I must consider that the Trewellian women have always been strong-minded."

"And most of all," Roland said, hoping to finally sway her, "you are my mother and I would be made very unhappy to wed without your presence."

"But you'd do it anyway?"

"Yes, I would. Lady Viola is for me, and I am for Lady Viola.

Did you know, she actually prefers my hair color? She has a preference for red hair. She calls mine copper-colored."

"Does she?"

"You will go, then?"

The dowager sighed. "I suppose I will have to. I cannot imagine the talk if I were not to go along. You know how much I dislike it when there is talk about the family."

CHAPTER NINETEEN

THOUGH THE DOWAGER did not like to hear talk about the family, she found herself rather pleased with the talk when word of the Bennington-Trewellian caravan to Scotland went round and became widely known.

The *ton* was soon apprised of what would eventually be named an "all-parties elopement" with parents and siblings included. As Conbatten was involved, and as it was seen as an original idea, it became exceedingly popular with young people recently engaged. It somehow took on the mantle of elegance and sophistication, most likely because it was an unwieldy and expensive thing to arrange. Were anyone involved to really look at it, a wedding in Town would have been just as quick and a deal simpler.

The allure of the difficulty managed to paint the trip with an aura of romance. Unfortunately, few of the young couples who were keen to do it could talk their respective sets of parents into it, and so the idea of an all-parties elopement soon died out.

As for the original Bennington-Trewellian all-parties elopement, the journey to Scotland was every bit as eccentric and interesting as any Bennington trip ever was.

The departure from Portland Place was comprised of so many carriages that it had even drawn a small crowd on the pavement. Onlookers guessed it must be for some important event, especially since the duke's carriages were among them.

Juliet, who was exceedingly enthusiastic about the trip, helpfully leaned out her carriage window and told Mrs. Hankin of the "all-parties elopement," thereby sending it by swift messenger throughout London.

Viola and Lord Baderston took one of the earl's carriages, chaperoned by Miss Mayton. Then, Darden and the earl, Juliet and Cordelia all went together. Conbatten and Rosalind took their own coach. The dowager rode in Lord Baderston's carriage. Tattleton, various valets, footmen, and ladies' maids, and of course, Chester, were accommodated in their own carriages.

The only two persons who were missed were Beatrice and Van Doren.

As it took a full week to settle the marriage contract and make all the arrangements, Juliet had written to Beatrice to see if she might be enticed into making the trip, even though she found herself with child.

A response was received, though it was not the response Juliet had hoped for. It said,

> *My darling sister, what a mad scheme and kiss Viola for me! I knew Lord Baderston should prove himself. I wish you all the fun in the world in Scotland. As for me, I am nesting at the moment, a veritable hen awaiting the arrival of my chick. I've just informed Van Doren that all the curtains and rugs in the nursery must be changed. As for the preserving of fruits and vegetables that is going on just now, well, I suppose we will never go hungry. Best of luck to Viola and all my love to the rest of you, Bea.*

Below Beatrice's jolly words, was the inevitable grim postscript from Van Doren.

> *Juliet—be so good as to refrain from sending any more of your lunatic proposals to my wife while she is in her delicate condition. If you all are actually going to Scotland, I pray Lord Baderston can hold up against what is bound to be a journey*

full of delays and ridiculous happenings. I, myself, have barely recovered from the last I experienced.

Van Doren was well known to be crochety and had little patience for the Bennington style of family travel, however, it could not be denied that he was accurate in his assessment.

Though the Benningtons had always been slow in traveling from Taunton to London, going further afield and adding more people, a parrot, and carriages into the mix slowed the caravan exponentially.

Juliet spotted a new and compelling vista every few miles or so and the odes that resulted were read after dinner at the various inns they stopped at. There was much written about blazing orbs, fence posts, lonely farms, and a particularly striking rabbit.

Then, of course, Chester was not known to be a very good traveler. What could they do, though? They certainly could not leave him behind when he had so recently joined the family—he would become confused and depressed.

The footmen had been charged with looking after the parrot and there were frequent stops for Chester to regain his equilibrium until Johnny found a way to secure his cage from swaying so much.

Conbatten appeared entirely perplexed at how slowly the whole caravan made progress, but could not put his finger on how to speed them all up. He was learning the lesson the earl had learned long ago—there was no way to speed them all up.

The duke was stopped from being in a temper about it only because he had the company of his wife to entertain him.

The dowager went on stoic and near silent for some days, but after riding alone for hours during the day and then being assaulted by Juliet's odes after dinner, she one evening found the earl's offer of a game of piquet to be appealing.

This seemed to break the ice between them. After some further forays into civility, the earl began to fret that it was not seemly for the poor dowager to ride alone when so many others had conversation. He took to riding part of the day in her carriage, so that she might have company.

What they talked about, nobody knew, but the dowager's sharp edges began to soften and round out.

When Juliet had finished reciting her odes of an evening, Miss Mayton continued on reading aloud from *The Harrowing Homecoming at Harrowbridge Hall*.

It seemed that the duel between Duke One and Duke Two did not come off. Unlike Lord Baderston's duels, in which all parties fired into the air, the two dukes found they had nothing to fire.

The gentle governess had hidden all their weapons so there would not be bloodshed on the lawn. She took the further precaution of hiding all the knives in the kitchens, swords on the walls, and anything else that might be a likely weapon.

As they had nothing to kill each other with, the two dukes ended up rolling around the lawn in hand-to-hand combat. Who got the worst of it was hard to tell—they both came out of it with scratched up faces.

The real duke would eventually be revealed as Duke Two. Duke One made the mistake of leaving a bit of correspondence laying on a table. That letter was addressed to Martin Tinglewink and sent from Mrs. Peggy Tinglewink, wishing to know when her husband was coming home and pointing out that the family farm was falling to ruin.

The earl was pleased as anything to discover that the real duke had prevailed, the false one had been run off, and the duke and his gentle governess were wed and lived happily ever after.

As was inevitable when the Benningtons were on the move, a new creature somehow made its way into their carriages. Just as they were passing through Weatherby, Chester had another of his fits of dizziness.

The carriages stopped and a footman brought the cage outdoors for the parrot to take in some fresh air. Juliet and Cordelia rushed to his side to say soothing and kind words.

In the usual circumstances when Chester was dizzy from the rocking of the carriage, he was very quiet. Sometimes nearly lifeless. This time, however, he started screeching, "Charming Chester! Murder!"

A faint voice shrieked back. "Shut it, old man! Shut it!"

Juliet and Cordelia instantly noted that the order to shut it came from a bird in a cage in a shop window. They determined that Chester was eager to go inside and say hello, in his own interesting fashion.

It surprised nobody that they emerged from the shop carrying Chester's cage, and another one housing the small, green parrot. The bird had only cost them one pound, as the shopkeeper said her customers were getting tired of being told to shut it. The parrot's name was purported to be Jemima.

How the footmen made out under the barrage of parrot conversation that was had in that carriage all the way to Scotland and back was not at all known.

As for Viola and Baderston, all these hiccups passed by largely unnoticed. Miss Mayton proved herself to be a most genial chaperone, as she was asleep most of the time. When she was awake, she entertained Lord Baderston with stories of her tragic youth spent on the continent, losing one love interest after the next.

Roland, for his part, was alarmed to discover that Count Tulerstein had gone over the side of a cliff and then very surprised at how much he was able to say regarding his love for Miss Mayton as he hurtled down the mountain. He was perhaps even more than alarmed when he heard about some of the other tragedies—a hanging, a deadly blow, and an unfortunate impalement.

At least Miss Mayton's recounts of her bad luck in love were only short interludes. Mostly she snored and they were left to themselves.

What they did when left to themselves was probably not something they would advertise. Viola would later tell her sisters that every time the carriage stopped or Miss Mayton awoke, there was a mad scramble to locate her hairpins and straighten her clothes.

As the carriages trundled north, leaving Leeds behind, Viola said, "I have not settled on what I shall call you."

Roland said, "You can call me anything you prefer."

Viola leaned back into the crook of his arm. "I think I like Baderston. Bea calls her viscount Van Doren and Rosalind naturally calls her duke Conbatten—I do not suppose anybody calls Conbatten by his given. It's Balthazar and Rosalind says he does not like it. Also, your mother calls you Baderston."

"Baderston it is then."

"However," Viola continued, "I ought to have something all my own. Something only your dear wife calls you."

"My dear wife," Baderston said, seeming to like the sound of that.

"Roland, hmm. No, I will call you Rolly. You will be Rolly when we are alone and I am delighted with you."

"And what will you call me when we are alone and you are not delighted with me?" Baderston said, laughing.

"I will always be delighted with you," Viola said.

"I will make sure you are, as I will deny you nothing."

"Tell me about your house in Dorset, Rolly," Viola said.

"Soon to be *your* house, the mistress of it all. Well, let us see, I would call Trewellian Hall a distinguished older gentleman. He is composed of gray stone and was built in the fourteen-eighties in the Tudor style. As you might imagine, additions have piled on through the centuries. The great hall, though, has been there from the first—it is three stories high, with the long walls lined with stained glass. It is positively magical in the late afternoon sun."

"We might hold a ball there," Viola said.

"As many as you like. Now, as to the drawing rooms, there are two—one that is rather small and cozy for family and then a larger one when people are expected. The east drawing room, the larger, has a fireplace it is no trouble at all for a grown man to walk into. The library contains more books than I will ever read, the kitchens are commodious, and the bedchambers all have an attached sitting room and wardrobe."

"It sounds divine."

"I think you will like it. I think you will appreciate the gardens and the greenhouse too."

"Tell, me, Rolly, how far is the dower house?" Viola said with a mischievous smile.

Roland smiled back. "Whoever built the dower house knew what they were about. It sits nearly a mile off. Though, I believe the dowager is warming to you."

"Mmhm, I think you might be right, and she seems to be warming to my father too."

"All will be well," Roland said. "I will make it so. We are to have a charmed life."

"I believe you."

By some mysterious twist of fate that had been doused in buckets of good luck, the Bennington caravan eventually stumbled into the area of Gretna Green.

As they were such a large party, they all began to think they should have sent somebody ahead to warn of their arrival. As it turned out, there was nowhere in the village that could accommodate them all and they were further directed to nearby Springfield. They arrived to the King's Head Inn, though even there the servants could not all be housed. The footmen ended up sleeping in the hayloft, though Tattleton, due to his refusal to share a room, stayed with a local couple who owned a shop and had a spare bedchamber.

By the time everyone was settled into their respective places, it was determined that they would visit the blacksmith on the following mid-morning, before setting off for the earl's cousin's fishing lodge, which had been left at their disposal.

That night after dinner, Juliet recited a moving poem she

called *Ode to Three Duels* that was to be framed as their wedding gift.

After that, and seeing a pianoforte tucked in a corner, Rosalind performed one of her travels through the world of music until the proprietor asked her to stop. They had all enjoyed it so much that they really had not noticed how late the hour had grown.

All through it, Viola kept reflecting on the fact that it was her last night as Viola Bennington. On the morrow, she would be Viola Trewellian, Countess of Baderston.

Now in her bedclothes, she gazed out the window at the stars. What a miraculous thing had happened. She and Lord Baderston would wed.

Of course, she did recognize that events had not at all transpired as she'd thought they would.

Viola had imagined that she would come to Town, she would dance with Lord Baderston, they would talk over dinners and perhaps slip into corners at routs. All was to go along very smoothly. Something or other would present itself for Lord Baderston to prove his loyalty.

She really had not expected to have raced to Hyde Park to rescue Lord Baderston, and she certainly had not thought that their families would escort them to Gretna Green.

What a man he was! To challenge three different gentlemen in her defense, when another man likely would have challenged none.

"Come my dear," Miss Mayton said, taking her hand. "To bed with you, as you will marry on the morrow."

"Oh Aunt," Viola said, "I only wish you had found the same happiness as I have found."

"Never mind it, I do have my memories. Tonight, I will dream of Count Tulerstein's last poignant sentiments to me as he plummeted down the side of the mountain."

⟫⟫⟫✕⟪⟪⟪

THE DAY HAD dawned bright and the wind was gentle, which for Scotland must be seen as a particularly auspicious sign.

Roland had sent Markson out to alert the blacksmith priest that his services would be required.

His valet returned with the news that the blacksmith had been paid and Roland would likely be pleased with his mien. His name was Mr. David Lang, though due to his very formal style of dress he was called Bishop Lang. He was a serious fellow who could out-grim any vicar.

As they were doing things quite unorthodox, rather than have the wedding breakfast following the ceremony, they had it beforehand. It was a jolly affair. The earl cheered the happy couple, and the dowager went so far as to say that her son could have done far worse.

Juliet capped the whole thing off by reading her wedding present ode again.

Ode to Three Duels
One, two three, I challenge thee
You did not know but now you see
Pistols blazing and heart on fire
Willing to perish on a funeral pyre.

"Mind you, Lord Baderston," Juliet said, as the applause died down, "I'll have it framed so you can hang it properly."

"Hang it where?" the dowager said, for some reason appearing alarmed by the idea.

"It might look nice in the great hall," Viola said, "under the stained-glass windows."

The dowager gulped down her champagne and held her glass out until it was refilled.

Shortly after, they piled into carriages and trundled their way to Gretna Green. For once nobody, not even Chester, needed to stop for anything.

Mr. Lang joined Viola and Roland's hands and wrapped them in a silk scarf that had been Viola's mother's. In a deep and sonorous voice, he said, "In the joining of hands and the fashion of a knot, so are your lives now bound, one to another. By this cord you are thus bound to your vow."

He swung the hammer upon the anvil, alerting all in Gretna Green that a new marriage was set to commence.

Roland took Viola in his arms and kissed her. She kissed him back rather enthusiastically, despite so many people being about.

"Come, my love," Roland said. "Let us fly to this fishing lodge where we are to take our wedding trip."

"With no chaperone in our carriage," Viola said.

"And no stopping along the way, I hope."

"It is said to be four hours away."

"Four hours," Roland said. "Just us."

"We can pull the curtains," Viola said.

"Gracious," the earl said, interrupting, "we'd best set off, then."

And so they did. Viola could not have said in which carriage Miss Mayton ended up riding in. She could not have said what anybody's arrangements had been outside of her own.

Her own had been rather marvelous. What secrets Bea and Rosalind had kept from her. But then, of course they had, as she did not have the first idea how anybody would explain it. It was not a thing to be explained, but experienced.

The fishing lodge turned out to be a rather large, rambling, and ramshackle sort of place. Neither of them minded it a bit. After taking stock of the accommodations, Roland and Viola promptly took possession of the steward's cottage, while that fellow helpfully took himself off to relations in the village.

The cottage was made of stone and comprised just one large room, nestled in a wood and a five-minute walk to the lodge. It was not, perhaps, the grandest of accommodations, but the bed was marvelous and topped by a luxurious goose down quilt. What went on under that goose down quilt was rather marvelous too.

They reveled in rainy mornings, when the wind howled out of doors, and they lay abed in front of a fire, drank strong coffee, and spoke of all the things to come.

Roland even managed to make breakfast. He'd spent a lot of his youth hanging about Trewellian Hall's kitchens and had watched eggs being cooked a thousand times. After a few unsuccessful tries, he had mastered it well enough that it was at least edible. The eggs may have looked unsightly, the bacon was most assuredly burned, and the slices of bread roasted, but they did not mind it.

If the weather were not too bad, they might set off with fishing poles and march across fields. No fish were ever returned with, but they did discover some charming dry corners in the landscape where one might have a picnic and admire the rolling hills in the distance.

In the early evening, Roland and Viola would walk up to the lodge and dine with their relations.

Juliet had written so many odes that she'd run out of paper and had begun writing crosswise over what she already had.

Cordelia's Desdemona was inspired by the setting and her dramatics reached new heights of creativity. If the Scottish accent she applied to it was not precisely accurate, nobody mentioned it.

The earl and the dowager had fallen into a routine of playing piquet after dinner and seemed content with each other's quiet company.

The duke had located a tub from somewhere and had it hauled up to his bedchamber so that he and Rosalind could continue taking baths and having marriage conversations. The local servants did not know what to make of it and it did not seem as if the bathwater was ever able to reach ninety-eight degrees.

Darden spent most of his days out with the steward, fascinated by the workings of the land.

Miss Mayton had brought another book to read aloud, now that the false duke had been revealed at Harrowbridge Hall. *The Monstrous Mix-ups at Mondrian Castle* was turning into a nerve-wracking tale and nobody could guess if the duke were alive or a ghost, not even the gentle governess.

Tattleton surveyed it all and spent many a night regaling the local servants with stories from London and the eccentricities of the *ton*. Perhaps he might have even hinted that a certain powerful lady by the name of Hightower had at once recognized his stature as a top butler just by looking at him.

Chester shouted murder for any and all reasons. Jemima, the small green parrot, was thought to be exceedingly bold in telling Chester to shut it.

Chester ended up gaining quite the reputation in the local village. What could be more spinechilling than hearing of the exotic creature up at the lodge who was always portending a violent end for some unknown victim? In the ensuing years, his presence in those weeks would transform into a local legend. Parents would scold their naughty children with the warning—"lest the cursed macaw speak your name."

Roland and Viola joined the party for dinner, and then slipped away to their own little place. They might have been driven there for food, but it was their time to be alone before the world and its concerns intruded. Nobody made comment on how fast they ate, how little they spoke to anybody else, or how ungraciously they took their early leave.

The party stayed a fortnight before setting off home again and the trip back was even longer than the trip up. They did finally make it back to London and it is presumed that Tattleton was relieved that they'd only arrived with one extra parrot.

Roland and Viola stopped at his house in Town for a week before departing for Trewellian Hall in Dorset.

They had wondered what the dowager would do, but in the end she said she would accompany them. She had begun to make various forays into conversation with Viola and now she claimed there was much about the house and its environs that a new mistress should be apprised of.

It would turn out that she was right about that. There were hidden passages and disguised doors, priest holes, and a rather temperamental cook. There were the villagers to get to know—who could be hired to reliably do a job, and a few who could be hired but would somehow never finish a job. There was the neighborhood society to be explained—Lady Ivy would talk one's ears off regarding her roses, and Mrs. Dalkin had a secret recipe for peas that must always be complimented. The dowager was also very knowledgeable about the apple orchards and the greenhouse.

After she was assured that all was well in hand, the dowager countess returned to the dower house. The lady had very slowly made herself so agreeable that Roland and Viola settled to having her to dine three days a week.

These initial dinners were mostly comprised of ham, which the dowager would have liked to complain bitterly about, but she had learned to keep her own counsel.

Finally, Roland admitted to his wife that while he liked ham well enough, he did not wish for it so often. This prompted Viola to mention that sometimes ham even made her feel a bit sick, but she had claimed it was her favorite as a child and had felt bound to stick with it out of loyalty.

Ham eventually faded from the forefront and sank to being of equal importance to every other sort of meat.

Very predictably, Roland and Viola's children were blessed with shades of red hair. Some darker, some lighter. They somehow got the idea, probably from their mother, that red hair was a mark of a true and loyal heart. Whether or not that was factual was beside the point. Armed with the idea of loyalty, the four offspring formed a cabal of sorts, no less tightknit than the Bennington sisters had ever been.

The dowager would be instrumental in assisting them with

creating their motto—*cross one and cross us all.*

Viola continued with her efforts at painting, and Roland was often alarmed at the finished product. In fact, he had a terrible time even knowing if a particular canvas *was* finished or not. Fortunately, during the very next season after their wedding, Conbatten gave him a helpful hint. He advised that Roland dedicate one room of the house as the "family room" where such things as paintings and odes might be housed away from a peering public.

This worked out wonderfully well, as Viola took it as the highest of compliments. The portraits of the Earl of Baderston, if that's what they were, hung proudly next to the framed copy of *Ode to Three Duels*—their wedding gift from Juliet.

Viola had come to London for her season determined to test Lord Baderston's loyalty. He proved himself beyond anything she could have imagined. He would be loyal all his life, which he found exceedingly easy to accomplish, as there was nobody he preferred over his wife.

That next season after their marriage would be Cordelia's turn at love and Viola was certain it would be a straightforward affair, as Cordelia had rather straightforward preferences.

Cordelia Bennington had watched her eldest sister Beatrice set London's gentlemen on impossible quests, only to marry their staid neighbor. Then she'd helped Rosalind stage her own ill-advised kidnapping. And of course, she'd been exceedingly interested when Viola set a rumor going round that she'd almost eloped to Gretna Green, only to then actually elope to Gretna Green.

The Bennington ladies were in the habit of defining which qualities they must require from a gentleman and then going forth boldly to secure such qualities. So far, it had met with rousing success.

Cordelia could not be more ready to carry on where Beatrice, Rosalind, and Viola had left off. She was in no doubt what she looked for—her man will be all physicality.

He will be prepared to sweep her up in his arms and carry her off at the slightest provocation. If there is even the smallest puddle anywhere in the vicinity, she must fly into his arms. Those arms she's been thinking about are unusually muscular and tailors are finding it devilish difficult to even encase them in sleeves.

This miracle of a man spends his days racing his horse, boxing, and crossing swords. He will be a man of all action and leave the thinking to her.

He is a true Corinthian and the only thing that can take his attention away from his adventurous pursuits is Cordelia Bennington. His sporting heart beats with passion for her.

What Baron Harveston, erudite intellectual, esteemed member of *The Royal Society*, and founder of *The Society for Serious Literary Examination* will make of Cordelia Bennington's plans remains to be seen.

The End

About the Author

By the time I was eleven, my Irish Nana and I had formed a book club of sorts. On a timetable only known to herself, Nana would grab her blackthorn walking stick and steam down to the local Woolworth's. There, she would buy the latest Barbara Cartland romance, hurry home to read it accompanied by viciously strong wine, (Wild Irish Rose, if you're wondering) and then pass the book on to me. Though I was not particularly interested in real boys yet, I was *very* interested in the gentlemen in those stories— daring, bold, and often enraging and unaccountable. After my Barbara Cartland phase, I went on to Georgette Heyer, Jane Austen and so many other gifted authors blessed with the ability to bring the Georgian and Regency eras to life.

I would like nothing more than to time travel back to the Regency (and time travel back to my twenties as long as we're going somewhere) to take my chances at a ball. Who would take the first? Who would escort me into supper? What sort of meaningful looks would be exchanged? I would hope, having made the trip, to encounter a gentleman who would give me a very hard time. He ought to be vexatious in the extreme, and *worth* every vexation, to make the journey worthwhile.

I most likely won't be able to work out the time travel gambit, so I will content myself with writing stories of adventure and romance in my beloved time period. There are lives to be created, marvelous gowns to wear, jewels to don, instant attractions that inevitably come with a difficulty, and hearts to break before putting them back together again. In traditional Regency fashion, my stories are clean—the action happens in a drawing room, rather than a bedroom.

As I muse over what will happen next to my H and h, and wish I were there with them, I will occasionally remind myself that it's also nice to have a microwave, Netflix, cheese popcorn, and steaming hot showers.

Come see me on Facebook! @KateArcherAuthor